W9-AOJ-489

Rock With Me

Book Four in the
With Me In Seattle Series

By
Kristen Proby

ROCK WITH ME - Book Four in the With Me In Seattle Series
Kristen Proby

Copyright © 2013 by Kristen Proby

All rights reserved. Without limiting the rights under copyright reserved above, no part of this publication may be reproduced, stored in or introduced into a retrieval system, or transmitted, in any form, or by any means (electronic, mechanical, photocopying, recording, or otherwise) without the prior written permission of both the copyright owner and the above publisher of this book. This is a work of fiction. Names, characters, places, brands, media, and incidents are either the product of the author's imagination or are used fictitiously. The author acknowledges the trademarked status and trademark owners of various products referenced in this work of fiction, which have been used without permission. The publication/use of these trademarks is not authorized, associated with, or sponsored by the trademark owners.

The following story contains mature themes, strong language, and sexual situations. It is intended for adult readers.

Cover Art:
Photographer: Linus Pettersson of Photo by Linus
Models: Sulan Von Zoomlander and Katerina Lotus
Graphic Artist: Renae Porter of Social Butterfly Creative

Sunshine © 2013 by Kristen Proby and Nicole Brightman, co-writers.

Dedication:

This book is for the readers.

Thank you, from the bottom of my heart.

Prologue

"You know," Meg announces to the room at large. "You didn't all need to come help. I don't have that much stuff. Leo and Will could have handled the big stuff."

We are gathered at Will Montgomery's house, helping him move his girlfriend, Megan in with him. I've grown to love these people. My brother marrying into the Montgomery family might have been the best thing he ever did.

Damn Luke, for always getting it right. I glance across Will's impressive living room where I'm trying to decide where one of Meg's brightly colored paintings should be hung and eye my brother as he kisses his pretty brunette wife on the cheek. Natalie is the best, and I'm so happy that she's forgiven me for being a bitch to her when I first met her. Not that I'm all that sorry for it. I had my reasons. But Nat is fantastic.

She's my best friend.

"Thanks so much for volunteering me," Leo, Meg's brother, mutters. "Why didn't we hire a company again?"

I grin to myself and turn my back on the room, focusing on the wall and the artwork in my hands. I'm in a room with Leo Nash. *The Leo Nash.* He's only the hottest rock star in the country. And he's sexy as hell.

And he's been watching me all day.

Will and Leo continue to grumble about doing all the heavy lifting, earning glares from Meg. God, she's funny.

And I guarantee not one of us girls is going to complain about watching Leo, Nate and the Montgomery brothers lift heavy objects. Holy hot men.

"So, Sam," Leo saunters over to me. I can feel him move up behind me, just a few feet away, and damn if I can't smell his musky sweat and the soap from his shower. "What are you doing later?"

I take a deep breath and keep my face blank. I learned a long time ago to keep my emotions in check.

"I won't be doing you," I mutter and hammer a nail into the wall. As attracted as I am to him, and really, who wouldn't be, Leo is off limits. He's Meg's brother.

He's famous.

He's cocky as hell.

"Uh, I wasn't offering, honey." I turn around to see Leo smiling smugly. "I was wondering if you'd like me to take you to have that stick pulled out of your ass."

The girls gasp, and Luke's eyes go hard as stone.

Okay, that hurt.

Don't touch the stick in my ass, you jerk.

Before my brother can rip Leo to shreds, and despite his usual sweet demeanor I have no doubt that he would in a heartbeat, I paste a smile on my face and laugh.

"Nope, I like my stick right where it is."

"Let me know if you change your mind." Leo grins and shoves his hands in the pockets of the worn jeans that sit low on his hips.

"You'll be the first to know." I turn back to the wall and hang the painting. "But just so you know," I turn back to him, "I don't date famous people."

"Neither do I." He winks and saunters into the kitchen, pulls a beer out of the fridge and takes a sip. His biceps flex under those amazing tattoos covering his skin as he lifts and lowers the bottle to his lips. He swallows and smiles over at me, his eyes shining with interest, and for the first time in five years I regret my no celebrity rule.

Damn him.

Chapter One

"You okay?" Luke murmurs in my ear as he hugs me before we leave Will's house.

"Of course, why wouldn't I be?" I smirk as I look defiantly into Luke's happy blue eyes.

"Leo's not really an asshole." He frowns and glances back at the house.

"He was being funny, Luke. I can take a joke." I wave him off and sink into my little white Mercedes. "I'll see you at mom and dad's on Sunday?"

"Yeah, we'll see you there." He waves and joins Nat in their car and drives away. Everyone has left except Leo who hung back to help Will lift a few more boxes, and I'm relieved to get away from him.

He's too good looking for my comfort level.

Okay, that's not it. I pull out of the driveway and toward my downtown condo.

I see something in Leo that disturbs me. Not in a creepy, what the hell is he thinking way, but because he's so… virile. He pulls to me in a way no one ever has before. It has nothing to do with his band or his money, and everything to do with those gray eyes and sweet smile.

He's got baggage, and he's probably a bit of a rock star jerk. I don't have time to deal with an arrogant attitude.

I have my own to deal with.

Suddenly, a couple miles away from Will and Meg's house, my car jerks and drops in the front.

Fuck, I have a flat.

I pull to the side of the road and jump out of the car. It's started to rain, that thick, cold, biting rain that Seattle is famous for in the winter. Thank God I was dressed for unpacking, in my jeans and sneakers and a hoodie.

Not my every day attire.

I stand in the rain, my red hoodie over my hair, and stare at the tire. This is the perfect end to the week from hell. I sigh and look up and down the street around me and then give the tire a quick kick, managing to stub my toe in the process.

Shit! I hop around in a circle and then scowl at the tire again. Fucking tire.

Well, I could call roadside assistance, but it's just a flat tire, and I could have it changed before the guy got here to help.

I open the tiny trunk of the car and remove the small donut spare, jack and lug-nut-removal-thingie. I don't know what the tools are called, but I'm sure as hell thankful that my dad made me learn how to use them.

Just as I lean the spare against the car and set the jack under the axle, a familiar car pulls up behind me, and I sigh deeply.

Leo.

Sonofabitch.

He unfolds his lean body from his black muscle car and walks to me, black Converse crunching over the gravel, seemingly unfazed by the rain. He's wearing a leather jacket, open in the front, over his white t-shirt and loose jeans. He's covered his head with a black knit beanie.

"Problem?" He asks with a half-smile, that lip piercing catching my eye.

Why am I attracted to a lip piercing?

I don't know, but I am.

"Just a flat. I'm gonna change it. You don't have to stay." I start working on the lug nuts.

Leo hasn't moved.

"You don't have to stay," I repeat more firmly and look up into his handsome face.

"Do you honestly think I'm going to leave you here, at the side of the road, to change out a flat by yourself?" He asks, his eyes have gone colder, and I frown.

"I have this handled."

Instead of stalking back to his car and driving off, he leans his ass on my car, crosses his arms over his chest, and watches me with those stormy eyes the same color as the clouds currently dumping cold water on us.

"Suit yourself." I shrug and return to the task at hand. God, the rain is cold and the wind has picked up now, making my hands throb and I wish for gloves, but refuse to let Leo see my discomfort. The nuts come off smoothly until I get to the last one, which is on too tight.

I struggle with it, grunting, and fall on my ass with the effort. The nut didn't move.

"Damn," I mutter and glare at the tire.

Strong hands wrap around my upper arms and lift me to my feet. "God, you're a tiny thing," he mutters and moves me aside. He squats beside the tire and easily loosens the stubborn nut.

"I loosened it for you," I tell him with a stubborn set to my chin.

"Of course," he chuckles and pulls the flat tire off the axis. "Are you always this stubborn?"

I cross my arms over my chest, burying my hands against my ribs to warm them up. "Pretty much."

He laughs and shakes his head, his tattooed fingers mounting the new tire and tightening the lug nuts. I can't look away from his hands, the vivid colors of the ink.

His body art is gorgeous.

I wonder what he's got under his clothes? He's typically shirtless in publicity shots, so I know he has sleeves on his arms, a tat across his chest, stars on his hips, but I'd love to see under his pants.

I take a deep breath, close my eyes, and force the shirtless image out of my head just as he lowers the jack and gathers my tools and replaces them in the trunk with the flat tire.

"You didn't have to do that you know." I offer him a half-smile and then laugh out loud when he scowls at me.

"Sam, I'm not about to leave you here at the side of the road by yourself to change a tire in the rain. Your brother would put his foot up my ass."

Of course. He's only being nice because of Luke. Just like every-one else.

I systematically school my features, blank canvas, straighten my shoulders and put the walls back up.

People can't hurt me if I don't let them.

"You're probably right." I back away and move to walk around the white car to climb inside and escape. "I'll be sure to tell him you were a big help. Thank you."

"What the fuck just happened?" His eyes are narrowed on my face, his thumbs tucked in the loops of his jeans.

"I don't know what you're talking about."

"Yes you do. You'd loosened up a bit, and then suddenly you turned back into the ice queen."

I'm not an ice queen! I'm a fucking human being, but I'll never let you or people like you see me as vulnerable ever again!

"Have a good day, Leo."

"Hey." He blocks my path to the driver's door, and tips my chin up to look him in the eye. "What did I say?"

I shake my head and back away, needing the space. God, he's like an effing magnet.

He watches me closely for a moment and then shrugs. "Okay. Drive safe. Take that in to the shop tomorrow." He walks back to his car, lowers himself gracefully behind the wheel and waits for me to drive off ahead of him.

Who knew that a rock star as famous as he is could be a gentle-man?

Weird.

I offer him a wave and drive away, exhaling for the first time in thirty minutes. That is one sexually potent man. No wonder he's so damn famous.

And I am never going down that path again.

* * *

Olivia is perhaps the most perfect baby ever born, and she gets all her charm, intelligence and good looks from her auntie

Sammie.

And no one else on the face of the Earth had better ever call me Sammie.

I'm not usually one to cuddle babies, but oh how I adore this little girl. We are all gathered at my mom and dad's house, and by all, I mean the whole crew. All of the Montgomerys are here with their kids, Luke and Nat and Livie, my youngest brother, Mark. Even Brynna is here with her girls.

Will has tugged Meg into his lap on the couch and they're laughing intimately. He glances up at me and winks and I feel a glow in the pit of my stomach. To think that just two years ago family dinners consisted of just the five of us. How boring! Now we have this beautiful extended family. I wouldn't change a thing, even if it did lose me my job last week.

"Livie, you're the most beautiful girl in the room. Yes, you are." The sweet nine-month-old giggles as I blow raspberries on her neck and clutches my hair in her tiny fist. "Uh oh... let go of my hair, sweetie."

She giggles some more and tugs my blonde strands into her mouth. "Ew. Do you know how much product is in my hair, girl-friend? It's definitely not edible."

"Everything is going in her mouth these days," Nat mutters and sits next to me on the floor, our backs are resting against the love seat. "She's also slobbering like it's going out of style. I think she's cutting more teeth."

As if on cue, Livie offers us a big grin, proudly showing us her four front teeth and we laugh at her.

"She's so sweet." I kiss her cheek.

"Yeah, she is." Nat's green eyes shine as she looks from her daughter to me. "I hope the next one is too," she whispers.

What? I gasp and almost drop the baby. "You're not...?" I whisper back to her and she offers me a small smile and a tiny nod, and then smiles lovingly over at Luke who has been watch-ing us.

"When are you going to announce it?" I ask. Another baby!

"After dinner, I think," she replies as Luke sits next to me on my other side and takes Livie from my arms.

"Hi baby girl," he kisses her forehead and Livie lights up from the inside at seeing her daddy. "So, did she tell you?" he asks softly so only I can hear.

"Yeah. Luke, I'm so happy for you."

His soft blue eyes turn to mine, and I can read his thoughts. He waited so long for this kind of happiness. He deserves every smile, every wonderful moment his family brings him.

"Thank you," he murmurs and kisses Liv's head again. "I can't wait anymore, baby."

Natalie giggles. "Go ahead then."

"Everyone, I have news." Luke stands easily, the baby propped on his forearm and addresses the room. Everyone quiets and turn their attention to him.

My gaze catches Leo's from across the room. This is the first family event Meg has talked him into attending. I wonder how he's coping.

He winks at me, but I can see tension around his eyes.

We are one overwhelming group, even if you're used to big, loud families, and I know he isn't.

My mom has already started to cry, anticipating what the news is. She's right, as usual.

"Natalie and I," he pulls on Nat's hand so she's tucked into his side. "Are expecting again."

"Holy shit!" Caleb exclaims first, and the room explodes into activity of voices and hugs and cheers.

"Jesus, what are you, a baby factory?" Jules asks with tears in her eyes as she jumps up to hug Nat. "This is what happens when you keep doing all that gross stuff."

"Yeah, well, we want a lot of kids," Natalie murmurs with a grin, her eyes happy. Luke laughs at Jules and kisses Nat square on, no-holds-barred, just for her benefit.

"Ew," she scowls and backs away.

As everyone continues to celebrate the good news, I decide to slip out back and get a breath of fresh air.

I love them all, but they are seriously a lot to take in, and I spend ninety percent of my time alone, so the noise starts to get to me.

I grab a sweater from the mud room and slip out onto the covered back porch on my parents' house, take a deep breath, and lean on the railing looking out into the woods at the back of their property.

"You needed a break too?"

* * *

~Leo~

"Holy shit!" She jumps and spins to look up at me, hand pressed against her chest, bright blue eyes wide, and I have to grip the railing at my hips to keep myself from crossing to her and kissing the hell out of her.

"Sorry, didn't mean to scare you." I smile at her and watch the dialogue of decisions running through that sexy head of hers. Should she smile? Scowl? Straighten those shoulders?

I would love to try to knock that chip off her shoulder.

"I just needed a minute away from the noise." She swallows and looks back out at the trees. "Are you having fun?"

I smirk and cross my arms over my chest. "You have a great family, but it's a lot of activity for me."

"You're used to fifty thousand screaming fans in one room, Leo. I can't imagine this is too much activity for you."

"That's different. It's my job." *It's my life.*

"Well, this group is a lot to handle. Especially at one time." She smiles softly at me and then seems to remember to gather herself and look away.

Interesting.

"Meg wanted me to come, so here I am." It's the truth, and I'd do it again. Meg belongs to this family now, so I'll do what I can to fit in and make her happy.

Aside from my band, Meg-pie is my only family.

"That was nice of you." She sneers over the word *nice* and I can't help but laugh out right and cross to her.

"Believe it or not, doll, I can be nice."

17

She shrugs and watches my hands as I grip the railing again. She watched my hands the other day too, and I can't help but wonder if the tats turn her on, or turn her off.

There is usually no middle ground there, and I don't give a fuck either way.

She takes a deep, shaky breath and looks up into my face, her eyes a little brighter and pink lips slightly parted. Definitely turned on.

I can work with this.

I lift my hand to her cheek but she flinches, and I can't help the surge of pure anger at her reaction. *Who the fuck put that in her?*

"Easy." I pull some lint out of her hair and show it to her before letting it drop to the ground.

"Sorry," she whispers.

"So, what do you do for fun?" I ask.

"Why?" she asks, her eyes narrowed.

"Because I don't know you very well, and we're sharing a porch, so we might as well have a conversation." *God, she's so cold.*

What would it take to warm her up?

"I run." She shrugs.

"Run?" I ask.

"Yes, you know, where you put on sneakers and move quickly in a forward motion?"

She's fucking adorable when she's being sarcastic. She has a great, raspy voice, lower for a woman. She's not squeaky at all. I can't imagine her ever yelling, "Wooot!" when she's drunk.

Her voice is fucking amazing.

"I do understand the concept, yes, but what kind of running do you do?"

"Marathons."

My eyes travel down her small, firm body. She's skinnier than I usually like, but she's toned. I remember how her slim arms felt in my hands the other day and how light she was to pull to her feet.

She loves to run.

So do I.

Maybe we have stuff in common after all. I wonder what kind of music she listens to.

"How long have you been running marathons?" I ask and motion for her to sit beside me on the stairs.

"Since high school. I ran track, and there are some great marathons here in Seattle throughout the year."

"I know, I've run in some of them." I nod and lean back on my elbows.

"You run too?" Her eyes are wide and happy, and I see those walls slowly begin to come down.

"When I find time, yeah. I prefer running outside, but when we're on tour I have to take advantage of the hotel gyms."

"I run outside too. Running on a treadmill is not the same thing." She nods and offers me a half smile and my breath leaves me. Samantha Williams is beautiful, with her light blonde hair and big blue eyes, but when she smiles, she could make the gods weep.

I might have to write a song about her smile.

"I usually run in the mornings before the city wakes up," she adds and I frown down at her.

"Where do you live?" I ask.

"Downtown," she replies vaguely.

"Downtown in which city?" I ask with growing impatience.

"Seattle," she responds and scowls at me. "Why?"

I have to take a deep breath before I yell at her. "Do you mean to tell me that you run in downtown Seattle in the early morning? Do you have a partner?"

"Yes, I run in the early morning. Alone."

I shake my head and run my hands down my face, trying to push down this sudden need to protect this little spitfire.

"That's dangerous," I mutter.

"What, are you gonna be my bodyguard, Mr. Famous Rockstar?" She asks, her voice heavy with sarcasm, and I can't help but laugh at her. She's funny, and smart.

"Actually, yeah, I think I will." Well, that wipes the smirk off her face, and she flounders for a second, her mouth dropping open and then closed, not sure what to say, until finally she pulls herself together and eyes me warily.

"Sure. Okay, you wanna run with me, that's fine. But I won't slow my pace for you, just so you know. You'll have to keep up."

"Okay." I smile at her softly and inch closer to her.

"I usually run at 6:00 a.m., but," she loses her train of thought as her eyes settle on my lips, on my piercing. Yeah, she likes the tats and the metal.

And I like her. A lot.

"But?" I prompt her.

"Huh?" She looks up into my eyes, and then clears her throat and I can't stop the wide grin on my face as I watch her cheeks redden. "But since I don't have to be at work anymore, I figured I'd run at about seven. Is that too early for you? I figure you probably go to bed around that time."

"No, I'm a morning person," I run my finger down her cheek, happy that this time she leans into me rather than flinch. "I'll be at your place at seven. Text me your address."

"I don't have your number," she whispers.

"I have yours," I murmur. "I'll text you so you have mine."

"Why do you have my number?" Her eyes are back on my mouth now, our breathing ragged.

"I asked Meg for it. I was going to call you to check on your car."

"Oh."

She licks her lips and I can't stand it anymore. I cup her smooth neck in my hand, my thumb firmly planted on her chin, and nibble the side of her mouth, sweep across those plump, pink lips and nibble the other side and wonder if the lips of her pussy are this pink.

She sighs with a low moan as I sink into her, persuading her mouth open with my tongue and enjoy her. She's sexy sunshine and I soak her in, enjoying every breath, every tentative flick of her tongue against mine.

She grips onto my hips, anchoring herself against me, and I wrap my other arm around the small of her back, pulling her tightly against me.

Her nipples pucker against my chest and I grin as I slow the kiss down, rub my nose on hers, and kiss her forehead, still holding her.

"What was that?" she whispers.

"If you have to ask, I didn't do it right."

She chuckles, leans her forehead against my sternum and then leans back to look up at me.

She's so small.

"You know what I mean."

I shrug, suddenly uncomfortable. All the men just inside the house would kick my ass if they saw me holding her, kissing the shit out of her, and I couldn't blame them.

But I can't seem to stay away from her.

"You're kissable."

"There you are!"

We jump apart guiltily at the sound of Meg's voice in the doorway. She's smiling happily, not at all angry for finding me in a compromising position with her friend, and I exhale in relief.

"Dinner's ready," Meg tells us.

"Good, I'm starving." I wink at Sam, enjoying the blush on her cheeks. "Seven tomorrow."

"Seven," she murmurs as I saunter inside, looking forward to tomorrow.

Chapter Two

~Samantha~

I plug my earphones into my ears, que up the playlist that I've titled *sweat* on my iPhone and tuck it into my bra, pin my condo key in there as well so it doesn't fall through my cleavage and pull my front door closed behind me. I'm in black yoga pants, a pink tank and a light pink hoodie to ward off the chilly Seattle winter day. I've already stretched, so it's time to run and clear my head.

As I jog down the stairs, rather than take the elevator, I can't help but think of Leo. I knew he wouldn't show up this morning to run. Who the hell was he kidding last night? And what in the name of Moses was up with him kissing me like that?

It's best if I just forget all about that kiss and focus on finding a job.

I jog through the lobby of my building and wave at Frank the doorman; turn left on the sidewalk and set out, Adam Levine's smooth voice heavy in my ears, asking me to give him one more night.

No problem, Adam.

Suddenly, there's movement on my right and I startle, my heart climbs into my throat and I let out a yelp and stumble. Strong hands grip my upper arms, keeping me upright, and I look up into humor-filled gray eyes.

"What the hell?" I stammer and pull the plugs out of my ears.

"I told you I'd meet you this morning."

"I didn't think you'd show," I respond and resume running, tucking my ear buds in my bra.

"Interesting storage system you have there," Leo remarks with a grin, blatantly looking down at my breasts and I can't help but laugh with him.

"I can't carry a purse while I run." I shrug and look at him out of the corner of my eye. Really? Does he have to look this good at seven in the damn morning?

He's much taller than my five foot two; at least a foot taller. He's in basketball shorts and sneakers and a black long-sleeved t-shirt under a red short-sleeved t-shirt. I'm a little disappointed that only the tats on his hands are visible.

I'd like to trace his tattoos, with my fingers and my tongue. *Enough!*

We run in silence for about four blocks.

"Do you want to know how far I'm going?" I ask him, pleased that I'm barely panting.

"Doesn't matter," he responds. He's also barely panting.

Well, hell.

"Why?" I ask.

"Because I'll run as far as you want."

"Okay." I smirk and pick up my pace, my body warmed now and ready to just go. He easily matches my pace. I wouldn't admit it to him right now, but it feels good to have someone next to me while I run. No one has ever been interested in running with me before. It does make me feel safer, even if we aren't talking, just breathing and running side-by-side.

"You can plug your tunes back in if you want." He smiles over at me.

"It's okay." I wave him off and continue running. I kind of like hearing him breathe.

"What were you listening to?"

"It was a Maroon5 song." I smile at him. What is it about this guy that makes me feel so comfortable?

"Maroon5 fan?" He asks.

"Yeah."

"Who's your favorite band?" He asks with a curious grin.

Nash.

I am so not telling him that. Instead I shrug again and try to think of another band. Damn, it's hard when he's so close I can smell him.

He smells bloody fantastic.

"I like all kinds of music. No one band in particular."

"Me too," I hear the smile in his voice. "You were right, running at this time in the morning is great."

"I know. It's relatively quiet, and I don't even mind that it's rainy. Are you ready to speed up again?"

"Of course, I'm just following your lead."

I pick up the pace once again, and we are now running at a fast clip. My breathing is coming fast enough that it's difficult to talk, and I can hear that it's the same for him, so we fall silent and just enjoy the run, the constant thud, thud, thud of our feet hitting the pavement in perfect sync. I don't care that it's drizzling lightly, that my cheeks and the tip of my nose are cold. I wipe my nose on my hoodie and keep going.

I told myself last night while in bed thinking about this sexy rock star and his delicious kisses that I'd give him a run for his money today, but damn if I'm not enjoying myself.

Three miles in, I start to slow down, feeling the burn in my thighs.

"Are you okay?" he asks, concern on his face.

Why is he so nice?

"I'm fine, I thought you might be getting tired," I lie. I'll die before I tell him my thighs burn.

"I'm fine," he frowns.

"Okay," I shrug like I'm fine and pick the pace up again. My thighs and calves cry in protest, but I keep my face blank and instead concentrate on my breathing and sound of our feet.

If he can do it, so can I. I'll go another two miles.

Finally, I breathe an inner sigh of relief when I start to slow. My legs are a little rubbery. I do usually run every morning, but I haven't trained for a marathon in a long time, thanks to my job.

My ex-job.

My body shows the lack of training.

Leo slows with me and leads me into a park with picnic tables. He leads me to the nearest table.

"Sit on top of the table," he directs me, his voice hard.

I follow his orders and frown up at him. "Why?"

"Why did you do that?" He pulls my right leg straight and

begins working his thumbs and fingers into my thigh muscles and I barely hold my moan of pleasure in.

Dear God he has great hands.

"Do what?"

"You obviously went farther than you're used to. Your legs are shaking."

"I'm fine." I set my jaw and try to pull out of his grip, but he leans in and braces himself on his hand at my hip, his face a few inches from mine and tight with anger.

"Don't ever lie to me, sunshine. I don't ever want you to run until your legs give out on you like this again. The only time your legs will shake like this is if I'm inside you."

My mouth drops open and my eyes go wide. He glares down at me for another heartbeat and then resumes his work on my legs, pampering them and massaging them.

When was the last time someone wanted to take care of me? I don't even remember.

If I'm inside you.

Damn.

As tempting as that sounds, that just can't happen.

He rubs my other leg, and as I start to feel better, I pull away from him and stand up.

"Thanks, I'm fine." I can't meet his eyes. It's too easy to like this guy, to want to give in to his touch and his kindness.

He's family.

He's a celebrity.

Not going there.

He walks with me back toward my condo. We ran in a circle, so my place isn't far. As we pass my favorite café, Leo grips my elbow to pull me to a stop and I can't help the flinch as I pull away.

His eyes go hot as he scowls down at me. I clear my throat. He's watching me, like he wants to ask me something, but he just sighs.

"Let's grab some breakfast." He gestures to the café and loses his scowl. I shouldn't spend any more time with him. But the thought of going home with no job to go to and really nothing planned for today doesn't excite me.

"Okay."

He leads me to a booth and we settle in across from each other.

"Coffee?" the waitress asks as she approaches the table.

"Sure," Leo responds.

"No thanks," I murmur and grab the menu. "Just orange juice."

"No coffee?" Leo asks as the waitress leaves.

"No," I wrinkle my nose in disgust and read the menu, as if I don't already know what I want. "I hate coffee."

"You do realize that you live in Seattle, right?" He chuckles and takes a sip of his black coffee. "I think enjoying coffee is a law."

"Don't call the coffee police. I never developed a taste for it. I love this place." I close the menu and sit back in my chair and can't avoid looking at him anymore.

My insides do a double flip. It should be illegal to look like him. His hair is wet, but his style is a messy feaux-hawk anyway, so it looks fine. He's casual in his running clothes, tattooed hands wrapped around his mug, and it's easy to forget that he's a celebrity.

He's just a guy.

The waitress brings my juice and takes our orders and leaves us.

"So." He leans back and braces an elbow on the back of the booth. "Why aren't you working today?"

"How do you know I'm not?" I ask.

"You said last night that you're not working any more. Why not?" His eyes narrow slightly, and he's watching me closely.

No lying.

"I got fired," I answer and take a sip of juice, trying to clean the bad taste that word left behind.

Fired.

His eyebrows climb into his hairline in surprise. "Why?"

I shrug and look down at my juice. I don't want to tell him this.

He leans in and takes my hand in his and I can't stop the instinctual jump that comes with being touched.

What is wrong with me?

"Why do you flinch every time I touch you?" he asks in a low, tight voice.

"I don't know," I whisper.

"Look at me." His voice leaves no room for argument, so I look up into his angry gray eyes. "Tell me."

I shrug again and shake my head. "It's stupid. I'm no victim, Leo. You don't know me well, but I would think you'd know me well enough by now to know that I don't take shit from anyone."

"Okay, go on." He keeps my hand in his and rubs his thumb over the back of my hand.

God, that feels good.

"I don't want to talk about it." And that's the truth.

"Okay, fair enough. We'll save it." He smiles reassuringly, but doesn't release my hand.

Where is our food?

Not that I'm hungry now, but I'd really like to have my hand back. He runs his thumb over my knuckles again, sending a tingle through me. I slide my hand out and away from his against the table and grip my juice in my hands. My hand is cold not just because of the cool juice but because of the loss of contact.

He smiles softly, and I find myself smiling back.

"You are beautiful when you smile, Sam."

"Um, thank you."

"Tell me about your job," he demands and sits back as our food is delivered.

"I was the editor at Seattle Magazine for eight years." I sprinkle pepper on my omelet and take a bite.

"That's a long time."

"Yeah, I liked it. I was good at it."

"So what happened?"

"About a year ago, my boss wanted me to run a piece on Luke. He figured since Luke's my brother, I should be able to get an exclusive with him, his new wife, run a spread in the magazine."

"But you're not a reporter," Leo interrupts with a frown.

"No, but he wanted me to make an exception, since he knew I wouldn't let anyone else do it." I lower my fork to my plate and take a sip of juice. "I told him absolutely not." I shake my head as I remember the anger on my boss's face when I told him I wouldn't do the piece.

"What made you tell him no?" Leo asks.

"Luke is fiercely private. There is no way in hell I'd put him in my magazine. Besides, it's insulting to ask me to write a piece on my family, and then get pissed when I say no." I scowl, pissed all over again.

"Okay, so what does that have to do with you getting fired now?" He asks and eats his pancakes.

"How can you eat pancakes and stay thin?" I ask before thinking.

He smirks, that piercing catching my eye. "Genetics."

"Lucky bastard," I mutter, earning a belly laugh from him and my whole being just stills.

My God, he's amazing when he laughs.

"Anyway," I continue, shaking myself awake. "Last week the same boss came to me and ripped me a new asshole for not telling him before that I'm linked to Will Montgomery through my family."

"Fuck," Leo whispers.

"He wanted me to pull some strings, get an exclusive set up for the magazine, and again I refused." I shake my head and push my plate away, too angry to eat. "Leo, they're my family. I'm not ever going to use them to further my career. Ever."

"What did he do to you?" He asks quietly. His fingers have gripped his coffee mug tightly in anger on my behalf.

"He yelled, called me a pussy." I smirk as Leo takes my hand in his again. "I said, 'No, Bob, I *have* a pussy. I understand if you don't know the difference.'"

"Good for you." Leo chuckles. "I bet he didn't like that."

"No, he wasn't impressed." I sigh and absently trace the letters on Leo's fingers. "He said that I wasn't a team player, and if I'm not willing to go the extra mile for the good of the magazine, then maybe I shouldn't be with the company anymore."

I bite my lip, tracing the ink on his hand now. "Maybe he's right," I whisper. "I loved that stupid job."

"What does your family say?"

My gaze jerks to his and my stomach twists painfully. "They don't know. Please don't say anything."

"Why don't they know?" He frowns.

"Because, they don't need to worry about me, and I don't want them to feel obligated to help me. I'm fine. I'll figure it out. I have job offers in other cities, but I don't want to move away from my family. Stupid, huh?"

He turns his hand over and grips my own tightly. "It's not stupid. This is your home. I missed it too."

"Why are you home?" I ask, enjoying him. He's so damn easy to talk to. Maybe too easy. I probably shouldn't be talking so much, but I can't talk to my family about this stuff.

They'd freak the hell out.

"I missed Meg. Tired of the road. I needed a break."

"How long since you had a break?" I ask and sip my juice.

He laughs humorlessly. "We've been going non-stop for the better part of five years. The three last tours were back to back, three years long."

"Three years of traveling?"

"Yeah."

"No wonder you're tired."

He nods and smiles, but his eyes suddenly look bone-tired. Weary.

"You ready?" He asks.

Not really.

"Sure." He pulls me out of the booth, pays the check and leads me back out to the sidewalk and toward home.

"How are your legs?" He asks casually as we walk down the busy sidewalk. The city is waking up.

"Better, thanks."

"I mean it, don't do that again."

"I'll do whatever I please," I retort.

"Stubborn woman," he mutters and glares down at me. I can't help but laugh.

"Gee, I've never heard that before. I'm so easy going." I flutter my eyelashes at him playfully.

"Smart ass."

We approach the front door to my condo.

This could be awkward.

He just pulls me in for a hug, wraps those strong arms around me and pulls me into him, against his chest and rocks me back and forth for just a moment. I feel him kiss my head and frown.

What is this?

"I'll see you tomorrow morning," he whispers and pulls away, his gray eyes soft and a smile on those lips. "Are you sure you don't have a favorite band?" he asks hopefully as he backs toward his car.

I laugh and shake my head. "Yeah… Matchbox Twenty is pretty good."

"You slay me." He grips both hands over his heart.

"Go home," I tell him with a smile and pull the door open, step into the warm lobby and look back as he lowers himself into his car. He winks and waves as he pulls away.

I am in so much trouble.

Chapter Three

~Leo~

"What are your weekend plans?" I ask Sam as we jog up her street. It's Friday, and we've run together every morning this week. Monday set the tone. We run, we have breakfast, I walk her home and leave.

Jesus, I want to kiss her again.

But I think she needs a friend more than anything, and damn if I don't like her. When she forgets to keep those walls erected around her and loosens up a bit she's funny as hell and fun to talk with.

And it's certainly not a hardship to watch her run in her little yoga pants and tank. She has a strong, lean body.

I wonder what those legs would feel like wrapped around my waist.

"Every day is a weekend, Leo," she responds dryly, bringing me out of my fantasy. "But I think I'm meeting up with Nat and Jules for coffee tomorrow afternoon."

"You don't drink coffee."

She laughs; her big blue eyes light up and she wrinkles her adorable nose at me. "You clearly don't understand the girl definition of having coffee."

"Enlighten me." We're both starting to breathe heavily now. When we started this on Monday I was sure that our little runs wouldn't challenge me, but Sam is a strong runner.

"We'll meet at a coffee shop, buy a beverage, and gossip for a few hours."

"What do you talk about?" I ask, although I really don't care. I just want to hear that sexy, raspy voice of hers.

"I can't tell you that. It's girl stuff."

"C'mon, I won't tell anyone. Swear." I cross my heart and

grin down at her.

"Nope." She shakes her head and smiles some more.

"Fine. Then I won't tell you my gossip." I shrug nonchalantly and grin.

"What gossip?" She asks.

"Not telling."

"Fine." She shrugs and glances at me from the corner of her eye, trying to hold a smile in. Finally, she laughs and shoves me in the shoulder. "You don't have any gossip, you jerk."

Before I can respond, my toe catches on a raised portion of the sidewalk and I feel myself pitch forward, face-first onto the sidewalk.

"Shit!"

My knee catches the most grief from the fall, and I roll out of it and back onto my feet.

"Are you okay?" Sam grips my upper arms in her strong, little hands, her eyes wide and worried, searching my face, panting.

Fuck, she's gorgeous.

"I'm fine. No big." Her eyes take a journey down my body and she gasps when she sees my knee.

"No you're not! You're bleeding."

"It's just a scrape, Sam."

"You're bleeding," she repeats and squats in front of me, examining the tiny scrape. I didn't even know it was there until she said something.

"It doesn't hurt. Come on, let's keep running."

"No way, I'm taking you home and patching you up. I'm so sorry, I didn't mean to push you that hard." She stands and her eyes find mine again, her brows pulled together in a frown.

I laugh and run my thumb over her frown lines, ignoring her little flinch. "I'm fine."

"Come on. Run's over." She takes my hand and turns us back toward her apartment, walking quickly.

Could she be any more adorable?

We reach her building, and for the first time this week, she leads me in with her, waves at the doorman and pulls me into the elevator.

"This is a nice building," I comment, watching her face.

I can't get enough of her face.

"Yeah, I like it."

She's suddenly digging around in her bra, and unfastens her key from her tight sports bra.

"I do love your storage system." And I want to dig around in there.

Sam smirks and leads me to her apartment.

I am not prepared for Sam's apartment.

The space is open and surprisingly big. Light. There are large windows, offering in plenty of sunshine.

I smirk to myself. Appropriate.

But instead of the modern, sleek, cold home I was expecting, I'm met with big, inviting furniture in reds and blues, plants and flowers, fashion magazines on the coffee table, her laptop closed on the couch. There is a gas fireplace in the corner and filmy white curtains on the windows. A piano pushed upright against the far wall.

She plays?

"Come on in. We'll go back to the master bathroom, that's where my first aid kit is." She smiles and throws her key in a bowl by the door.

"This is a great place."

Her smile is wide and as inviting as her home. "Thank you."

"Did you decorate it yourself?" It's so feminine and sweet.

Like her.

"Yeah, it's all me." She laughs and looks around with me. She takes my hand in hers and leads me down a hallway, through her bedroom, all full of soft pillows and fluffy bedding and more reds and grays and white.

Her bathroom is the same. Soft and pretty, but not disgustingly so. It's comfortable.

"Sit on the side of the tub and I'll grab my stuff." She turns her back to me, unzips and removes her pink hoodie, leaving a skin-tight tank over her yoga pants.

My hands clench into fists at my hips on the tub. Fuck, I want to touch her, cup her ass in my hands, push my face between her legs. She turns back to me, her hands full of supplies.

"Okay, this could sting a little," she bites her lower lip and looks up at me as she squats in front of me, just inches from me. "I'm sorry."

"Sam, I'm fine. It doesn't hurt. It's stopped bleeding."

"I don't want it to get infected. I'll just clean it up." She starts gently rubbing it with a warm cloth, cleaning the blood that has already begun to dry on my shin. Her sweet blonde head is bowed over me, concentrating on her task.

And my cock is stirring with every little touch from those amazing white-tipped fingers.

She grips my calf firmly in one hand to steady me, and I flinch, imagining her gripping my dick in the same way.

"Did I hurt you?" She backs away, eyes wide and glances up at me with worry.

"No, sorry."

"I don't think you need a Band-Aid or anything."

"No, I don't think so," I murmur and chuckle. "See? It's no big deal."

"I'm sorry I pushed you," she mutters.

"Sam, I'm fine. I've had much worse, trust me." She sets the cloth aside, and I take her hands in mine before she can stand and move away. I like having her this close.

She smells fucking amazing.

"Why do you flinch when I touch you?" I murmur and tilt her chin back to look her in the eye. She frowns and a light pink blush moves over her cheeks. I run my fingers down her face and trace her bottom lip with my thumb. "Tell me. I enjoy touching you."

She swallows and briefly frowns again. "I guess I'm just not used to it."

"What do you mean?"

"I spend most of my time alone, Leo. Unless I'm around my family, which isn't often, I'm not touched much." She shrugs and looks down. "I'm just not a touchy-feely person."

"Okay." God, she breaks my heart and makes me want to scoop her up and keep her in my arms all the time.

34

That wouldn't go over well with this independent, stubborn woman.

"I bet you're touched all the time." She smirks.

"Why?" I ask. We're still face-to-face, inches apart. I don't want to move.

"Fans. Groupies. People who want a piece of you."

"The fans are great, and yes, can be a bit gropy." I smirk. "I haven't paid attention to the groupies in a long time."

Her wide eyes find mine again. Does she think I fuck every woman who comes on to me?

Okay, I used to, but I was a kid.

"Really?"

I run my fingers down her cheek again and smile down at her. "I let the roadies have them."

"Perk of the job," she returns with a chuckle.

"They don't complain." I agree. "You smell good," I whisper. Her sweet, light scent is all around me. She smells like vanilla with a hint of lemons.

Sunshine.

Her breath catches and her eyes fall to my lips and I know I'm a goner.

"I'm going to kiss you, Samantha," I whisper.

~Samantha~

"Thank God," I whisper, watching his lips, that piercing. He's been touching me all week, a brush here, a hug there, but he hasn't kissed me since that moment on my parents' porch.

I never knew I could crave a kiss so much.

He smirks, his eyes happy and hot, runs those calloused fingertips down both of my cheeks and tilts my head back.

I brace my hands on the tub at his hips as he leans down and lightly, softly brushes his lips over mine. He nibbles the corner of my mouth, and then moves in, grips my ponytail in one fist to keep my head tilted back, his other hand wraps around my neck and cheek and he kisses me like I've never been kissed before.

Like he just can't get close enough to me.

The feeling is entirely mutual.

I wrap my arms around his neck and hold on, moving from a squat to my knees, and lean into him. I swear someone turned the heat up in my apartment. I'm hot and bothered, literally.

He moves his hand from my hair, down my back, and cups my ass in his hand.

He backs away, breathing hard, eyes shining with lust. "Are you seeing anyone?"

I shake my head no and lean in to kiss him again, but he pulls back, his face still so serious.

"Fucking anyone?"

"Brandon moved."

"Who's Brandon?"

"Former fuck-buddy." Why are we talking?

"How long?" He asks, eyes narrowed, watching me.

"A few months." I take his face in my hands and frown up at him. "What's this about?"

"I don't want to move in on another guys territory, and I don't share."

Wow.

"I'm single." I frown again. "But we aren't…"

"Oh, I think we are," he interrupts, his gaze challenging me. He grips my ass harder and stands, easily pulling me to my feet. "I can't let go of you," he whispers.

"You have to let go of me," I whisper back and try to pull away but he scowls and tightens his arms. "Let go," I repeat, stronger.

He sighs and lets go and steps back. His face is grim. His tall, lean body is in his usual black t-shirt and running shorts but the shorts are tented just a bit. I bite my lip and then offer him a small smile before pulling my tank and bra over my head and toss them to the tile floor.

I hear his breath catch, but stay on task, peeling my yoga pants and panties off and onto the floor with my shirt.

He's frozen in place, his stormy eyes wide and his mouth agape, taking me in. His hands are fisting in and out, like he wants to touch me but is trying to hold himself back.

"Your belly is pierced," he whispers almost to himself and I chuckle.

"Yeah." I look down at the diamond hanging from my navel and grin. "It was my one rebellion when I was in high school. *Aerosmith's Cryin'* had just come out, and most girls just had to have their navels pierced."

"It's fucking hot."

"Get naked." I step toward him, but he puts his hand up, his eyes pinned to my own.

"Are you sure?"

"Leo, I don't invite many men to my home. I certainly don't invite many men to get naked. I think I mean it."

He searches my face for a moment longer and then instead of taking off his clothes as directed, he rushes to me, picks me up and sits me on my sink and kisses me silly.

This man can seriously fucking kiss.

I catch his piercing in my teeth and pull gently, making him laugh.

"You like it rough, sunshine?" he asks me.

"Yeah, actually, I do."

"Good, you'll get it. You'll get it soft too." He traces my ear with his tongue, sending shivers down my spine.

"Rough works for me."

He bites my ear, hard, making me yelp, then soothes it with his tongue.

"I'll take you hard, and soft, and every way in between." He grips my face in his hands and looks down at me, his nose touching mine. "I'm going to fuck the shit out of you."

Oh God, yes!

"And I'm going to make love to you until you're shaking and don't remember who you are."

His big hands glide up my arms and then cup my breasts gently, his thumbs tweak my nipples, making them pucker even more than they were, and I didn't think that was possible.

He's found a direct line to my pussy, and I squirm.

I push my hands under his shirt and find warm skin and smooth muscle.

37

"Want to see you," I murmur and nibble his bottom lip, next to his piercing.

He steps back and reaches an arm over his head, grips his shirt at the shoulder blade and pulls it over his head in that sexy way men do. He shucks off his running shorts, toes off his shoes, and there he is.

Buck ass naked.

He steps back between my knees, resting his hard erection against me and kisses me some more. I don't think I've been kissed this much in my whole life.

I like it.

"God, you're beautiful," he murmurs. I look up to find him staring at my back in the mirror and smile.

"So are you."

"I'm a guy."

"So?"

"I'm not beautiful." He gives me a mock glare and then bends down to suck my nipple.

"Your art is," I reply breathlessly and twine my fingers in his hair. "You know, I have a bed."

"Good idea."

Before I can hop off the sink, he lifts me easily and carries me to the bed, pulls the covers back and climbs onto the bed still cradling me to his front, my arms and legs wrapped around him.

He lays me down and latches on to my nipple again, his hands roaming over my torso, my arms… *everywhere.*

Suddenly he flips me over.

"Good idea," I mutter and try to lift my ass in the air, but he laughs and pushes me back down.

"Not yet, sugar, I'm enjoying you."

"Just do it. I'm ready." I squirm under him, ready to feel him inside me, but he covers me with that lean body of his, kisses my shoulder, and nibbles my ear.

"Relax."

"Just fuck me, Leo."

He lifts off of me and turns me onto my back again, his face serious. "No. I'm not going to *just fuck you.*"

"Fine." I try to roll away, but he holds onto me.

"I'm going to enjoy you, damn it." He kisses me hard, demanding, rough, pulls my hair free of its band and plunges his fingers into it as he makes love to my mouth. I can't help but run my hands over his arms, his shoulders, reveling in the smooth skin, despite the riot of color of ink that covers them.

"Enjoy this, Sam," he whispers and kisses me softly, completely different from his kiss a moment ago, sending me spiraling into a tailspin.

Just when I think I've figured him out, he changes it up on me.

I can't have sex with him in this position.

He kisses down to my breasts, nibbling and sucking and then moves down to my navel.

"I fucking love this," he mutters and kisses it chastely.

"I'm glad." I smile down at him. He grins back, kisses it again and then moves south.

"Pink," he whispers.

"What?"

"Your pussy is pink. I've wondered if your pussy is as pink as your lips since the day I met you."

"What?" I lift up onto my elbows and stare down at him, open-mouthed.

"It is," he assures me and nuzzles it with his nose, and then spreads my thighs wider, opening me up to him, and licks me from my folds to my clit, in one long lick.

"Oh God," I groan and lay back, flinging an arm over my face. Oral sex always makes me nervous.

It's too intimate.

But I don't want to tell him to stop. He's too damn good at it.

He pulls my labia into his mouth and sucks with little pulses, pushes his hands under my ass to tilt my pelvis up for him, and plunges that delicious tongue deep inside me.

I cry out and grip the cool sheets in my fists, writhing against his face. He gentles his strokes, and then closes his mouth and rubs that metal against my lips and up over my clit, catching it in the loop, and pulls up, then sucks my nub into my mouth and sucks.

Hard.

I plant my heels on his back and come apart, pushing my pelvis up, and begging him to never stop.

Holy fucking hell that piercing is going to kill me.

He releases my clit and kisses it gently, and as I come down from my high, he gently kisses and massages my pussy with his fingers, crooning to me, but I can't understand the words.

Finally, he climbs back up my body, leaving wet kisses in his wake, and settles himself between my legs. He pushes my hair off my face and kisses me softly.

I can taste myself, and it turns me on all over again.

"I taste good on your lips," I whisper. His eyes flare in lust.

"You are amazing, sunshine."

"Why do you call me that?" I ask and slowly thrum my fingers up and down his back. He looks like he's thinking about it, a small frown forming between his eyebrows, but he smiles down at me.

"Because of your pretty blonde hair."

"Huh." I rotate my hips, and feel his erection against my core. "You need to wrap that bad boy up, my friend. There are condoms in the bedside table." *And I need you off of me.*

"I thought you didn't invite men here." He pushes off of me and opens the drawer, pulls out the condom and rolls it on.

"I *rarely* invite men here, and it's good to be prepared." Before he can climb back on top of me, I straddle his lap; knees planted at his hips and wrap my arms around his neck. His hands immediately roam all over my back and I moan softly.

It feels so good to be touched!

He grips my hips and lifts me gently until the head of his beautiful cock is poised to sink inside me.

"Are you ready?" He asks against my lips.

I kiss him and push down slowly, groaning with him as he impales me all the way to my cervix.

"Fucking A you feel good, sunshine."

"Mmm." I agree and begin to move, clenching around him, riding him.

"Fuck," he whispers again and looks down to watch. "That's

sexy."

He leans back on his elbows, bends his knees, and begins to buck, pushing in and out of me hard.

It's the most intense thing I've ever felt.

"God, Leo," I cry and lose myself in him; riding him so hard my legs start to shake. He pushes one hand between us and worries my clit with his thumb, and I cry out.

"That's it, baby, come for me." He pushes harder with his hips, presses harder with his thumb, and I come undone at the seams, crying out his name.

He sits up again and grips my hips firmly, impaling himself all the way, and follows me into his own orgasm, growling as he spills himself inside me.

"Damn, baby," he whispers and pushes my hair behind my ears. "You are incredible." He kisses my breasts, my collarbones, and then my chin.

"You're no amateur yourself," I murmur and chuckle when he bites my neck playfully.

"Let me stay," he whispers, his eyes happy and on mine. I can't resist him.

I nod happily and twine my arms around his neck. "Stay."

Chapter Four

I wake to my bedroom falling dark with shadows and a cold bed. We fell asleep after a particularly vigorous round of crazy sex, but I didn't plan to sleep so long. I sit up and glance around the room, spying Leo's shirt still on the bathroom floor and suddenly realize I smell bacon.

Bacon in the evening?

I climb out of the bed, throw on a black silk robe and follow my nose. My feet come to an abrupt stop at the entrance to the kitchen, and I'm mesmerized.

Leo Nash, rocker superstar, is in my kitchen cooking.

Half naked.

He pulled jeans on -*where did he get those?*- but they're loose as though he didn't button them, and he's clearly not wearing his underwear. He has the most amazing dimples above his ass.

His shoulders are wide, but lean, like the rest of him. He's muscular, although not like the Montgomerys. He has a runner's body.

His hair is a mess from my fingers, and I want to bury them back in there and hold on to him.

He glances back at me with a half-smile and my stomach clenches.

Shit, I'm in so much trouble.

"Hey, sleepy-head."

"Hey." I walk to him, wrap my arms around his waist and kiss his back, between his shoulder blades. He's so tall next to me. Or I'm short. "You cook too?"

"A bit. You had breakfast stuff, so I dug in. I hope that's okay."

"Mmm, I'm starving."

Don't get used to this, Sam.

"Meow."

"Hey, little one," I grin and scoop my fluffy white cat into my arms, nuzzling his face.

"You have a cat." He glances at me, one eyebrow raised, as he scrambles the eggs.

"I do. Leo, meet Levine."

"Hello there." He pauses and smirks. "Levine as in Avril or Adam?"

"He's a boy, Leo."

"How did you come up with that name?" He asks with a laugh, scooping the eggs onto our plates.

"I guess I just have a thing for tattooed rock stars." I grin and shrug.

"What was wrong with Nash?" He asks with a mock scowl.

"Oh, nothing. They're okay, I guess."

"I will hurt you later," he laughs and then shakes his head.

"What?" I ask and set the cat on his feet.

"Never pegged you for a cat owner."

"It's one cat. I'm not the crazy cat lady or anything." I hop up onto the counter next to the stove and watch his tattooed hands as he deftly makes our meal and the cat threads his way through Leo's legs, purring.

"Well, the jury's still out about the crazy part," he winks at me and I slap his arm.

"Don't be a douche bag. I was thinking about having sex with you again."

Leo laughs and plates our food, handing me mine. "Wanna sit at the table?" I ask.

"I'm fine." He leans against the island opposite me, crosses his jean-clad legs and digs into his food. He's watching me as I eat, but we don't say anything; just watch the other with a smug smile on our lips.

"What are you thinking?" he finally asks.

"How'd you get that scar?" I ask and point to his abdomen with my fork. He has stars tattooed on his hips, right over those incredibly sexy V lines, and he has a surgical scar just above the one on the right.

"Appendectomy," he shrugs. "Not a very exciting story."

"I bet it hurt."

"It almost killed me."

"What?" My eyes find his and I stop eating. "What do you mean?"

"I was a teenager, in a foster home. I told the lady I lived with my stomach hurt, but she told me to just go lie down." He shrugs again and takes a big bite of bacon. "When I started throwing up and ran a temp of about one-oh-four, she took me to the ER. I had to have emergency surgery."

He's concentrating on his plate, not looking me in the eye, trying to play it off like it's no big deal, but I can see that it is a big deal.

Of course it is.

I set my mostly-consumed plate into the sink and hop off the counter top, take his plate from him and set it on the island behind him and wrap my arms around his middle, rest my cheek on his chest, and hold him.

Aside from Olivia, I've never felt the need to cuddle anyone in my life.

He wraps his arms around my shoulders and hugs me close, plants his lips on the top of my head, and takes a deep breath.

"I'm sorry," I whisper and kiss his chest. I lean back just a bit so I can see his tats up close while I'm not in the throws of passion.

Who has time to examine tats when he's inside me?

Not I.

There's script that says *Never Kill What Burns Inside* over a heart held in two hands with flames. It's totally rockstar, but I have a feeling it means more than that. Maybe I'll ask him about it later.

My eyes travel down his torso, over his sculpted washboard abs, to his stars, and damn, I just want to lick them.

I look up into his face to find him patiently watching me with those stormy gray eyes. His teeth are clenched, a muscle twitches in his jaw, but otherwise his body is completely calm and quiet, watching me explore him. In this moment, I forget about Leo Nash the rock god, and he's just a man, standing in my kitchen with me.

I pull my hands around his waist, brushing along the top of his jeans, and follow the outline of the stars with my thumbs.

He sucks a breath in through his teeth and his stomach seizes, and I grin to myself and sink down to my knees, so his hips, and the erection straining against the zipper of these sexy, ripped jeans, are eye level with me.

"Sam," he begins but the words catch in his throat when I lean in and lick the star on the right side, following the path my thumbs took moments ago, and then lave the scar from his surgery. "Sonofabitch," he whispers.

I plant tiny kisses over the blue and red ink, over the white scar of the incision, like I'm kissing it better. I kiss my way along his lower belly, over his pubis, and switch sides, paying equal attention to the other star, enjoying the muscular line of his hip.

Any woman who says that V in a man's hips isn't sexy is a fucking liar.

Leo gently tucks my hair behind my ears as I run my hands up the outside of his thighs and to the zipper of his jeans and lower it slowly, allowing the denim to fall off his hips to his ankles and his impressive cock to spring free.

He pushes my robe apart and I let it fall off my shoulders and to the floor.

I grip his cock in my fist and pump up and down loving how it continues to harden in my hand, and lean in to lick a drop of dew off the end.

"Samantha," he whispers and buries his hands in my hair, gripping the strands in his strong hands as though he needs an anchor. I look up as I sink down over him, pushing him all the way to the back of my throat and then I grip him tightly with my lips and pull all the way up.

His eyes are on fire, watching me intently, panting as if we'd just run three miles. I smile up at him and repeat the motion, up and down on him, teasing him with my tongue and the tips of my teeth, and then sucking vigorously.

"Fucking A, Samantha," He pulls me to my feet and into his arms, stomping out of the kitchen.

"Where are we going?" I ask with a chuckle as I wrap my

arms around his neck and nuzzle his neck.

"Bedroom. I'm going to have to stock every room of your apartment with condoms," he mutters and sets me down on the bed, pulls a foil packet out of the drawer and makes quick work of suiting up as he crawls onto the bed beside me.

I straddle him and run my hands up his arms to link our fingers and pin them to the bed beside his head, raise my hips and impale myself on his hard shaft.

"Fuck, you're wet."

"You sort of turn me on," I respond with a sassy grin.

"I'm so happy to hear that, sunshine," he replies sarcastically and chuckles and then groans as I grip my intimate muscles around him and pull up, then push back down and begin to ride him, circling my hips, grinding my clit against his pubis, and I feel the pressure begin to build, my stomach tightens, and I break out into a sweat.

"Damn you feel good," I whisper and move faster, chasing the orgasm that's almost in my reach.

"Let go of my hands, Sam."

I comply and he palms my breast with one hand and his talented thumb finds my clit and sends me over the edge in an overwhelming climax. Before I can resurface, he lifts me off him and flips me onto my stomach, pulls my ass in the air and shoves himself into me roughly.

"Oh God, yes!" I cry and push my palm against the headboard as I rock back onto him. He grips my hips tightly and fucks me hard, growling and panting, in the most deliciously primal way I've ever experienced.

"Fuck, fuck, fuck." He chants as he pulls me back onto him and empties himself inside of me.

I don't think I've ever come that hard in my life.

Jesus, what is he doing to me?

He collapses on top of me, pushing me into the mattress, and I don't even care if I can breathe. I think he may have just killed me anyway.

And what a way to go.

He slowly pulls out of me and rolls to the side and off the bed to discard the condom, then crawls onto the bed and covers us both with the blankets, tucking me against his side, with my head on his chest.

"Meow." Levine jumps onto the bed, eyeing Leo for a second and then nudges Leo's hand with his head.

"He likes you," I whisper and smile as Leo pets his head.

"Are you okay?" He asks.

"I'm fantastic, thanks. You?"

Leo laughs and shoos the cat aside, who then flips his tail at him and curls into a ball at the end of the bed and begins to take a bath.

"Fantastic is a good description." He kisses my forehead lightly.

"Are you leaving now?" I ask, ready to put some distance between us, yet hoping he says he wants to stay.

He stills for a moment, and then tips my chin back so I'm looking him in the eye. "Do you want me to leave?"

"You can stay." I shrug. "I might have a use for you in the morning."

He lowers his face to mine and nibbles my lips softly, then rubs his nose against mine. "I want to stay."

"Okay." He's running his fingers up and down my back, making me sleepy.

"You don't have any tattoos," he murmurs sleepily.

"Nope," I confirm.

"No desire to?" He asks.

"Nope."

"Gee, you're so chatty." He chuckles. "Why not?"

"I don't know, I guess I just never found anything that I wanted on me forever." I shrug and trace one of his stars again with my fingertip. "I like yours. I've seen them in photos, of course, but they're better in person."

"Thanks."

"Are you gonna get more?" I ask.

"Maybe." He shrugs. "Probably."

"They photograph well."

"That's what I'm told." He chuckles and kisses my forehead again.

"Are you starting to miss it?" I ask, and he doesn't even pretend that he doesn't know what I'm talking about.

"Sometimes, but I'm enjoying the break. I'm writing music, and I talk to most of the band just about every day."

"You're close to them." It's not a question.

"Yeah, they're my brothers." He turns on his side so we're facing each other, wraps his arm around my low back and holds me close. "We spend a lot of time together."

"Are any of them married?" I ask, although I already know the answer. Nash is my favorite band. I've seen interviews.

"Yeah, a couple are. It's not easy for them to be away from their families for long stretches. We're all enjoying the break."

"Can't they take their families on tour with them?"

"They do part of the time."

I nod and trace his jaw with my finger. "How have you managed to stay single?" I ask. "You're the most eligible rockstar bachelor in the US right now."

He frowns and then laughs and me. "Whatever."

"You are." I push his shoulder and smile at him. "Spill it."

"I don't ever want to get married," he replies, his eyes sobering. This surprises me.

"Never?"

He shakes his head, watching me closely.

"You don't necessarily have to be married to be committed to someone," I remind him.

"My job is really hard on relationships, Sam. Trust is hard to maintain, on both sides. I'm gone a lot." He shrugs and looks sad for a second, but covers it up with a grin. "Why are you single?"

I just had to go there, didn't I?

"Never been even close to marriage, and don't intend to be." I withdraw automatically, school my features, and give him a bland look.

And piss him the fuck off.

"You're lying." His gray eyes heat.

"No, I'm not." I shake my head and focus on tracing the letters on his chest.

"Why did you just pull away?" He asks, watching me closely.

KRISTEN PROBY

I continue to trace the ink on his chest, and he stills me by gripping my hand in his.

"I'm sorry I asked," I whisper.

"Sam, we're just having a conversation." I shake my head, but he leans in and kisses me softly and I relax instinctively.

He calms me, and that makes me nervous.

"I was in a relationship that ended very badly," I whisper. "I don't trust people easily, and don't see myself ever trusting anyone enough to commit to them like that."

"Look at me."

Instead, I lean in and rest my forehead against his sternum.

"Look at me, sunshine." His voice is almost light and I risk a peek.

He's smiling.

"Am I funny?" I ask and give him a mock glare.

"Actually, yes, you can be." He continues to grin, and I just want to lean in and grip that piercing in my teeth and tug. "This might sound selfish, but I'm glad it didn't work out with the other guy because then I wouldn't be here with you, and I've never enjoyed myself more."

I feel my mouth drop and eyes widen. That might be the nicest thing anyone has ever said to me.

How pathetic am I?

"But I also want to kick the shit out of him for hurting you."

"Maybe I hurt him," I reply with a smirk.

He watches me closely and then exhales as he shakes his head. "No, he hurt you." He pulls me against him and wraps his arms around me tightly. "Did he ever hit you?" He asks, his voice just a whisper.

"No," I respond immediately. "And I don't want to talk about it."

"Okay."

"So, who's your favorite band?" He asks, making me laugh.

"Who's *your* favorite band?" I ask.

"I asked you first."

I squint my eyes like I'm thinking really hard. "U2."

"You are so gonna pay for that." He attacks me with tickles,

49

and I shriek with laughter, and then moan in pleasure as his hands roam over my body.

"I think I like this payment system you have."

"I'm just getting started, sunshine."

Chapter Five

I'm a moron. What the fuck was I thinking? Since when do I let my loins make the decisions?

Because that's exactly what happened yesterday. And last night. And again this morning.

I shift uncomfortably in the drivers seat of my car, the soreness between my legs reminding me exactly where Leo spent the majority of the past twenty-four hours.

The man is just sex on a stick.

So much for not getting involved. I'd been doing so well all week, keeping him at a distance. And then he had to go and look so right there in my apartment, and I just couldn't keep my hands off of him.

But not again. No, for the sake of my sanity, and keeping my family relatively drama-free, last night was a one-time deal.

I'll find another fuck buddy to play with once in a while and things will go back to normal.

So why does the thought of that make me sick to my stomach?

I park outside the coffee shop near Alki beach in West Seattle. We decided to meet near Nat and Luke's place this time, which suits me just fine. The view here is amazing, even on a dark, gloomy day like today.

I wrap my black scarf around my neck and move quickly through the wind and rain to the café and immediately spot Nat, Jules and Meg at a table near the back.

"Hey!" I wave at them and order a chai tea and then join them.

"How's it going?" Jules asks and sips her latte.

"Good. How are you guys?" I ask and take a seat.

"We're good, we're talking about Nat and Luke's big move." Meg replies and points to Natalie.

"What big move?" I ask and sip my tea.

"We're moving." Natalie responds and bites her lip.

"What?" *What the fuck?* "Where the hell are you moving to? If you say L.A., I'll kick your ass."

"No." She waves me off and shakes her head, a wide grin on her pretty face. "We're just moving to a bigger house."

"When?" Jules asks and takes a bite of a scone. How can she eat like that and stay thin? I think I hate her.

"We just started looking. I don't know." Nat shrugs. "I'm hoping before the new baby comes because I won't want to deal with it after it's born."

We all nod in agreement and sip our drinks.

"I'll help you look, if you want," I offer. "I like to shop for anything."

"Me too!" Jules agrees happily.

"Not me." Meg shakes her head. "I love you guys, but I hate looking at houses. It's like buying a car. Boring as hell."

"I'll let you guys know when and if there's something to look at. So far Luke hasn't found anything he likes, so he's making noises about having something built."

"Sounds like my brother," I mutter with a chuckle. "He'll build you guys something fabulous."

"Yeah, but I want to move in the next six months, so we'll see how that goes." Nat shifts in her chair and pushes her muffin away without taking a bite. "Enough about that, it makes me nervous. Meg, how's Leo settling in? Luke mentioned he's staying at your old place?"

Great, my turn to be nervous.

I take another sip of my tea and keep my face blank. I'm so not telling my friends what Leo and I have been up to.

No way.

"He's good," Meg replies and then frowns. "But he's been really moody the past week or so."

"Broody musician?" Jules asks with a wink.

"Not usually." Meg shrugs. "He usually acts this way when he's stuck on a girl. But he's even more moody than usual. If he is seeing someone, and I meet her, I'm gonna kick her ass for making him so grouchy."

I choke on my drink, sputtering and coughing, and Nat leans

over to smack my back.

"You okay?" She asks.

"Fine," I choke out and take another sip. "Sorry, just went down wrong."

"So, you think he's seeing someone?" Nat asks Meg.

Please, God, change the subject!

"I don't know, he won't tell me. So, I told him to stop being a moody asshole." Meg smiles smugly.

"I think that you might be the only person on the planet who can tell Leo Nash to stop being an asshole," Jules remarks.

"He's my brother. Sam can relate." She smiles at me and I nod, trying to push down the guilt.

Why the fuck do I feel guilty?

Okay, maybe because I just let her brother fuck my brains out and I'm not gonna tell her.

This only confirms for me that not seeing Leo any more is the best decision for everyone.

"It's different when it's your brother."

"Do you ever tell Luke to stop being an asshole?" Nat asks me, her green eyes laughing.

"All the time." I salute her with my cup and take a drink and we all laugh.

"How long is he in town for?" Jules asks.

"A while." Meg shrugs and smiles. "I like having him here again. He's staying at my townhouse for now. We actually started working on a song together last week."

"That's awesome, I'm so happy for you." Nat pats Meg on the shoulder.

"Jules, how's Nate?" I ask and effectively change the subject.

"Sexy," she replies and flips her blonde hair back over her shoulder.

"That we knew." Meg rolls her eyes.

"We're good. Busy." Jules shrugs. "Nothing really to report."

During the next hour we gossip about mutual friends and catch up with each other, and I'm relieved that the conversation stays clear of Leo.

I don't like lying to my closest friends, and by not telling them about Leo, I'm lying. It doesn't sit well with me.

"Sam, how's your job?" Meg asks.

Oh good, another lie to feel guilty about.

"Fine. The usual." I shrug nonchalantly and smile.

I am so going to hell for lying to my family.

***

"Hi, baby, did you guys have fun?" Luke asks Nat as we come through their front door and greets her with a kiss, Livie perched on his hip. Livie squeals in delight and reaches for her mama, and I can't help but smile as I watch their little family.

They're adorable.

Nat showers her daughter with kisses and then passes her along to me and then Luke dips her low and plants a big one on her.

I have a very Jules-like compulsion to gag.

"Ew, don't watch that, Livie. You're too young." I carry her to the kitchen, put her in her chair and she immediately reaches for the Cheerios spread on her tray.

"Mmm," she grins as she sticks a Cheerio in her mouth.

"Mmm," I agree.

God, she's adorable.

"Did you put the pretty pink bow in her hair?" I ask Luke with a smirk.

"Uh, no."

"I did before I left." Nat laughs and kisses her baby on the head as she walks past. "Did you two have fun?"

"Always." Luke smiles. It's good to see him smile so much.

He didn't for far too long.

"Nat invited me for dinner." I plop in a chair next to Olivia and push her cereal around on the tray.

"Cool. We're having liver and onions."

"I'm leaving." I brace my hand on the table to stand and Natalie smacks Luke on the arm.

"If we are, I'm leaving with her."

"What are you making?" I ask and give him the big blue-eyed look he can't resist.

"I guess I'm making alfredo." He sighs, knowing it's my favorite.

"Yes!" I pump my fist in the air and offer Olivia a high five, but she just giggles at me.

"So, what do you know?" He asks me like he always does and leans on his elbows on his countertop.

"I know you're a pain in the ass," I reply with a grin.

"Why did you invite her?" He asks Natalie.

"I like her." She shrugs and winks at me.

"She likes me more than she likes you," I tell him smugly.

"No, I guarantee that isn't true, is it baby?" Luke grabs her from behind and nuzzles his nose in her neck and pushes his pelvis against her ass and this time I do gag.

"God, stop it. There's a baby present." I shake my head. "You're disgusting."

"He can't keep his hands off me." Natalie laughs and points at her still-flat belly. "Hence, baby number two."

"You do know what causes that, right?" I ask.

"What?" Luke asks innocently.

"I'm so not having this conversation with you." I shudder violently. "Gross."

He laughs and we settle into a happy, relaxed evening of good food and conversation. I love my brother more than just about anyone else in the world. I trust him. I can be myself with him, and he loves me back.

And I've grown to feel the same about Nat.

I needed this tonight.

When dinner is cleaned up, Nat takes Olivia upstairs for a bath and bed, and Luke hands me a glass of white wine. We're sitting at the breakfast bar of their really impressive kitchen.

He's so damn spoiled.

"So, what's up with you?" he asks.

"Nothing." I take a sip of the crisp, sweet wine. "What's up with you?"

I'm not fooling him. He just stares at me for a minute and then takes a sip of his own wine. He runs a hand through his always-messy blonde hair and scratches his head.

"Don't wanna talk about it?" He asks.

I hate it when he can see through me.

Dumb brother.

And I want to tell him, so badly, about my job and Leo, because I know he'll understand and listen, but I just can't.

"Nothing to talk about."

"Do you need help?" He asks softly, the blue eyes that match mine serious and worried.

"Nope." I repeat and shake my head.

"You worry me, you know."

"I thought I was the older sibling." I wrinkle my nose at him and pat his back. "I'm fine."

"Okay. I'm here." He exhales and tugs my ear and then takes another sip of his wine.

"I know." I'm mortified to feel tears trying to gather in the corners of my eyes, so I quickly change the subject. "So you guys are moving?"

"Yeah, if I can find a place that doesn't suck."

"Which means if you can find a place you love more than this one," I respond with a smirk. "I know you love this house."

"I do." He nods thoughtfully and then his eyes turn to the top of the stairs. "I love them more, and we'll out-grow this house soon."

"I'm not helping you move. You have too much shit." I finish my wine and laugh at his scowl.

"Well, it's a good thing I can afford a moving company."

"Good thing." I agree and smile smugly. "But I'll babysit."

"You're just using me for my kid." He laughs and refills his wine. "Want more?"

"No, I have to go."

"You're leaving?" Nat asks as she jogs down the stairs.

"Yeah, your husband is boring me." I wink at her and pull my jacket and scarf on.

"You're so charming," Luke mutters.

"I know."

I hug them both and head out to my car and feel my phone vibrate in my pocket.

My heart rate picks up at the sight of a text from Leo and I have to remind myself that I don't get to keep him.

He's not mine.

I climb in my car, start the ignition and buckle my belt before I check the text, just to prove to myself that I'm not dying to see him again.

Because I am.

Where are you, sunshine?

God, I love it when he calls me sunshine.

I'm out.

Maybe, if I'm less than warm and friendly, he'll go away.

Can I see you tonight?

Or not.

I do not want to be mean to him, but I can't see him again. The longer I let a physical relationship progress, the harder it will be to stop seeing him later.

I don't know how long I'll be out. I may not come home tonight. You know how it is.

I take a deep breath and shift the car into drive and head toward home. Did I seriously just insinuate that I was with another man while I can still feel the after-effects of having him inside me every time I move?

When I can still practically smell him?

I am not that girl.

My phone chirps with another text and I raise the phone in my shaking hand.

I'll wait.

He'll wait?

Okay, if he wants a fight, I'll give him a fight. Who the hell does he think he is, anyway?

I feel better with my anger simmering to the surface and make the drive home in record time. I park under the building in my spot and take the elevator up to my floor and find Leo leaning against the wall next to my door, his legs crossed at the ankles, reading something on his phone.

He has a plastic bag full of take-out.

"How long have you been here?" I ask as I move past him and

unlock my door.

"Not long," he answers, his voice calm. I refuse to look him in the face.

"*Why* are you here?" I hate how cold my voice sounds.

"I thought I'd bring you dinner." He follows me inside my apartment and closes the door behind him, sets the bag of food on the coffee table and turns to me, shoves his hands in his pockets and rocks back on his heels.

"You should have called earlier. I already had a dinner date." I swallow and look everywhere but at him, my stomach rolling.

"Look at me."

"Leo…"

"Look at me, damn it." My eyes find his and my knees almost buckle at the pain in his stormy gray gaze.

Fuck.

"What do you want from me?" I ask and plant my hands on my hips. "I don't recall making any promises last night."

"What's up with the ice queen act?" His voice is stone hard now. Anger is good. I can work with anger.

"This is just who I am, Leo." I smirk and turn away and he stomps after me.

Just leave!

"Bullshit." He grabs my arm and spins me around to face him. "Talk to me."

"What is there to say?" I pull my arm out of his grip and back away from him. The more distance the better. "Last night was a one time deal, Leo."

"What?" He frowns at me, not believing what I'm telling him.

"Did you think we were starting a relationship?" I smirk at him. "You don't do relationships, remember?"

"You're pissing me off, Samantha." His hands ball into fists at his sides and his eyes are shooting daggers at me and I have to mentally square my shoulders to keep from sinking to the floor.

"I don't know what to tell you," I wave him off like he doesn't matter. "You knew the score. It was just sex. Really good sex," I concede, "But just sex. I finally fucked a rock star. Thanks."

I wink at him and quickly turn away so he can't see how badly it hurts to talk to him like this, to put that hurt his is amazing gray eyes. I pull a bottle of wine out of the fridge and pop off the stopper in the neck, but am suddenly spun around to face him. His eyes are feral, his breath coming in harsh pants, and his hands are gripping my shoulders hard.

"You wanna fuck a rock star, sugar?" Before I can react, he plunges his fingers in my hair and pulls me to him. He kisses me hard, demanding me to open my lips and accept his tongue. He licks and sucks my mouth, bites my lips, and takes some more, and I push on his chest, trying to shove him away, but he holds firm. His hands slide down to cup my face and he pins me with my back against the fridge.

"I didn't fuck you last night," he growls. "But I'll sure as hell fuck you now."

He attacks my mouth with more violence than before, yanks my button down shirt apart, scattering the buttons around the room, and pulls it down my arms and tosses it onto the floor. He unfastens my jeans and peels them down to my knees, spins me around the kitchen until I'm bent over the island and gasps when he sees my underwear.

I'm wearing black lace underwear with ruffles on the ass, and he deftly rips them into two pieces and tosses them aside.

"What the fuck? Those were brand new!"

"I don't give a shit. They were in my way."

"You'd better have a condom on you; I don't know where your dick has been," I bite out, deliberately trying to hurt him, and I know I hit the target square on when he sucks in a breath through his teeth.

I hear him rip open a foil packet, and the next thing I know, he grips my hair hard in one fist and pushes my face down to the counter top, spanks my right cheek, hard, and plunges inside me, all the way.

He spanks me again and then grips my hip, bruising me, and does exactly what he promised. He fucks me.

Hard.

Angry.

Hurt.

And I hate myself for loving the way he feels inside me. For being so damn wet and ready for him that had I not already been sore from him earlier, it wouldn't have hurt me.

But, oh God, it does hurt.

He releases my hair to grip my other hip and pumps himself into me, growling, as he comes, shuddering behind me.

He pulls out, yanks off the condom and tosses it into the trash, zips up and stands behind me, panting.

I can't look at him. I'm so ashamed, and I just want him to *go*.

"Now you've fucked a rock star. How do you feel?"

"Like everyone else you fuck. Used and ready for you to leave," I respond without looking at him.

"Jesus," he whispers, and I hear him scrub his hands over his face. "Stand up."

"Go away, Leo."

"Sam…"

"Go away," I whisper and lean my forehead on the countertop. I will not look at him. I will not talk to him.

If I do, I'll beg him to stay and forgive me, and it's just better if he hates me.

After a long minute, he sighs and walks to the door. I don't look up when I hear the door open, or for a few long minutes after it closes.

I just stay here, leaning against the counter top and let the tears come.

Chapter Six

~Leo~

I shouldn't have left her.

I shouldn't have fucked her against her kitchen island like a complete arrogant asshole.

She shouldn't have been such a bitch. How can someone who looks so sweet turn up the bitchiness so fast? Who the fuck does she think she is?

No woman is worth this bullshit.

I've been sitting in the townhouse for two days. I can't write. I can't sleep.

I'm fucking sick of myself.

So I climbed into my Camero and have been driving around the city, windows down, the hard metal sounds of *The End of Grace* blaring through my speakers, with no destination in mind.

I just need to drive.

I turn a corner and pull through an open gate and stop the car, throw it in park, and cut the engine, the sound abruptly cutting off with it, and stare straight ahead for a few minutes.

Jesus, I can't even think straight.

I blink and look around and realize that I've driven to Meg's place, and she's standing in the doorway, leaning against the door-jamb, arms crossed over her chest, watching me with a frown.

Shit. She's going to bust my balls. But I need to talk to someone, and she's the only one I trust with this.

The guys in the band would razz me for the rest of my life if they knew I was this hung up on a woman.

What is wrong with me?

I climb out of the car, and slam the door. "Why is your gate open?"

"Why do you look like shit?"

"Fuck you." I push my hand through my hair and glare at her and she smirks back at me.

"You're not my type." She loses her pretty smile and holds a hand out for me. "Come on."

I take her hand and follow her into her house. She moved in with Will Montgomery last weekend. I'm glad she's happy. She deserves happiness more than just about anyone I know after the shitty way her life started.

But if he hurts her, I'll fucking kill him with my bare hands.

"Are you hungry?" she asks.

"No, mom," I reply sarcastically, and she sticks her tongue out at me.

"Coffee?" she asks.

"Yeah."

She pours us each a mug of coffee, black, and we grab a stool at her breakfast bar.

"Gonna tell me who she is?" she asks.

Damn, she's perceptive. She always was. I'd forgotten how much I missed that over the past few years.

I shake my head and look down into my coffee. Isn't this why I drove here?

"I've been seeing Sam." I mutter softly and take a sip of coffee, ignoring her look of shock.

"Samantha Williams?" She asks.

"That's the only Sam I know."

"I just saw her on Saturday."

I shrug at her. *I did too, and it went from bliss that morning to the biggest fucking mess that night.*

"So what's the problem?" Meg asks.

"We both fucked up," I respond and laugh humorlessly. "Big time."

"I need more info. Start at the beginning. Don't leave out any of the sex." She pulls her feet up under her in her stool and settles in for a story.

"I'm not telling you about my sex life."

"Okay, tell me the rest."

"I've been running with her every morning," I start and she

nods thoughtfully.

"That sounds like a good thing."

"It's been great. And then we sort of fell into bed and now she won't speak to me." I clench my hands into fists as the frustration returns full force.

"From what the groupies said back in the day, you were a better lay than that." Meg laughs, and I know she's trying to be funny, but it's like a slap in the face all over again.

"I don't fuck groupies, Megan."

She flinches at my hard voice and I swear under my breath. "I'm sorry." I take a deep breath.

"Don't tell me Sam thinks you sleep your way through the line of groupies at your door."

"I don't know." I shrug.

I don't know where your dick has been.

"She pissed you off," Meg comments soberly, and she's right. She fucking pissed me off.

"She has such a fucking stick up her ass." I can't sit still any more, so I start stalking around her kitchen. "We had a good week, and she was loosening up, and I enjoyed being with her. She's funny as hell, and she can be sweet, and God, she's fucking sexy." I run my hands through my hair again.

"What happened, then?" Meg asks with a frown.

"I left Saturday morning, and by the time I saw her again that night, she put her fucking walls back up and told me that she didn't want to see me anymore. We both tried to hurt each other and it worked." I can't get the image of her crying on her countertop out of my head. Bent over, jeans around her knees, arms folded under her body, shaking.

Fuck, I'm an asshole.

"I don't need her shit."

Meg's phone rings and she frowns at the display, then holds her finger up to me to hold on a minute and takes the call.

"Hello?"

I lean against the granite and listen half-heartedly.

"Sounds like you have the flu. What's your temp?"

Someone is always calling her for medical advice. I'm so damn proud of my little sister. She's excellent at her job.

"You need fluids and rest. It's a virus, but you need to take some Tylenol and watch that temp." Her eyes flick up to me and she shrugs and then ends the call. "Sorry."

"It's fine." I shrug her off.

"So, you don't need her shit," Meg prompts me.

"No, I don't. I don't know what the fuck her problem is, but I don't need it."

"So don't see her again."

Is it that easy? The thought of not hearing her laugh, not sinking into her soft body, just… hurts.

And that pisses me off too.

"I don't do relationships," I remind Meg and she shakes her head at me in disgust.

"I think you like her."

"When she's not being a cold bitch, yeah, I like her."

"I think she has trust issues, Leo." Meg looks down at her coffee in thought.

"Don't we all?" I ask sarcastically.

"I suppose." She shrugs. "Remember, her brother is super famous, and she had to watch him deal with that. It's probably not easy being related to someone that famous." She raises an eyebrow at me. "I bet a lot of people have used her to get to him."

"Are people using you to get to me?" I ask, pissed all over again.

"No." she waves me off. "Until recently, most people didn't know you and I are connected. But she and Luke are tight, and people suck."

"But I have no reason to use her to get to Luke. I knew Luke before I knew her."

"I'm just saying that could be why she's so difficult to get to know, and why she's not quick to make friends."

I cross my arms over my chest and frown.

"I don't think she has a lot of friends," Meg murmurs, and I silently agree.

"I don't need her shit," I state again, firmly.

"Okay, so then why are you so pissed?" She asks. "You would

typically flip her the bird and go about your life."

"I don't know."

"Don't lie to me, Leo." Meg's eyes are as soft as her voice, and she smiles gently at me, and I know I can't fool her.

"She's different," I mutter with a scowl.

"Go apologize."

"It's going to take more than that."

"Leo, if you pursue something with her, are you ready to tell her everything about before?" My stomach clenches at the thought.

Fuck. That should never touch her.

But, I remember her reaction at the story of my surgery, how she just held me, the first person to do so since my mom died, and my chest suddenly feels heavy.

"Not yet, but she's the first person since you who I would consider telling."

Meg's eyes go wide, and to my horror, fill with tears. She blinks them away quickly.

"Okay." She nods. "Don't make me regret telling you this…"

* * *

~Samantha~

I'm dying. God is finally punishing me for being such a bitch, and is killing me slowly.

I deserve it.

My stomach heaves again, and I'm not sure if it's because I have the flu, or if I can't stop thinking about the horrible things I said to Leo the other night. The horrible things we said to each other.

It's clearly best that we don't see each other again. Any relationship between us would be toxic.

I'm an idiot.

No it wouldn't because he's not really an asshole and I'm not really a bitch, we're just two people who have baggage and don't trust anyone.

More heaving.

Jesus, what is coming up? I haven't eaten anything since dinner at Luke's house on Saturday. There's nothing left in me except my internal organs.

Although, I'm pretty sure I just threw up a kidney.

I wash my face and rinse out my mouth for the fortieth time today and look for a clean sleep shirt. I sleep in concert t-shirts. They're soft and big and comfort me. And today I need a Nash shirt.

I may never see him again, but I want him wrapped around me.

I pull a large, grey t-shirt out of my drawer and slip it over my head. The band's photo is on the front, Leo in the center. It's been washed a millions times since I bought it during their first major tour, and it's my favorite.

I slip into another pair of clean panties and move toward the bed when someone starts pounding on the door.

Are you fucking kidding me?

I pad through the apartment to the front door and open the door without looking through the peephole and almost pass out at the sight of Leo.

Leo.

"What are you doing here?" I ask as my stomach rolls again.

"You're sick," he murmurs and smiles hesitantly, like he doesn't know how I'll react, and then his eyes lower to my t-shirt and his smile widens.

It's so fucking good to see him, but before I can say a word, my stomach heaves again. I throw my hand over my mouth and run for the bathroom.

There goes the other kidney.

I hear shuffling around in the kitchen and then in my hallway and briefly wonder what in the world he's doing, but I throw up some more.

Finally, it stops, and I feel Leo move behind me and scoop my hair back and secure it into an elastic. He lays a cold cloth on my neck and rubs his big hand up and down my back.

"Are you okay?" He asks softly.

"It's stopping," I whisper. "I need the bed."

"Come on, I'll help." He takes my hand to help me to my feet, stands guard while I rinse my mouth again, and then scoops me into his arms and heads for my bed.

"You shouldn't be here, Leo. I'm a mess and I can't talk to you when I'm like this."

I rest my head on the soft cotton t-shirt on his shoulder and enjoy his warm, strong arms around me. He kisses my forehead and frowns down at me.

"Your temp is still high. Did you take some Tylenol?"

"I don't have any," I whisper, my eyes falling closed. I'm just so weak, I can't keep my eyes open.

"I brought some." He tucks me into the bed and leaves the room, returning quickly with a glass of water and pills. "Take these, and then I want to take your temp."

I comply, too weak to argue. I should kick his ass out of here, but I'm too weak for that too.

He takes the water from me and sticks the thermometer into my mouth, sitting at my hip on the side of the bed. His fingers are trailing down my cheek and then my neck, softly, soothingly. He'll put me to sleep.

God, I just want to sleep.

"One-oh-two," he mutters and exhales deeply. "Too high, sunshine. The Tylenol should work. Get some sleep. I'll wake you in a few hours for more and to take your temp again."

"Don't need you to stay," I whisper. "Don't want you to see me like this."

"I'm not leaving, and you're too weak to kick my dumb ass out of here, so deal with it, sugar." I feel his lips on my forehead again and then nothing as sleep finally claims me.

* * *

"Wake up, baby. Sam, wake up." A cool cloth is being rubbed on my forehead and Leo's smooth voice is calling to me. "Sam, I need you to take more medicine. Wake up."

I open my eyes and there he is. He wasn't a dream. His eyes look worried, and his hair is messier than usual.

He looks tired.

"What time is it?" I ask, my voice hoarse.

"About two in the morning. Here, take these." He hands me two small white pills and water and then takes my temp again. "One hundred even. It's coming down."

"I'm a sweaty mess," I mutter in disgust.

"Do you want a shower?" He asks.

"Yeah."

"Let's go." He pulls the covers back and helps me to my feet, but I'm wobbly with weakness.

Fuck, I hate feeling like this.

"A bath it is." He smiles down at me and scoops me into his arms.

"I thought I dreamed you," I whisper and bury my nose in his neck.

"That explains why you were telling someone they were sexy and talented and wonderful in your sleep." He winks down at me and I can't help the small smile that finds its way across my lips.

"That explains it," I agree. He sets me gently on the toilet while he runs the hot water in the tub, pulls the soaked t-shirt over my head, helps me out of my panties and scoops me back into his arms so he can lower me into the water.

"It feels cold." I frown at him.

"I can't give you a super hot bath, honey. I'm trying to break your fever." He scoops up my dirty clothes and tosses them into my hamper. "Where are you pajamas?"

"Sleep shirts are in the top drawer of my dresser. Panties are in the second drawer down."

He nods and leaves the bathroom and I just push my hands through the water, watching it fall over my knees. He's really good at this taking care of someone stuff.

"Where did you learn to be a caretaker?" I ask him.

"I took care of Meg for a long time." He shrugs and smiles down at me sweetly, that piercing catching my eye, and I can't help but remember what he can do with that little piece of metal. He holds up another Nash t-shirt. "What's with all the concert t-shirts?"

"I see a lot of concerts." I look back down at the water, embarrassed that he's seen all of my Nash shirts. "I always get a t-shirt and use them for pajamas."

"You have quite a Nash collection."

"They're my favorite," I whisper, my eyes falling closed again. "Happy now?"

"Getting there," he whispers and kisses my forehead. "Come on, baby, let's get you back in bed." He scoops me out of the bath and I gasp at the cold air that feels even colder on my over-heated skin.

"So cold." I watch him wrap a towel around me as I start to shiver. "I'm sorry."

"Why are you sorry?" He asks.

"That you're taking care of me."

"I'm not sorry about that." He briskly dries me and slips the soft cotton t-shirt over my head, lifts me in his arms again and delivers me to the bedroom. "I *am* sorry about the other night, Samantha. Jesus, I am so sorry. I would never use you."

"I know. I'm sorry too. I'm so mean when I'm scared," I whisper and snuggle down in bed. He brushes his fingers through my hair, rhythmically, gazing down at me softly.

"I'll sleep in the spare room," Leo offers and starts to stand, but I grab his wrist to keep him next to me.

"I don't have a spare room."

"This is a two bedroom apartment." He frowns down at me and I offer him a small smile.

"I converted the other bedroom into a closet. No bed there. Sleep here." I yawn, sleep pulling me back down. "Where's my cat?" I ask.

"He's been following me around. I fed him. Just sleep." I feel the bed dip as he climbs under the covers behind me and pulls me against him, his arms around me, fully clothed, and let sleep take me over.

* * *

Sunlight is spilling over my face as I wake and look about the room. I'm in bed alone again, aside from Levine, curled up at my feet, snoring.

I feel better. I don't feel like a night out on the town, but I think my fever has broken and I don't need to throw up.

Progress.

I can hear someone playing my piano and I smile. Leo is still here.

I use the restroom, brush my teeth and drape a throw blanket around my shoulders before I go find him sitting in my living room, in the same black t-shirt and jeans from last night. His feet are bare and he has a pen gripped in his teeth.

His hair is standing on end from his fingers.

Leo is here.

I cross to him and kiss his head. He shifts to the left, making room for me on the bench, and I join him.

"Hi."

"Hey. How are you feeling?" He leans down and kisses my forehead twice, checking for fever and must be happy with what he feels because he backs away and grins down at me.

"Better. I don't want to be in bed anymore." I look down at his long-fingered hands resting on the piano keys.

"Okay, hang out with me."

"What are you playing?" I ask.

"Something new." His brow wrinkles as he concentrates on the keys, playing a soft melody that I've never heard before.

God, he's so talented.

"I didn't know you played the piano," I murmur.

"Not well, but I don't have my guitar here."

"You didn't have to stay," I whisper and lean my head on his shoulder as he plays.

"Yeah, I did. I thought about taking you to the ER there for a while." I look up into his stormy gray eyes in surprise. "But you came through."

"Thank you."

"You're welcome."

We sit in companionable silence as he plays the melody. Every so often he'll stop and write something down, or switch the notes to suit him.

It's fascinating.

"I can't get the hook," he grumbles, fumbling over the song. He stops and backtracks and tries to play it again, but he's still not hearing it.

But I do.

I start to hum it and his eyes shoot down to me in surprise. "You play it," he says and pulls his hands away from the keys.

And I pick up where he left off, playing what I hear in my head for the hook of the song.

"Your turn," I mumble and lean my head back on his shoulder as he mimics what I just played and smiles down at me.

"You never stop surprising me." He kisses my head and keeps playing, humming along.

I'm completely content here, sitting on my piano bench, with this complicated, moody man. As the song comes to a close, he rests his hands in his lap and leans his cheek on my head.

"Did you write the whole thing while I slept?" I ask.

"Yeah."

"Leo?"

"Yeah, sunshine."

"So not a one night thing," I whisper.

He chuckles softly and drapes an arm around me, pulling me closer to him.

"I'm glad you're catching up."

Chapter Seven

"What did you pick?" I ask as I wander into the living room from the bedroom. I'm fresh out of the shower, finally feeling normal again in fresh clothes, my hair washed, and belly full of soup from my favorite deli down the block that Leo fetched me for dinner.

And I don't even need to throw up.

If I don't watch it, I could get used to being pampered.

The opening credits of a movie are paused across the TV.

"The new *James Bond*," he grins at me from the couch and I plop down next to him. "Feel better?" he asks.

"Much, thank you."

"No Nash t-shirt?" he asks with a raised eyebrow.

I look down at my shirt and back up at him with a sassy grin. "The Goo-Goo Dolls are my favorite."

"Right. That's not what you said last night." He pushes play on the remote and Adele begins to sing the opening song to the movie.

I love Adele.

"I was delirious with fever," I mutter and settle in next to him, leaning my head on his shoulder.

"Liar," he whispers with a chuckle and kisses my forehead.

I enjoy having him here, in my space, among my things. I never thought I could be so comfortable with someone for long stretches of time. People usually annoy the hell out of me.

Hell, sometimes *I* annoy the hell out of me.

Leo and I have settled into a rhythm. The conversations are interesting. The silences aren't uncomfortable.

And he likes to have me near him, which is a comfort to me, not just because I've been sick.

I link my fingers with his and rub my thumb over the ink on his skin. I love his tattoos. I can't stop looking at them. I wonder what these on his hands mean to him?

I wonder if he'd tell me if I asked?

Leo clears his throat, and I realize I've been lost in thought. I look up into his smiling gray eyes. "What?"

"The movie isn't playing on my hand."

"Sorry," I mumble and pretend to watch the movie.

"Don't you like *James Bond?*" he asks.

"Sure, I like it."

"Why aren't you watching it?"

I climb onto his lap and wrap my arms around his neck. "You know," I begin and kiss his chin. "I haven't made out during a movie since Ethan Middleton took me to see *Toy Story* in the eleventh grade."

"What kind of a douche bag takes his date to see *Toy Story?*" Leo responds, wrapping his arms around my back.

"I had a big crush on Ethan," I reply with a laugh and kiss his cheek. "I didn't care what he took me to see."

"Did he score that night?" Leo asks, his eyes happy and laughing.

"Hell no, but he got to second base. Play your cards right, and I'll let you score a home run, sexy man."

"Where is Ethan now?"

"I have no idea." I shift so I'm straddling him, my knees planted on the couch at his hips. "The point is, I think we should make out."

"You *are* feeling better," he kisses my nose and then lifts me off his lap and dumps me back on the couch beside him. "Watch the movie."

"I wanna make out," I pout and cross my arms over my chest, earning a belly laugh from Leo, and my stomach tightens at the sound.

Even his laugh sounds musical. God, I could eat him with a spoon.

"You wanna make out, sweetheart?" he asks and shifts toward me, pushing me down onto my back on the couch.

"Well," I shrug nonchalantly. "You know, if you want to."

"You are so sassy," he mutters and stares down at my lips.

"I'll make out with you if you want."

"Oh good, I was afraid I was going to have to track down Ethan."

"I'm the only man for this job, baby."

He plants his elbows on the cushion beside my head, rests his lower body against mine and leaves tiny kisses on my chin, my jaw, and then slides his nose against my neck, making me shiver and squirm.

"You have great lips," I whisper and feel him grin against my ear. I run my hands down his firm back and pull his t-shirt up so I can feel his warm skin beneath my hands.

"Clothes stay on," he whispers and continues with the small, sweet kisses.

"Why?" I ask and gasp when he bites my ear.

"We're just making out."

"For now."

He pulls up to brace himself on his hands and stares down at me with shining gray eyes. "No, we're just making out. No farther than second base."

"Uh, Leo, Meg's the one with the three date rule, not me. Remember?"

His face splits into a wide smile and I feel myself smile back at him.

"She has a three date rule?" he asks.

"Yeah, she about killed Will."

"That's my girl," he chuckles proudly. "And I do believe you made me wait through about five dates."

"Running isn't a date." Holy Mary Mother of God, if he licks my neck like that again, I'll tear his shirt off his body and attack him.

"I bought you a meal each time. It was a date," he whispers and moves to the other side of my neck to wreck the same havoc on the sensitive skin below my ear.

"Leo?"

"Mmm hmm?"

"Kiss me, please."

"I am."

I pinch his ass, and he bites my ear and glares down at me. "Please."

My eyes fall to his lips, his silver metal in his lower lip, and I've never wanted anyone to kiss me as much as I want him to right now.

He loops his fingers in my hair, tilts his head, and gently lays his lips over mine. I tighten my hands on his back, holding him tightly against me, and sigh deeply as he begins to move those talented lips. He nibbles and sucks, from one corner of my mouth to the other, leaving no piece of skin untouched.

My hands begin to travel, over his back, down his arms, up to his face, slowly and lightly exploring him, until I'm so consumed by him, I don't hear the movie, or feel the couch under me. All I know is Leo.

I thread my legs through his, not able to get close enough, and rotate my hips against him, but he abandons my lips and slides down to my ear.

"Samantha, I'm not going to make love to you tonight. But I'm going to kiss the fuck out of you."

My lips meet his again with a moan and this time he deepens the kiss, teasing my lips and the tip of my tongue with his.

I've never been kissed this thoroughly in all my life.

One of his hands leaves my hair and journeys down my face, my shoulder, and just when I think he's going to cup my breast, his hand glides down to my hip, and he just rests it there.

He's seriously just going to kiss me.

I moan again and run my fingers down his stubbly face. Despite the stubble, his skin is smooth and he just smells so damn good.

He slows the kiss down; nibbling my lips again, and then nuzzles my nose.

"You make me forget how to breathe," he whispers.

"I love the way you kiss me," I whisper back.

"Good," he murmurs and offers me a half smile, his stormy eyes are lazy and heavy-lidded. "Because I plan on kissing you a lot."

"Okay," I agree shyly.

Why does he make me so shy?

Suddenly, he stands and pulls me into his arms, cradling me against him, and carries me into the bedroom.

"The TV is still on," I remind him.

"I'll get it later."

* * *

~Leo~

She's beautiful when she sleeps.

She's beautiful period. Even when she was hurling and sweaty with fever, she was a sight to behold.

I'm in trouble.

We slept late this morning, but neither of us has anywhere to go, so I'm lying next to her, enjoying the view.

I've never just kissed a woman and not made love to her. I rarely kiss women at all. Sex is great, but kissing leads to all kinds of attachments and feelings, and it's just best if I don't go there, especially given that women I've been with in the past ten years were a quick lay. I certainly don't kiss the way I kissed Sam last night. I wanted to sink into her and make love to her all night, but she had been sick.

Maybe I'm turning into a pussy in my old age. The kicker? I don't give a shit.

Sam stirs and yawns, opens her sapphire-blue eyes and smiles softly at me.

"Good morning." I kiss her soft cheek and enjoy her sleepy moan.

"Mmm… mornin'." Fuck I love that raspy voice of hers. It's sexiest when she first wakes up and when she's just about to come.

"What do you want to do today?" I ask and brush a piece of her hair off her cheek.

"I want cupcakes."

"Cupcakes?" I ask with a laugh. "It's only ten in the morning, sweetness. Isn't it a bit early for cupcakes?"

"Clearly you've spent too much time abroad," she pushes her hand through my messy hair and gives it a yank, which immediately makes my dick stir. "Cupcakes are appropriate at any time."

"Can I have coffee with mine?"

"Sure."

"Okay, I'll take you for cupcakes."

"That was easy," she grins.

I just shrug. Fuck, I'd give her just about anything she wants right now.

"Let's go."

"Should we run first?" she asks with a frown.

"You're not ready to run yet. You were sick twenty-four hours ago," I remind her and climb off the bed.

"Then maybe I shouldn't have a cupcake."

"Samantha, let's go get cupcakes and anything else you damn-well want." I scowl down at her, and clench my hands into fists to keep from reaching out to her and tumbling her back into that bed when she offers me a wide smile.

"Cupcakes it is then."

We dress quickly and I hold her black coat up for her to slip into before pulling on my own and sliding my beanie over my head.

"Leave the beanie off," she's grinning at me. "I like touching your hair."

"It's just easier if I wear it." I kiss her forehead and usher her out the door.

"So, is it your disguise?" she asks sarcastically. "Pull the beanie down over your trademark sexy hair and eyebrow piercing and cover your tats and pray no one recognizes you?"

She may be joking, but I can hear the edge to her voice. My being recognized doesn't excite her any more than it does me.

I push the button for the lobby on the elevator and pull her into my arms for the trip down.

"I don't get recognized often, sugar."

She relaxes against me and sighs and I can't help but smile. The difference in her from when we first started running together and now is amazing. She's used to me touching her now, which is good because I can't keep my hands off her sexy little body.

"Where is the cupcake place?" I ask as we walk out of the elevator and through the lobby of her building.

"Just a couple blocks over. We can walk it."

"Are you feeling well enough for that?" I ask and frown down at her, but she just nudges me with her elbow.

"I'm fine. A few blocks won't kill me."

"Lead on then."

The Seattle sky is bright blue today, treating us to a rare winter sunny day. I twine Sam's fingers in mine and kiss them, and follow her into a little shop called *Succulent Sweets.* It smells like coffee and sugar inside, and Sam's pretty blue eyes light up as they fall on the glass case full of baked goods.

Damn, she's cute.

"What do you want?" I ask.

"Chocolate, of course," she laughs and my gut clenches. I love her laugh.

She orders her chocolate cupcake and a hot tea, and I place my order and the little brat reaches for her wallet.

"What are you doing?"

"Buying you a cupcake."

"Right, 'cause I'm going to let a woman buy me breakfast." I roll my eyes and push her aside and pull my wallet out of my back pocket.

The redheaded cashier glances up at me casually and then does a double take.

"Holy shit, are you Leo Nash?" she asks and I scowl at her as if she's nuts.

"I get that all the time," I laugh. "No, I'm not. That band sucks."

"I like them," the redhead shrugs and I instantly like her. "But yeah, sorry, I can see now that you're not him."

"I'm better looking, right?" I wink at her and she laughs and hands us our drinks and cakes and we find a table.

Sam is smirking and trying not to laugh out-right.

"What?"

"That's seriously how you thwart unwelcome recognition? By dissing your own band?"

"It worked." I chuckle and take a bite. "Damn, that's good."

"You got lemon! Can I have a bite? It's my second favorite."

I hold the cake up to her lips and she takes a tiny bite and closes her eyes as she moans in happiness, and I have to readjust myself on my chair.

Jesus, I'm like a randy teenager with her. I thought I had better control over my dick than this.

"Can I have a bite of yours?" I ask.

"Hell no, get your own," she pulls her cupcake closer to her and scowls at me.

"Selfish brat. I shared mine."

"Sucker," she smirks and continues eating her chocolate.

I glance across the street and grin. "Do you know what that building is across the street?"

She follows my gaze and shrugs. "Just a red brick building."

There is no signage, and it's non-descript.

"Nope, it's a recording studio. It's owned by a famous female duo from Seattle. They've owned it since the early eighties." Excited, I lean forward and cup my coffee in my hands. "Sam, Johnny Cash recorded there. Nirvana, Sound Garden, Pearl Jam. God, too many to count." I look at the building again, an idea forming in my head.

"Have you recorded there?" she asks, staring at the building.

"No," I shake my head. "I have been inside, though. When I first moved to Seattle, I won a radio contest and got to go to a private Pearl Jam concert there. There were only twelve of us in the audience, all sitting in a semi-circle. It was the coolest thing I'd ever been to."

"Wow, that's awesome. You guys should do that."

I nod, the idea taking more shape. "I wonder if we could record the next album there," I murmur and Sam's eyes widen.

"Really?" she asks.

"Yeah, I don't see why not. I don't know how far they're booked out for studio time, but that way I wouldn't have to go back to L.A. to record. Most of us live up here anyway."

I grin at her, excited to start making calls and she grins back.

"Could I come listen?" she asks.

"Of course. Anytime." The thought of having Sam in the studio with us as we lay tracks makes my stomach clench.

The thought of fucking her in the studio is even better. I've never done that before because work and personal shit have always been separate for me, but damn, I've already blurred all my lines for her, why not this one too?

"How many songs do you have written?" she asks and licks her fork.

"I've written three by myself and two with Meg. Some of the other guys have written a few. I'm working on one more now. We have a list of songs that the studio wants us to consider. I figure we'll start pulling it together in a few weeks." Her big eyes are on me, listening intently. It makes me proud that she's so interested, and she asks intelligent questions, not the typical fan questions.

She's definitely a fan of the band, and that's just one more thing that draws me to her.

Of course, I'd be drawn to her if she hated the band too, but nothing long-term could come of it. My band is my family.

"You have frosting on your lip," I murmur.

She licks the wrong side and smiles knowingly. "Did I get it?"

"Nope, other side."

She licks again, her pink tongue running along her lips and my cock instantly comes awake. She missed.

"Now?"

I reach out and brush the frosting with my finger, but before I can pull it away, she grips my wrist in her hand and pulls the finger in her mouth, sucking the frosting off and nibbling lightly on my skin.

Fuck.

"We need to get the fuck out of here," I growl. I hear the need in my voice, and her eyes dilate with lust.

"I'm not done with my tea," she mutters and her eyes fall to my piercing.

"Yeah, you are. Let's go."

Chapter Eight

~Samantha~

Well, I guess I'll work that cupcake off this morning after all.

Leo pulls me into the elevator of my building, after practically dragging me the two blocks home, and jabs the button for my floor.

As soon as the doors close, he's on me. He lifts me against the wall, holding me in place with his pelvis pressed to mine, my legs wrapped around his lean waist, and he's kissing me like crazy.

I yank the beanie off his head and dig my fingers into his hair, holding on, as he plunders my mouth, biting and sucking and then plundering some more.

God, he can kiss.

The bell dings, signaling that we've arrived at my floor, and he's suddenly pulling me along behind him.

My fingers are fumbling with the keys as he folds himself around me from behind, kissing my neck, his thumbs tweaking my puckered nipples.

"I can't open the door," I mutter and gasp as he sucks on the soft skin beneath my ear.

"Give me your keys, baby."

He makes quick work of the door, guides me inside, shuts and locks it and begins to lead me toward the bedroom.

"The couch is right here," I remind him, and he stills, turns to me, his gray eyes on fire and breath coming fast. He steps to me and cups my face in his hands, holding my eyes with his own.

"I haven't been inside you in days."

"Satur…"

"Saturday was nothing more than us hurting each other. It doesn't count. I haven't been with you, been inside you, for days. I'm not fucking you on your couch. I want to spread you out on your bed and drive us both crazy. I want you trembling and wet."

Holy shit.

"Can't argue with that." I grin at him and suddenly I'm caught up in his arms again. I unzip his hoodie and pull it down his arms, and pull his shirt over his head. We quickly undress each other, leaving a trail of clothing through the living room, down the hallway and to my bedroom.

When we're standing by the bed, him completely nude, and delicious, he steps back and sweeps his eyes up and down my body, over my pink lacy bra and matching boy-short panties.

"Jesus, do you always wear underwear like that?"

I smile smugly. "I like pretty underwear."

"You wear underwear like that every day and old concert t-shirts to bed?"

"Don't knock my shirts. I love them."

And suddenly I'm on my back on the bed and Leo is peeling my panties down my legs. He throws them over his shoulder and plants a kiss on my belly, right above my piercing.

"I love this piercing," he mutters and kisses me again.

"It's just a navel piercing, babe." I chuckle and then moan when he licks down my belly to my pubis and over my clit.

"Don't knock it," he mumbles and licks further down through my folds.

"Fuck you're good at that." My hips instinctively thrust up, but he holds my hips firmly against the mattress.

"You taste amazing." He sucks my clit into his mouth and pushes two fingers inside me and I can't hold back, I come apart, shattering and shuddering, pushing my pussy against his face, gripping onto the sheets at my side.

He kisses the insides of my thighs, the crease where my legs meet my center, and with his fingers still inside me, he kisses his way up to my breasts. He swirls his tongue around a nipple, nibbles it, and pays the other the same attention, while moving his fingers, all four of them, in a rhythmic wave motion, tickling me and making me giggle.

"That tickles."

"Mmm." He grins and kisses my mouth, softly, playfully. I

grip that piercing in my teeth and tug gently, and he smiles some more, moving his fingers more quickly.

I moan and squirm beneath him, and gasp as he presses his thumb on my clit.

"I'm not a guitar, you know," I remind him as he continues to torment my labia with those talented fingers.

"Oh, but the sounds you make, sunshine," he whispers and buries his face in my neck. I wrap my arms around him. He's pressed against me, from hip to shoulder, his fingers playing me like an instrument, and to my surprise, I come again, violently.

He's going to kill me.

"Leo," I cup his face in my hand and look up at him, and for the first time in my entire life, the idea of having sex with him on top of me doesn't freak me out. "I've never done this."

"I know that's not true, sunshine, you've done it with me." He grins down at me, but I shake my head.

"Never in this position, on my back."

"What?" He frowns down at me and pulls his hand out from between my legs and braces himself over me. "What do you mean?"

I close my eyes, regretting my words, and take a deep breath. "Exactly what it sounded like," I whisper.

"Look at me," he murmurs softly.

My eyes find his as he slowly shifts between my legs, covering me with his lean body, and I love the feel of his weight on me. He just rests here, allowing me to adjust to him, his hard cock pressed against my folds, his legs between mine, and I raise my legs and wrap them around his waist. He drops his forehead down to mine and pulls in a ragged breath.

"Are you okay?" He whispers.

"Yeah," I breathe.

"Why?" His eyes are pinned to mine, and he looks worried and happy at the same time.

"I couldn't stand the thought of giving someone that much control over me." My voice is soft and I move my hips, sliding his cock against me. "God, you feel good."

"You have to stop doing that, sunshine, I'm trying to go slow here."

"Who said it needs to be slow?" I ask and brush my fingers down his face. "You can fuck me hard like this."

"It doesn't always have to be rough to be good, Sam."

I will not cry. I swallow and close my eyes. Jesus, what is he doing to me? He's seen me sick, pissed off, and now he's seeing me at my most vulnerable.

"Baby," he whispers and gently kisses me. "I've got you."

He reaches down between us and rolls on a condom, grips one of my hands in his, and pulls it close to our chests, and slowly, oh so slowly sinks inside me.

My breath catches as I look up into his eyes, at the look there that I'm not ready to label, and I hold him close as he begins to move, his cock strong and full, his pubic bone pushing against my clit with each gentle thrust.

I've never in my life had a man make slow, sweet love to me, and it's this moody, amazing man giving it to me.

"My God, Sam," he whispers. "You're just so tight."

His words, the tone of his silky voice, and the way his body is blanketing me is my undoing, and I feel the build coming from the base of my spine, my face flushes, and I cling to him as I fall over the edge, chanting his name.

"Yes," he mutters against my lips and his body stills and then jerks as he comes inside me.

"Don't cry," he whispers and kisses a tear on my cheek. "Did I hurt you?"

I can just shake my head and blink my eyes. "No."

"What is it?" His voice is soft.

"This is just new," I respond and offer him a watery smile. "But it's good."

"I was aiming for really good."

"You have good aim."

He grins proudly and my phone starts to play the old Twentieth Century Fox theme song.

"That's Luke."

"He can wait."

Leo kisses my nose, my forehead, and my cheek before settling his lips on mine again and brushing them back and forth.

And the phone goes off again.

"Something could be wrong," I whisper. "I should answer."

He regretfully pulls out of me and watches me move off the bed to find my phone that's still in the pocket of my jeans.

"Hello?" I turn to find Leo lying, face down, face propped on his folded arms, smiling at me. I stick my tongue out at him.

"What the hell, Sam?" Luke's pissed.

"What?"

"You were supposed to watch Liv today while Nat and I went to the doctor."

"Oh, shit! I'm so sorry, I forgot. I've been sick." Leo frowns at me and sits up and I turn my back on him.

"Are you okay?"

"Yeah, I'm feeling better."

"Well, I hope you're home 'cause we're bringing her to you, since the office isn't too far from you. I'm parking now. We'll bring her up."

He hangs up and I immediately panic.

"Fuck!"

"What is it?" Leo's standing behind me, his face worried, and my panic rises.

"Luke and Nat are on their way up here with Olivia. I'm supposed to watch her, and I forgot." I eye his hot naked self, and then start scooping up our clothes, throwing his at him as I go. "Get dressed! Damn, damn, damn!"

Leo starts to laugh, not helping the situation at all.

"You have to hide in the closet." I pull my shirt and jeans on and turn around to find him glaring at me.

"I'm not sixteen, Sam. I'm not hiding for anyone." He crosses to me and pulls me in his arms, and kisses my forehead. "We've established this isn't a one night thing."

"Right."

"Our families were bound to find out sometime."

I swallow hard. *Fuck.* "Right," I whisper.

"Don't worry." He smiles reassuringly just as the doorbell rings.

"Get your pants on," I hiss at his smiling face and cringe when

Luke knocks on the door. Leo pulls his jeans up and fastens them and I can't wait any longer for him to pull a shirt on.

I open the door to a grinning Livie, but a scowling Luke.

"Gee, thanks," he mutters sarcastically and hands me the baby, pushing past me into my living room. Natalie happily follows him, grinning at me, when she sees Leo in the kitchen washing his hands. Luke is struck dumb.

"Hi, Leo." Nat grins and waves.

"Hey Nat. How are you feeling?" Leo asks and kisses her cheek, drying his hands on a towel.

"If you're going to touch my wife, you'd better put a shirt on. Dude, what the fuck are you doing with my sister?"

Livie's eyes fill with tears at her daddy's harsh voice. I kiss her forehead and bounce her in my arms.

"Luke, chill out." I pin him with a glare, but he doesn't care.

"We're going to be late," Nat reminds him and offers me a sympathetic smile.

"We will talk about this." Luke kisses Liv and leans in to whisper in my ear. "Be careful."

"We won't be long," Nat says. "She has snacks, diapers and toys in her bag. She just had a nap so she should be fine until we get back."

"Nat, I'm fine," I assure her and guide them out the door. "Go."

"She's cute," Leo murmurs and runs his hand down Liv's plump cheek. The baby immediately grabs his finger and sticks it in her mouth.

"Here, take her and I'll get her some juice."

"Whoa, take her?" He takes a step back, his eyes suddenly scared. He's hilarious.

"She's a baby, Leo, not a weapon of mass destruction." I thrust the baby in his hands, pull Livie's sippy cup from her bag and head to the kitchen.

"Can I put her on the floor with her toys?" He calls out to me.

"Sure, just put a blanket down for her to crawl on."

Damn, he's funny.

"I think the baby is about to kill your cat," Leo says dryly and I hurry back to the living room while capping the cup to find

Livie with a handful of the cat's fur, trying to put it in her mouth.

"Or eat her," I agree and laugh as Leo tries to untangle Liv's tiny, and surprisingly strong, grasp from my poor cat.

We sit with her and entertain her with her toys for a while, chuckling at how cute she is.

"This isn't too hard," I tell him and he grins at me.

"Nah, not too hard." He runs his hand over her soft brown hair and then frowns. "Wait, do you smell that?"

"No." I stop what I'm doing and sniff. "What is it?"

Leo scowls and glances down at Liv, who's grinning widely at him, slobber dripping down her cute little chin. "I think she shit herself."

"Stop swearing in front of her."

"Me swearing is not our biggest problem right now."

We stare at each other for a minute and then he digs around in the diaper bag, pulls out a diaper and wipes and hands them to me. "Here."

"Why do I have to do it?" I ask.

"Because you're her aunt. Duh."

"I don't do poop." I scowl down at the little girl, like she's done this to me on purpose.

"What do you normally do when this happens and you're watching her?"

"My mom changes her."

"Haven't you watched her alone before?" Now he's laughing, Liv is laughing with him, enjoying the joke, and I'm scowling at both of them.

"Dear God, what did they feed her?" I hold my hand over my nose. "Don't you know how?"

"She's a girl. I'm not going to jail."

"Don't be an idiot. You won't go to jail for changing her diaper. You might go to jail for *not* changing her diaper."

"Come on, Auntie Sammie," he winks charmingly, "You got this."

"Leo is going to lose his manhood if he ever calls me Sammie again," I tell Liv and she giggles. Then, suddenly, it's as if she realizes what she's sitting in, her pretty face crumbles and she starts to cry.

"Shit, we need to change her."

"I'm calling Meg." Leo pulls his phone out and dials Meg's number.

"Why?"

"She's a nurse. She deals with crap all the time. Hey, I'm at Sam's. There's an emergency, and I need you to come here asap. Uh huh. No, no ambulance, just need your help. Okay thanks." He hangs up and stuffs the phone back in his pocket. "She'll be right here."

"You totally just lied to her."

"She'll be here in ten."

It's the longest damn ten minutes of my life.

Finally, the doorbell rings. The only reason I hear it is because Liv has taken a moment to take a breath, thus giving us zero point three seconds of silence.

"Thank God," Leo pulls her into the apartment and she scowls when she sees the baby in my arms.

"What's wrong with her?" She asks.

"She has a shitty diaper," Leo tells her.

"So change her."

"Leo's afraid he'll be considered a pedophile and I don't know how."

Meg takes the baby from my arms and stares back and forth at us, her face incredulous. "Are you fucking kidding me? You said it was an emergency. I worked all night last night, and you woke me up for this?"

"Don't you smell that? It is an emergency."

"Jesus, you two are worthless." Meg finds the diaper and wipes, lays the baby on the floor on her blanket, and gets to work. "This is nothing. At least she didn't blow out the diaper."

"What does that mean?" I'm not sure that I really want to know.

"When the poop goes up their back, into their hair, all over the place. Now that's gross."

"Isn't the point of a diaper to catch the poop?" Leo plants his hands on his hips, frowning at Meg. "I mean, if they don't do their job, what's the point?"

Meg laughs and snaps the baby's jumper back in place, all clean and happy. "There, all done."

Liv smiles and leans her head on Meg's shoulder when Meg lifts her off the floor.

"This is our secret," I tell her. "Luke will never let me live it down if he finds out that I couldn't change her diaper."

"It's fine." Meg waves me off and hands me the baby. "Have you fed her?"

And, as if on cue, Liv burps, spitting up whatever she had for lunch.

"I'm so not having kids," I mutter.

"Good call," Leo agrees and offers me his fist for a fist bump.

* * *

~Leo~

"Thanks again for coming to help." I lean on Meg's Range Rover and offer her a grin.

"You got me here under false pretenses." She glares at me and then laughs, shaking her head. "You both looked ridiculous."

"Yeah, maybe no kids for me."

"You'd do great." She shrugs and grins, her dimple showing. "Looks like things are going better."

I just nod and step back from the car, pushing my hand through my hair. "Yeah, things are better."

"Good. I'm going back to bed."

"Okay, get some sleep."

She grins wider, and I have the feeling she's about to say something that I really don't want to know.

"Will's home. I'm going back to bed, but not to sleep."

"Stop saying shit like that, Meg. I mean it." She laughs and pulls away from the curb, waving as she merges into traffic.

And now that I have visions of my sister shagging Will Montgomery, I want to poke out my mind's eye with something sharp and hot.

I turn back toward the building just as Luke and Natalie return

ROCK WITH ME

and park. As I approach them, Luke's gaze is on me, not friendly, and I feel the bro talk coming on.

"Hey baby, you go on up and get Livie. Tell Sam I'll call her later."

"Okay. See you later, Leo." She waves and walks into Samantha's building. Luke watches her until the glass door closes behind her.

"How is she?" I ask him.

"She's great, baby's great, now let's get down to it. What the fuck, man?" He crosses his arms over his chest and scowls at me. I glance around us, watchful of anyone with a camera or phone pointed this way. The last thing we need are photos posted on the internet of Leo Nash and Luke Williams having it out on a street in Seattle.

"Look, Sam's great…"

"I know, I'm her motherfucking brother."

"What's your problem?" This is more than brother overprotection. "You know I'm a good guy."

"You're a celebrity. Sam has been hurt by this industry enough."

"What are you talking about?"

"That's her story to tell." He shakes his head in frustration and paces away. "Your lifestyle isn't for her."

"Sam is a grown woman, Luke. She can make her own decisions. You and I both know how damn smart she is."

"You will hurt her, and I'll be damned if I sit by and watch." His index finger is pointing at me, and he's pissing me the fuck off.

"I'll fucking protect her. Luke, my band members have wives and families…"

"Is that what you want with her?" He asks sarcastically. "The womanizer Leo Nash wants a family?"

Fuck you, asshole. You don't know what I want.

"I'm crazy about her, dude. If you think I'll let anything hurt her, you're nuts."

"You can't protect her from this business, and you know that. You should leave her alone now, before it goes any further."

"I will do everything to keep her safe," I repeat, my jaw ach-

90

ing from being clenched so tightly. "I'm not going to stop seeing her."

Luke watches me rub my chest, where an ache at the thought of not seeing Sam anymore has taken up residence, just shakes his head and sighs. "I can't believe she's doing this again," he whispers. But before I can ask him what the fuck that means, he follows it up with, "I'm telling you, when you're done with her, she'll be a wreck. It took her years to recover from last time, and I don't know that she could do it again."

What the fuck happened?

"Ready?" Natalie asks as she comes out of the building, holding Liv on her hip. The baby's face lights up at the sight of her daddy.

"Yeah," Luke responds and watches me thoughtfully as Natalie settles Olivia in her car seat. "You better protect her, Nash, or I'll fucking kill you."

"I wouldn't have it any other way."

Chapter Nine

~Samantha~

"Ms. Williams, your references are impeccable, and your credentials are spot on. We'd love to have you come down to L.A. to meet with us and the other editors to see if this would be a good fit for all involved."

"Thank you, Mr. Foss." I grin into the webcam on my Mac and the handsome man on the other end smiles in return. "I'd like that."

"Would next week work for you?"

"Yes, I believe my calendar is open next week." I'm bouncing up and down on the inside, but manage to remain calm on the outside.

"I'll have my assistant email with the travel arrangements. I look forward to meeting you in person. Have a good week, Ms. Williams."

"Thank you, and likewise."

The screen goes black as Mr. Foss disconnects the Skype chat and I sit back in my chair, chewing on my lip.

I need new interview clothes.

Shopping helps me think. It may sound stupid, and my brothers tease me incessantly, but roaming through racks and racks of clothes and shoes helps me clear my head.

So I throw on a jacket and grab my handbag and set out for the shopping district.

I don't live far.

One of the reasons that I chose to buy this condo was the convenience of being downtown. It was close to my old job, shopping, the market, and I love being in the middle of the hustle and bustle of the city.

I'm a city girl.

I push my way into Nordstrom; the heat from inside the store is a deep contrast to the cold weather outside. I make my way to my favorite section of the store, the underwear, and let my mind wander.

L.A. Do I want to move to L.A.?

No.

But I desperately need a job. I have a mortgage and a car and a *life* to pay for. I'm blessed with a healthy savings, but it won't last forever.

And I will die before I ask anyone for a handout.

But leaving Seattle means leaving my family. My friends.

Leo.

I still, a pair of black panties with ruffles on the butt in my hands and feel my face flush. These are exactly like the ones he ripped off me that night in my kitchen.

I may as well replace them.

And grab some pretty new bras while I'm here.

It's been more than a week since our fight, since I was sick. Since we watched Olivia together.

I carry my undergarment finds over to the women's section to pick out a new suit for my interview next week and end up with three new outfits, all suitable for interviews.

Because even if the L.A. job doesn't work out, I'll have other interviews to go to.

I hope.

As I make my way home with my purchases, my mind wanders back to the sexy, tattooed man that has wormed his way into my life. And it feels natural to have him here.

He's attentive and caring. He's amazing in bed. He's funny.

And I just want to lick him.

But there will come a time, in the not-too-distant future that he'll be gone the majority of the time. He and his band will release the new album, and all the hoopla that goes along with it will begin: tours, promo, TV appearances. Lots and lots of travel.

He doesn't even have a home in Seattle. He's staying at Meg's old place. He owns a home in L.A.

Oh God, I don't want him to think that I'm considering a job in California just because he lives there. How mortifying.

The thought of Leo leaving makes me sad. Okay, it makes me feel like my heart is being torn from my bloody body.

But I'll survive it. And I'll enjoy him in the mean time.

I kicked him out of my apartment yesterday and told him to go home for a day. Time apart is healthy. We don't have to be in each other's pockets twenty-four-seven.

I don't want him to get sick of me.

He'd reluctantly gone, but then he'd called me at two a.m., complaining that he couldn't sleep.

I wasn't sleeping either.

And we had the most fun, sexy as hell phone sex I'd ever had in my life.

Yeah, I like him.

I drop my purchases on the ottoman in the center of my closet room and sigh happily. I love this room. Three walls are lined with clothes, separated by occasion; casual, work, formal. The fourth wall houses my handbags and shoes.

And in the center of the room is a long, plush sand-colored ottoman for dressing. Before I can begin putting my newest finds away, my phone rings.

The display reads simply, *Nash.*

I grin as I answer, "Hey there, ridiculously sexy rock star."

"Hey. What are you up to?" His voice is warm and deep and smooth and I have to lower myself to the ottoman before my knees buckle.

God, I have it bad.

"I had to go shopping, so I'm putting some things away."

"Shopping for anything special?" He asks.

"I got some new interview outfits and some new underwear."

"Hmm... I definitely wanna see the underwear."

I grin. "I'll see what I can do."

"Do you have dinner plans tonight?" *Why does he sound uncertain?*

"No, what's up?" I ask.

"Meg has invited us to have dinner with her and Will at their place." He exhales deeply.

"You don't want to go?" I ask.

"I'm fine with it, if you are."

"Okay, I'm in."

"Okay. I'll pick you up at six." He clears his throat and I hear voices in the background.

"What are you up to?" I ask, my curiosity piqued.

"I'm hanging out with a few of the guys. We're looking at song choices for the new album and they're being stupid."

I laugh and cradle the phone between my ear and shoulder as I stand and begin hanging my new clothes.

"What are they doing?"

"Jake is substituting dirty words for the regular words in the songs. I swear these guys are ten years old."

"You love them," I murmur with a grin.

"They're all crazy." There is mumbling in the back ground and I hear someone start to play an acoustic guitar, and I wish I was there to listen. "I'm gonna go finish with these guys and I'll see you at six."

"It's a date." I glance down at the black panties in my hand and think about how far we've come since that horrible night in my kitchen.

"Good. And baby?"

"Yeah?"

"You're not sleeping alone tonight."

He hangs up, leaving me with a wide grin and wet panties. *Thank God.*

* * *

"You look fantastic," Leo mutters and looks me up and down appreciatively, taking in my red sweater and black jeans. My red heels increase my height by four inches, and he's still way taller than me.

"So do you." And he does, in his faded blue jeans and black button-down shirt with the sleeves rolled up, revealing those hot tats on his forearms.

"Come on, Meg will kill us if we're late, and if I come in, we may not make it there at all."

He settles me in his car and pulls into traffic toward Will's home.

"So, you bought interview clothes. I suppose that means you have an interview?" He raises an eyebrow at me and offers me half a smile.

"I do. Next week." I clench my hands in my lap and pray that he doesn't ask me where.

No such luck.

"Where?"

"In L.A."

His head whips around to stare at me with his jaw dropped, and then he scowls deeply and turns back to the road, his knuckles going white on the steering wheel.

"Why L.A.?" He asks, his voice deceptively low.

"Because they offered." I shrug and look out my window, not paying attention to the landscape.

"But you don't want to move out of Seattle."

"Leo, sometimes what we want and what we get are two different things." I take a deep breath and frown. "What's the big deal?"

"You shouldn't have to settle." He glares at me.

"I need a job." I say the words slowly and clearly. "I'm going a bit crazy here, Leo. I need to work. I like to work. No one in Seattle is offering."

"I'll help you until you find something here."

He sounds so sure, and I want to soften, just at the thought that he wants to help me, but that is absolutely not going to happen.

"I don't need any help."

"Samantha…"

"Leo, I'm not thinking about the L.A. job because that's where you're based out of, if that's what makes you nervous. I may not even get the job, but they called, want to fly me there next week, and I'm going."

"That's what you think?"

"I just…"

"Sam, I just don't want you to take a job that you don't really want. There's no reason for you to."

I shake my head and rub my forehead with my fingertips. "I don't do anything I don't want to."

"Yeah, no shit."

"Like I said, I might not get it. It's good practice for the interview process."

"Hey." He takes my hand in his and kisses my knuckles. "You'll be great. They'd be stupid not to scoop you up."

"Thank you." I offer him a small smile. He still looks upset, but not angry. "How did it go with the band today?"

"It was good to hang out for a while and talk shop."

"How are they doing?"

"Good. Enjoying their time off." He pulls into Will and Meg's driveway and cuts the engine.

"Why did you sound nervous about bringing me here tonight?" I ask when he turns to me in the dark car.

"Because I'd rather be at your place, or mine, alone with you." He runs his hand down my face and cups my cheek gently. "I missed you last night."

"Me too," I whisper.

"Let's get this over with so we can leave and I can lose myself in you for about ten hours."

Damn, I love it when he says stuff like that. I feel the same way; when I'm with him, I lose myself in him.

"Can I lick your stars?" I ask and laugh when his eyes dilate and his breathing quickens.

"Fuck, you can lick anything you want."

"We'll start with the stars."

"Get out now, or I'll take you back home."

He escorts me to the door, his hand on my low back, and as we wait for our hosts to answer the door, he leans in and whispers against my ear, "As soon as I get you home, I'm going to fuck you until you can't walk."

I swallow hard, but grin sassily. "Promises, promises."

He swats my ass just as the door opens and spreads his arms for Meg to give him a big hug.

"Hey, Mag-pie."

"Hi, jerk." She snuggles into him for a minute, and then backs away and smiles over at me. "Any diaper mishaps lately?"

"No." I shudder and follow her inside. "I think I'll leave the babysitting to my mom."

"You'll learn." Meg grins.

"Hey, you're here!" Will looks delicious in his jeans and football t-shirt.

Will looks delicious in anything.

"Thanks for inviting us," Leo responds and shakes his hand.

"Come into the kitchen." Meg turns to lead us through the house to their pretty kitchen. "Dinner's almost ready."

I help her set the table and fill wine glasses.

"This smells delicious." She's prepared salmon with a rice pilaf and salad, and my stomach growls. "I haven't eaten today."

"Why haven't you eaten?" Leo asks from across the room.

"Because I had the meeting this morning, and then I went shopping and I guess I forgot."

"I do that too." Meg nods. "I made a ton of food, so please eat it up."

"You can count on me." I assure her and we all claim a seat at the table and begin dishing up.

"So Meg," Leo slides a big piece of salmon onto my plate and then one onto his. "What are your plans for your birthday?"

"The Montgomerys do a monthly birthday party for all the members of the family with a birthday that month, so we'll do that." She shrugs like its no big deal, but her eyes are happy.

She loves her birthday.

"I'm buying her a new car to finally replace that piece of shit that broke down on her a few months ago," Will adds and Meg shifts uncomfortably in her chair.

I feel Leo stiffen beside me.

"Why were you driving a piece of shit, Megan?" He asks her, his voice low.

"Because it's what I could afford." She takes a sip of wine, not meeting anyone's eyes. Will frowns down at her.

"That's bullshit," Leo snaps at her.

Will turns his confused gaze to Leo's. "No it's not."

Leo shakes his head and drops his fork to his plate. "Meg, I know for a fact that you could have bought anything you wanted. I made sure that you were set up to receive your fifty percent of the royalties from all the songs we co-wrote on the past two albums."

I can't help the gasp that escapes my lungs as my eyes widen and watch Meg's cheeks go red with embarrassment.

"What?" Will demands.

"Where is the money?" Leo asks.

"I donated it." She shrugs and continues to look down at her plate.

"Fucking A," Leo mutters under his breath and runs his hand down his face. "You mean to tell me that I spent the better part of fifteen years of my life taking care of you, and I'm gone for a couple of years, and while I'm making millions you're living paycheck to paycheck? What the fuck, Megan?"

"I didn't want the money!" She yells back at him and glares at him from across the table. "I just wanted you and you left and I was pissed!"

"So you gave away millions of dollars? Money that you needed?"

"I didn't need it." She shakes her head stubbornly.

"Babe," Will drops his arm around her shoulders. "Why didn't you tell me this before?"

She just shrugs again, and Will's face twists in pain.

"Okay, stop guys." I interrupt and three pairs of eyes, eyes filled with hurt and love, turn to me. "It's done. You can't change it." I take Leo's hand in mine and stare up at him. "She loves you, and she missed you," I whisper.

He clenches his eyes shut and then looks back down at me, his gray eyes full of worry. He releases my hand and wraps that arm around my shoulders and pulls me close to plant that magical mouth on mine, devouring me, and I forget that we're not alone.

"That looks like a good idea," I hear Will whisper, and assume he's kissing the shit out of Meg.

Leo pulls back and grazes my bottom lip with his thumb. "Thank you."

When we turn back to the table, Will plants a kiss on Meg's forehead, and her lips are full and swollen from being kissed, her eyes glassy from desire and unshed tears.

Her gaze finds mine, and she gets a goofy grin on her face.

"What?" I ask.

"I've never seen Leo kiss anyone before." Her voice is full of wonder, and her gaze travels between Leo and myself.

"Never?" I frown up at the man sitting next to me. He glowers at Meg.

"Nope, he's always had a strict no-kissing policy." Her grin widens as he continues to fidget.

"Shut up," he whispers.

"Interesting."

"Very," she agrees. "He always said, no kissing and no oral sex. Used to piss the girls off."

"Shut the fuck up, Megan." Leo's pissed all over again, and I'm struck dumb as I remember the night on my couch when he kissed me for hours, and held me and kissed me most of the night in my bed.

The times that he's gone down on me, like he can't get enough of me.

Megan laughs and I swallow hard as Will catches my gaze. He smiles reassuringly and winks, and for a moment, I want to run. This is too much. I'm coming to depend on the affections of a man who never used to kiss women.

Why me?

What am I going to do when it's over?

And then I feel Leo's hand on my shoulder, his grip firm and warm and I look up into his soft, sweet eyes and I calm. I lean in and kiss him, pull on his piercing with my teeth and grin.

"He kisses me all the time," I tell Meg smugly.

"Good. It's about time."

"You know, I have secrets I can tell too, brat," Leo reminds her and Will comes to attention.

"Spill it."

"No!" Meg shakes her head and giggles. "Story time is over."

"It's okay." Will and Leo share a look. "I'll get it out of him eventually."

"I think that you guys can never spend time together again," Meg decides. "Say goodbye now, and we'll go our separate ways."

"I don't think that's how it works." I chuckle.

"Damn."

"Come on." Will stands and pulls Meg out of her chair. "Let's go in the living room and have dessert."

Leo pulls me out of my chair too, but leans in to whisper, "You're dessert."

* * *

I wake with a start, sit upright in bed, and frown when I see that I'm alone. My eyes adjust to the darkness in Leo's bedroom, but I don't see him. He brought me here after our dinner at Will and Meg's, and I was excited to see what he's done with Meg's place.

It's small, messy and a total bachelor pad, but it suits him.

Where is he?

I climb out of bed and pull on his black button-down, buttoning just the middle two buttons, and on a whim, tuck a condom in the breast pocket.

The house is still. No music.

Something is wrong.

I find him in the dark of the living room, rocking quietly in a big recliner. It's too dark to see his face, but I know he's awake because the chair is moving rhythmically.

"Babe?" I ask quietly.

"Come here," he whispers.

I climb into his lap, and his arms close around me tightly, pulling me against him, and he buries his nose in my hair and takes a deep, deep breath.

"What is it?" I ask.

"Couldn't sleep."

"I thought I wore you out," I respond with a smile. When he said earlier that I was dessert and he was going to fuck the hell out of me, he hadn't been kidding.

I feel him grin against my hair. "I love making love to you."

"Hey," the wistful tone in his voice worries me. I lean back and take his face in my hands, making him look me in the eye. "Talk to me."

He tangles his fingers in my hair and watches them comb through it. His knuckles brush down my cheeks. He's softly touching me, and he's quiet for so long I don't think he's going to talk at all, when finally he starts to speak, so quietly that if I weren't just a few inches from his mouth, I wouldn't be able to hear him.

"When I met Meg, she was tiny. Underweight. She was all red hair and long limbs. And she was so scared." He closes his eyes and leans his forehead against mine, remembering the little girl he loved. "I was headed for bad things. Bad people. But then she came to the foster home I was in, and she became mine."

He takes a breath, swallows hard, and keeps talking. "She followed me everywhere, and I didn't mind. If my friends didn't want her around, they weren't my friends anymore."

"You're kindred spirits," I whisper to him and he nods.

"Yeah, and I knew what it was like to be thrust into foster care at her age. So I claimed her. I taught her how to play guitar. And when I got placed elsewhere, I made sure I always had a job so I could pay for her to have a cell phone."

He brushes my hair back from my face as he speaks, his eyes distant, lost in another time.

"We've always looked out for each other. Even when things were really shitty; and they did get really shitty, we had each other."

He swallows hard again and swears under his breath, and I feel his muscles tense even further under my hands.

"And now I learn tonight that she's been struggling for years and I wasn't here to take care of her."

"Leo, she's a grown woman. She made her choices for a reason."

"Yeah, because I hurt her." He shakes his head and growls in frustration. "I knew it would hurt her to leave her here, but damn it, she'd just started her career, and chasing this music thing can be unpredictable and brutal. I didn't want that for her." He kisses my forehead, as though he just needs the contact, and runs his hands up and down my back. "I made sure she was set to receive that royalty money so that I wouldn't have to worry about her financial situation."

"Meg doesn't care about the money. She's all about the people she loves," I remind him.

"I know." He sighs. "I love that girl more than just about anything. It kills me that she was driving an unsafe car."

"Sweetie," I whisper and kiss him softly, needing to comfort him. "She's okay."

His arms tighten around me again and he pulls me into a hug, tucking my face against his neck.

"And now I have you." His hands continue to run up and down my back. "Another stubborn woman."

He grips my shoulders and pulls me up so he can look me in the eye again. "I know you're strong and independent and I respect that, but this is who I am, Sam. I take care of what is mine. You're mine."

He waits for me to argue, but I can't. I feel tears prick my eyes, and I bite my lip.

"Don't cry," he whispers. "Just let me do what I do best, baby. Let me take care of you."

"It's hard for me to let people in, Leo."

"I'm already in," he reminds me. "And I'm not going anywhere."

Yet.

His hands wander under the shirt, making my body come alive. He lifts me so I'm straddling his naked lap and unbuttons the shirt, peeling it down my arms to throw it on the floor, but I rescue the condom from the pocket and grin at his raised eyebrow.

"I'm a planner."

"I see." He pulls the sleeves over my hands and throws it to the floor.

"That's better," he whispers and leans forward to capture a nipple in his lips.

"God." I grip his soft brown hair in my fingers and hold on as he wrecks havoc on my body. His hands cup my ass; his lips are all over my breasts and neck.

Finally, he lifts me, takes care of the condom, and slowly fills me, kissing me gently.

"You. Are. So. Amazing." His soft lips brush over mine, back and forth, over and over again as he begins to move inside me. "Rock with me, baby."

And we begin to rock in the chair, so the chair is doing all the work, pushing his cock in and out of me, our arms wrap around the other and cling, our faces touching from forehead to nose, and we just lose ourselves in each other until I don't know where I end and he begins.

"So close," he whispers and bites his lower lip, and I feel my own climax approaching, my body tightening, thighs beginning to shake.

"Me too."

"Go over with me," he demands softly and catches my lips with his as I cry out, my orgasm consuming me. He growls low in his throat and follows me over, panting and clenching his hands on my ass.

"Not going anywhere," he whispers.

Chapter Ten

~Leo~

"You made breakfast?" I ask as I stumble bleary-eyed into my kitchen. Sam is wearing my black shirt again, and damn if she doesn't look edible in it. Her light blonde hair is pulled into a messy pile on the top of her head, and her face is clean of makeup.

My dick twitches at the sight of her, and I agree. She's beautiful.

"Yeah, I didn't want to wake you," she grins happily and piles hash browns and eggs on a plate.

"I know I didn't have that stuff in the kitchen," I mutter and kiss her cheek before I fill a mug with hot coffee. "God, you even made coffee."

"I went to the grocery store this morning. You didn't have much of anything except beer and pizza boxes."

"You went to the store looking like that?" I'll have to kill every man she came across today, on principle alone.

She rolls her eyes and smirks. "No, jackass, I wore pants."

"Gee, that's reassuring." I take a sip of my life-affirming coffee and watch her set the table.

She looks good in my kitchen.

She looks good anywhere.

"I hope you like your eggs scrambled," she mutters and pulls bacon out of the oven. "I don't know how to make an omelet."

"You don't?"

"No, I always mess them up." She shrugs and motions for me to sit.

"This looks great, thank you." I lean over and kiss her softly, thoroughly, and then dig in.

"You're welcome." She smiles softly. God, I'd do anything to get her to smile at me like that.

"What's up for today?" I ask and shovel potatoes into my mouth. Damn, she's a good cook.

"I have to go to yoga. I haven't worked out much since I got sick."

"Okay."

"How about you?" She asks and sips some orange juice.

"I have to make some calls, do a little work." She fidgets in her chair and she frowns for just a second, but I catch it. "What's wrong?"

She looks up, startled. "Nothing."

"You frowned."

"I did?"

"You did."

She shakes her head and shrugs. "I didn't do it consciously."

"You're sure?"

"Yeah." She eats her bacon and licks her lips, and damn if I don't want to scoop her up and take her back to bed.

We clean our plates, and I clear the table and load the dishwasher. My eyes constantly move back to the beautiful woman sitting at my table, sipping orange juice.

"I noticed when I went through your t-shirt drawer that you don't have the shirt from our last tour," I mention casually.

"I don't. I couldn't go to the show. We were in Tahiti for Luke and Nat's wedding." She scowls then, and sticks her lower lip out in a pout and I can't help but laugh.

"It's just a concert, sunshine."

"I literally had a moment when I thought about telling them I couldn't go to Tahiti so I could go to the show." She shrugs, her cheeks going pink with embarrassment. I pull her to her feet and lead her to the stairs.

"Well, that's just crazy."

"I wanted to go." I look back at her, following me up the stairs, and her eyes are on my ass. "Besides, your drummer is hot."

I round on her when we get to the landing. "Excuse me?"

"The drummer. You know, the guy who sits behind the big round things that make noise?"

"Yes, I'm aware of what a drummer is."

"Well, yours is hot."

"You like Eric, do you?"

"Oh, is that his name?" she asks innocently. Little brat.

"You know it is," I respond and pin her against the wall. Her breathing increases, eyes go wide, and fall to my lips, to my piercing.

It's funny to me that the lip is what turns her on.

I drop my lips to hers and kiss her long and slow, thoroughly, press my cock against her belly as I lift her off the floor. She moans and wraps her arms around my neck, sinks her hands in my hair and pulls on my metal with her teeth.

I lower her back to her feet and turn away toward the bedroom.

"Hey!" she exclaims.

"What?" I glance back with a raised brow.

"What was that for?"

"For teasing me about my band. You can never meet Eric now. I'll have to kill him, and he's too good to replace."

She laughs her raspy, throaty laugh, and follows me into the bedroom.

"So, back to the original subject."

"Yeah, back to the kissing."

"No, sweetheart, the subject before that." I laugh. God, she's funny. I pull a gift bag out of my closet and hand it to her nervously.

Maybe this is a stupid idea.

Her eyes light up like it's Christmas morning at the sight of the red gift bag.

"For me?" She asks and bounces on the balls of her feet.

Note to self: she likes presents.

"I don't see anyone else here, baby."

"Gimme." She extends her arms, wiggling her fingers, her sweet face all happy and glowing and she looks like a kid.

I hand her the bag and stuff my hands in the pockets of the jeans I threw on before heading downstairs.

"Why are you nervous?" She tilts her head to the side, watching me.

"I'm not."

Her eyes narrow as she studies me. "Uh huh. Sure."

She knows me too well already.

"Open it."

She tosses the white tissue paper on the floor and pulls the soft white t-shirt out of the bag, snaps it open and stares at the front, her mouth gaping open.

"It's a Nash t-shirt," she whispers, her eyes traveling over the photo of me and the guys on the front.

"Yeah, you were in Tahiti." I shrug.

She immediately strips out of my shirt and pulls the tee over her head, looks down at it and back up at me with a wide smile. "I love it."

"Good. I love seeing my name on you," I whisper.

She launches herself into my arms and kisses me soundly. "It's really soft," she murmurs. "Do you have a sharpie?"

"Probably, why?"

"Will you sign it?" She's bouncing again, like a fan, and it makes me still for just a moment.

I don't need a crazy fan-girl as my girlfriend.

And then I remember; this is Sam. She's no one's fan-girl.

"Why?" I ask again.

"In case I want to sell it on eBay." She bats her lashes at me and my stomach loosens. I dig around in my computer bag and pull out a black marker.

"Where do you want me to sign it, smart ass?"

"Duh." She rolls her eyes. She's so getting spanked. "On my boob!"

"On your boob!" I pinch the bridge of my nose and laugh.

"Like you've never signed boobs before," she smirks.

"Oh, I've signed my share."

"I figured. So mine shouldn't shock you."

"I love your boobs." I lean down and kiss her cheek. She has great tits.

"So sign them." She steps back and thrusts her breast toward me and my cock immediately strains against my jeans.

I slowly sign her shirt, right over her breast, my eyes on hers.

She bites that plump bottom lip of hers and sucks in a breath, her eyes dilate.

God, she'll be the death of me.

"All done," I whisper.

"Thanks," she whispers back, and then blinks, pulling herself out of the sexy trance. She pulls the shirt over her head, folds it carefully and places it back in the bag and walks over to her clothes.

"Stop," I order her.

She glances at me with surprise. "What?"

"Come here."

She frowns and stands in front of me again.

"I'm not done."

"You signed the shirt."

"Yeah," my eyes follow her curves, her lines, and her nipples pucker under my gaze. "But I'd like to play."

"With the Sharpie?"

I shrug.

"You want to draw on me?"

"You are a beautiful blank canvas, sunshine."

She blinks at me, mulling the idea over, and then smiles slowly. "Okay but then I want something too."

"What would that be?"

"I want to lick your stars."

"You don't need my permission to do that, you know." My stomach clenches at the thought. When her little lips and tongue touch my hips I about go out of my mind.

She just shrugs happily. "That's what I want."

"Done. Come stand by the mirror."

"I don't get to lie down?" She pouts.

"Hell no, you get to watch." I grin and lead her to the full-length mirror that hangs on the bathroom door and turn her so her back is facing the mirror, but she can look over her shoulder to watch.

I uncap the marker and start on her shoulder blades, drawing clouds and birds, a sun, and she gasps, bites her lip and watches with fascination.

"You're good."

"I like to doodle," I murmur and keep focused on the task at hand. Once I turn her and start working on her breasts and sweet stomach, I'll lose my concentration.

I continue to move the ink over her skin, adding an ocean and palm trees, sand, starfish. Along the bottom, across the top of her ass, I draw a music bar and add the notes to one of my favorite songs that I wrote called *Wrapped In You*. It's a ballad, and one she'd know. We play it at every show.

"You're writing music?!"

"I've already written this one, just putting it below the picture."

I pull the marker down her legs in long swirls, drawing random designs on her white flesh.

"Wow, you're good. Did you draw your own tats?" She asks.

"Some of them. Some I had done."

"What's up with the tats on your hands?" She's watching my hand closely. She always traces the ink with her fingertip.

I shrug. "It reminds me to slow down."

"But the word implies going fast," she frowns.

"Exactly."

"Who knew you were so deep?" She smirks and I smack her ass hard. She squeals and laughs. "I like to have my ass smacked you know."

"I know," I grin up at her and smack her again. "Okay, turn around."

She obeys, and I smile in approval. The front will be a bit different. I draw another music bar, diagonal, running from her left hip, over her sternum, to her right shoulder, but low enough that her clothing will hide it.

I add the notes, from the same song on her back. When it's finished, I start on the flowers.

Cherry blossoms, looping around the music, down her stomach, over her ribs.

She braces her hands on my shoulders; her eyes are pinned to the mirror over my head, watching intently. Her breathing is shallow, and I can smell her arousal.

She's so fucking turned on. I can't wait to sink inside her.

I finish the petals that weave around her pussy, and then, on her hip, I sign my name.

Not because I'm the artist, but because she's mine.

I'm completely in love with her. I just don't know how to tell her because I'm afraid that as soon as I do, she'll run at full speed in the other direction.

"All done," I murmur and stand back, watching her turn in circles, admiring the art in the mirror.

"It's gorgeous. I thought you'd draw some stupid stick figures or 'Leo Was Here'." She laughs. Her face sobers when she sees my face in the mirror.

"I want you," I tell her.

"I'm right here."

I can't stop looking at her. At the stark black lines on her soft white skin. At her pink cheeks, flushed with lust. At her hot blue eyes, raking over my own naked torso. Her eyes still on the stars on my hips, and then jump back up to mine, and I can't stand it any longer.

I lift her in my arms and carry her to the bed, lower her gently to the mattress and shuck off my jeans to join her on the soft bed.

"It's my turn," she whispers.

* * *

~Samantha~

I push Leo onto his back and kiss his chest, his shoulders, down his ribs. I nuzzle his belly button with my nose, enjoying the way his muscles clench at my touch. Gripping his hips in my hands, I kneel between his legs and lower my lips to the blue and red star on his left hip, kissing and licking, tracing the lines.

"I fucking love these stars," I whisper, and switch sides, paying extra special attention to the scar above the ink, tracing the line of muscle that forms that sexy as fuck V.

Leo grips my head gently in his hands, and swears softly and I grin as I plant kisses down his happy trail to his hard cock.

I lick from the base to the tip and suck him in, grip him in my fist, and fuck him with my mouth. He tastes delicious, smooth yet hard at the same time.

"God, Sam," he growls and fists my hair in his hands, guiding me up and down his glorious dick.

I pull back and lick his scrotum, earning me another growl. He clenches his eyes shut and throws his head back, but I want his eyes on me.

"Watch," I whisper and smile encouragingly when his eyes find mine. I kiss the underside of the tip and then lick it and sink down over it again, until I feel him against the back of my throat, tighten my lips around him and lift up, and repeat the motion over and over again until I feel his balls tighten and lift, and his legs become restless. He's gasping for breath.

I fucking love the effect I have on him.

"Stop," he whispers.

I ignore him.

"Stop, Sam, I don't want to come in your mouth." He grips my shoulders and pulls me on top of him, and kisses me deeply. "Your sassy mouth is gonna kill me."

"Not a bad way to go," I murmur and nip his chin. I straddle his hips and sit up, slide my wetness over his cock, and moan. He's tracing the music drawn on my belly. "What is it?" I ask.

Wrapped In You." He smiles shyly and I gasp. That's my favorite Nash song. "Do you like that one?" He asks.

I smooth my face and shrug. "It's okay."

Before I can blink, he grips my hands in his and reverses our positions, pushing me flat on my back, my hands held in one of his large ones over my head and his pelvis pressed to mine. "Admit it," he whispers.

"Admit what?"

"You like it."

I smirk up at him and try to pull my hands down, but he presses them harder against the bed. "It's fine."

With his free hand, he gently brushes loose tendrils of my hair away from my face, lowers his torso until his face is just inches from mine, and softly, so, so softly, begins to sing.

You make me tremble
When I hold you like this
You skin glowing in the moonlight
You have me all wrapped in you…

His voice is incredible. Even when he's just talking, I can't get enough of it, but when he sings, I'm lost to him.

He releases my hands and I caress his face gently with my fingertips, and pull his lips to mine and pour how I feel about him into this kiss, my hands on his face.

I am wrapped in him.

When he pulls back, I offer him a small smile. "That's my favorite Nash song."

"Really?" he breathes, his eyes are happy.

"Really. Who did you write it for?"

He frowns for just a moment and looks down at my lips, then back to my eyes. "I didn't write it for anyone." He kisses my nose. "But I think it fits how I feel about you. I'll never sing it again without thinking of you."

"You are so good to me," I whisper.

"You deserve so much," he whispers and kisses me again, deeper this time and I feel him reach over to his bedside to grab a condom.

"I want you inside me, babe."

"I can do that." He grins and pushes inside me, until he's completely buried in me, and stops. "How's that."

"It's okay." I shrug and bite my lower lip, teasing him.

"Do you think you can do better?" He raises his eyebrows and then just as swiftly as he put me in this position, he reverses us again, so I'm straddling his lap and lying over his lean body. "Have at it."

I gladly sit up and begin to ride him, clenching around him with every push and pull, up and down, reveling in his hands firmly planted on my ass, guiding me. His eyes are feral, pinned to mine.

"Feels so good," I mutter and lean forward to brace my hands on his shoulders, bucking my hips, grinding my clit against his pubic bone, and I feel the energy gathering in my core, ready to be ripped from me.

"My God, you're so fucking beautiful." His hands cup my breasts and pinch my nipples, hard, and then he soothes them with the pads of his calloused fingers. He suddenly sits up, his face level with mine, and kisses me hard, bites my lip and slaps my right ass cheek.

I lean down and suck on his neck, bite the muscle at the top of his shoulder and go crazy when he pulls me down hard, circling his hips, and makes me come, my orgasm ripping through me.

"That's it, baby." He licks up and down my neck, and when I come down from the high, he slips his hand between us, and rubs my clit with the pad of his thumb, and I come again, making him groan.

I feel his body tighten, his arm clenches around me, and he comes with me, shouting my name as he lets loose.

"Holy fuck," I whisper and chuckle when all he can do is smile. "I guess I don't need that trip to yoga today."

"Let's go for a run later." He tucks my hair behind my ear. "I've missed running with you."

"Okay. Are we staying here tonight? I'll need some workout clothes."

"I want to be with you, at your place, if you don't mind."

"I don't mind." I grin. "I'll head out, and you can make your calls and stuff and meet me there later."

"Fuck that. I'll take you. I'll make my calls from your place later." He kisses my forehead and lifts me off of him.

We're not attached at the hip, and I start to tell him that being apart for less than an hour won't kill us, but when he leaves me to throw the condom in the garbage, and the cold air hits my warm skin, I know that I don't want to be apart from him.

I enjoy him too much.

Way too much.

Chapter Eleven

I stare at Leo as he drives through Seattle traffic late Friday afternoon. He looks hot driving this car. He's pulled the sleeves of his gray blazer up his forearms, and I watch the muscles tighten and relax under the inked skin as he steers his supped up Camaro.

Even watching him drive makes me wet.

He's dressed trendier tonight, with a gray blazer over a white Levi's t-shirt, dark blue jeans and black Converse. He's still sporting the beanie over his signature hair.

We're heading out to dinner and then to a club to catch a band he knows.

Or, as I like to think of it, our first real date.

"Why a Camaro?" I turn to face him in my seat.

"What do you mean?" He changes lanes and smiles at me.

"You could have any car in the world. Why did you choose a Camaro and not something higher brow, like a Porsche or Bentley?"

He chuckles and shakes his head. "I've wanted a Camaro since I was a kid. My dad had one." He frowns as the memory runs through his mind. "You don't like my car?"

"I like it, I was just curious."

Leo's phone rings as he stops at a red light and he pushes the hands-free button on the wheel.

"Nash."

"Hey, it's Eric."

Leo smirks at me briefly. "Wassup?"

"Do you have an hour? The manager of that studio you called the other day just called me, and they have time to show us around tonight, if you can make it. Jake and I are in."

He glances at me, his eyebrows raised in question, and I nod. "Sure I can swing over there. I have someone with me. Be nice."

"That's cool. I think Rick is coming too."

"Okay, see you soon." He disconnects the call and grimaces. "I'm sorry, babe. We shouldn't be there long."

"It's cool." I shrug and then can't help but tease him. "But I thought you didn't want me to meet your band."

"Are you going to flirt with them?" he asks with a sigh.

"Probably."

"Shit," he mutters under his breath and I laugh, enjoying him.

He pulls up to the curb in front of the red brick building just across from my cupcake place. Eric and Jake are climbing out of Jake's black Jeep Wrangler and cross to us.

"Hey, man." They all do the man hand-shake-hug-thing that's always confused me, and then both sets of eyes rest on me, waiting for an introduction. Leo wraps an arm around me and smiles.

"This is Samantha. Sam, these are a couple of the idiots in the band, Eric and Jake."

Jesus, Mary and Joseph, I'm meeting Nash.

"Hey, guys." I smile warmly and shake their hands and keep my face completely neutral. I'm used to celebrities. I'm related to them.

For Godsake, I'm sleeping with one.

But I can't help but do a little, tiny happy dance in my head.

"Come on, let's look around and see what's what." Eric leads us inside, where a middle aged, partially balding man in a plaid shirt and khaki pants is talking with a younger, super skinny guy in skater gear.

"Thanks for coming, Rick." Leo glances down at me and gestures to the balding guy. "This is Sam. Rick is our manager," he informs me with a smile. I nod and smile and we're all introduced to Skip, the skinny guy who manages the studio.

"So, what can I do for you guys?" Skip asks.

"We just want to take a look at the studio space, talk with you about setting up recording time, stuff like that," Jake tells him with a grin. The female fans adore Jake. He's tall and muscular, and has a killer smile. He always wears the same pair of sunglasses.

"No problem. There's no one here now, so feel free to walk around and just ask me questions when you have them." Rick turns to chat with Skip and the guys wander back toward the sound booths. Eric turns back and eyes me appreciatively, and I immediately realize he finds me attractive.

This could get awkward.

"So, are you from Seattle?" he asks with a grin. He really is cute. His jet-black hair is too long, and his eyebrow is pierced. He's slim with strong arms. He'd have to be built to play as vigorously as he does for up to two hours at a time.

"Yep, born and raised," I smile.

"Cool, me too."

"Yeah? What part?" I ask, truly interested.

"Bellevue area," he responds.

"Me too!" I lay my hand on his arm and grin. "What high school did you go to?"

"Excuse me," Leo interrupts and I glance up into angry gray eyes.

What the hell?

"Skip, is there an office I can quickly use? I need to speak with you," he murmurs to me.

"Sure, it's down to your right," Skip responds and returns to his conversation with Rick.

Leo links his fingers through mine and pulls me behind him to Skip's office, shuts the door behind us and locks it.

"What's the problem?"

He doesn't answer, he just grips my upper arms in his hands and kisses me, hard, ravenous.

And I'm immediately caught up in him. I practically climb him, trying to get closer to him, to feel his skin on mine.

God, it's always this way. One touch and I can't get enough.

He lifts me against the door and grinds his cock against my center, kissing me to muffle my moans. His hands are rough, harsh. Hurried.

This is new from him.

I grip his hair and pull his head back from mine, both of us panting and gasping for breath.

"What's wrong?" I ask.

Still no words, he spins with me in his arms and lays me across

117

Skip's desk, not bothering to move papers. He unfastens and yanks my jeans over my hips, freeing only one leg, frees himself and pulls a condom out of his pocket.

"You're going to fuck me here?" I hiss at him, shocked. "There are people thirty feet away!"

"Stop talking," he commands, his eyes feral and jaw tight, and damn if he doesn't turn me the fuck on.

I'm already soaking wet.

I lean up on my elbows as he grips my hips and pulls me onto him, ramming himself inside my wetness.

"Oh God," I whisper, my gaze caught in his as he pushes in and out, hard, fast, over and over.

"Mine," he whispers and clenches his eyes closed. "Mine."

"Damn, Leo," I grip his face in my hands.

He pins me again with those eyes. "You. Are. Mine."

And with that I come apart, biting my lip until I taste blood so I don't cry out, spasming around him, and he follows me, coming hard and grunting softly.

He gasps for breath and leans down to whisper in my ear, "Do you have any idea how twisted up you have me? You're mine, goddamn it."

"Leo," I begin but he pulls out of me and tucks himself back in, watching me stoically.

I adjust my clothes and clear my throat. "Were you trying to mark me?" I ask quietly, trying to understand what just happened.

"I don't need you flirting with my band, Samantha."

"Leo, I was being friendly."

"You touched him."

"So?" I look at him like he's gone mad.

"Eric will…"

"Eric isn't an issue," I interrupt, pissed off. "Unless you let him become one."

He raises an eyebrow and then laughs.

"Leo, I get along well with men. I always have. If you have issues with that, we need to talk about it now."

He eyes me for a minute, and with a muttered curse scrubs his hands over his face.

118

"I'm an idiot."

"Yeah, but you're hot, so I'll overlook it this time." I smirk and lean my ass against the desk, my arms folded over my chest.

"I didn't like it," he whispers.

"So noted." We eye each other for a minute longer until he steps forward and wraps his arms around my shoulders, trapping my arms between us.

He kisses my forehead softly and smiles ruefully down at me. "Is this how you'll feel about groupies?"

"Probably not," I respond with a frown. "I don't give a shit about groupies."

His eyebrows climb into his hairline. "You don't?"

"No."

"Why not?" He looks almost insulted and I can't help but smirk.

"Do I have a reason to worry about groupies?" I ask sarcastically. I know I don't.

"Hell no."

"That's why I don't give a shit about them, babe. They're nothing." I shrug and kiss his chin. "I've been around crazy women fans for far too long to let them worry me."

"That's right," realization dawns and he smiles. "I bet Luke had his share."

"Luke had a woman kill herself in his house, Leo. I know all about women fans."

"Holy fuck," he sputters, appalled.

"Yeah. I'm not a jealous person. I never have been."

"I never have been either, until you. Seeing you put your hand on him made me crazy."

"So noted. You could have calmly talked with me about it later, you know."

"I liked this better." He winks and kisses me playfully just as there is a knock on the door. "Come on, let's finish this so we can get out of here."

Leo opens the door to find Eric standing on the other side, about to knock again. "Are we going to work, or are we going to fuck?" He asks with a scowl.

"Fuck off," Leo mutters and pushes past him. Eric grins down at me suggestively.

"I could take you back in that office…" he begins.

"Stop," I tell him and face him square-on. "You and I will be fine as soon as we get one thing straight: I enjoy you visually, but I don't now, nor will I ever, want to fuck you. I'm with Leo. He's your friend. That's it."

Eric sobers and shoves his hands in his pockets, rocks back on his heels and then a slow grin spreads across his face. "I like you."

"Glad to hear it. Get to work."

"I like her," he announces happily as he turns down the hall-way.

"I do too," Leo's eyes are dancing, watching me.

I roll my eyes. "You get to work, too."

"You're awfully bossy," he grins.

"A little," I concede.

"We'll do something about that later." He swats my ass and leads me to join the others, discussing the space and schedule.

"So, we can begin in about two weeks." Skip is consulting his iPad. "You can have the studio three times a week, four hours a day."

"We'll take it," Leo pulls his phone out of his pocket to add the appointments to his calendar.

"Great. Thanks, guys. I'm looking forward to working with you." Skip shakes their hands and shows us out.

"Have you talked to Adam and Jason about coming up here from L.A. for recording?" Jake asks.

"Yeah, they're good." Leo exhales. "They're going to bring the families with them and rent out some houses."

"Good," Eric nods. "It's good to be writing and recording at home again."

"It is," Leo agrees and waves as Jake and Eric pull off.

"I want to talk to you," Rick begins when it's just the three of us left.

"Okay," Leo frowns.

"Alone," Rick clarifies, gesturing toward me.

"I'll wait in the car." I begin to walk toward the curb but Leo interrupts.

"No. Stay here." He glowers at Rick. "Whatever you have to say can be said in front of her."

"Is she going to be a problem?" Rick asks bluntly.

"What are you talking about?"

"You weren't even here five minutes before you had to pull her into a locked room and fuck her. This album is a big deal. Your cut alone is over ten million, and that's before royalties." I feel my cheeks heat, and my mouth drop.

"Hold it." Leo holds up a hand, shutting him up and my wide eyes find his before he turns back to the asshole. "You may have forgotten, but it's never been about the money for me, Rick. It's the music. The fans love the music. If you have a problem with my girlfriend, I'll find another manager."

"I've been with you since you were singing in dumpy little clubs in Bothel," he sputters.

"Yeah, and you've gotten greedy." Leo gets in his face. "Don't ever disrespect my girl again, Rick. She's not the problem."

"Are you threatening me?"

"No, I'm laying it out for you, man. She's not just one in a long line. Get used to seeing her around."

Rick glares at me and then wipes his mouth with the back of his hand. "Fine."

Leo tightens his hand around mine and leads me to the car, settles me into his front seat, and climbs in himself, and speeds away from the studio.

"I'm sorry," I murmur when I find my voice.

"Why?"

"I don't want to cause any issues for you."

He laughs humorlessly and shakes his head. "You are not an issue. Half the guys in the band are married, Sam. Rick's just an asshole and doesn't like change."

"Okay," I whisper and clasp my fingers in my lap. He's right. Rick is an asshole. But I really don't want to be the cause of any issues in the band. In one hour I managed to make Leo jealous, set his drummer straight and piss off his manager.

I'm just a real charmer.

"Stop it," he murmurs and pulls my hands apart, links his fingers with mine and kisses my fingers. "Trust me, you're not an issue."

"Okay," I mutter and trace the tats on his fingers when he rests our hands in my lap. "Are you excited to get back into the studio?"

"Yeah, it'll be fun."

I nod and look out the window. Darkness has fallen. It gets dark quickly in the winter in Seattle.

"So, I don't think we're going to make it to dinner before we go to the club." Leo gives me an apologetic smile. "But I'll buy you bar food."

"I love bar food!" Just the thought of it has my stomach growling. "I want potato skins and buffalo wings and nachos."

"Is that all?" He asks with a laugh.

"And deep fried mozzarella sticks. I'll share with you."

"Okay." He shrugs and laughs again.

"How do you know the band we're going to see?" I ask.

"I met the lead singer back in the day when I played the Seattle circuit. He's had opportunities to come to L.A., but his family is here, and he's content here. I haven't seen him in years."

"Cool. Are they good?"

"Pretty good, yeah. They do mostly covers, but they throw in some original stuff too."

"Does he know you're coming?"

"Yeah, I called him the other day." Leo frowns and glances at me.

"What?"

"I'll probably be recognized tonight."

"I figured. You're not in your usual disguise." I snicker and kiss his hand.

"You're okay?"

I love that he's worried about me.

"I'm fine."

"Really?" He looks surprised.

"I don't trust the fame," I remind him. "You know this. But it's part of who you are. I'm excited to go listen to the band with you. I'll be fine."

"Okay, thank you."

He parks, pulls his beanie low so it covers his eyebrow and exhales deeply. "Here goes nothing, sweetheart. Let's go get your bar food."

"Don't touch my nachos."

123

Chapter Twelve

"I'll open your door," Leo pins me with a firm look. "Wait for me."

I frown and watch him pull himself out of the car and walk around the front end to my door. He pulls it open and grasps my hand firmly, pulling me close to his side.

Two tall, bulky men are standing stoically on the sidewalk, waiting for us.

"This is Stan and Henry. They're security for tonight," Leo murmurs and turns to the men. "You don't let her out of your sight, ever. Got it?"

"Got it, sir," Stan replies and they both nod.

"Uh, Leo…" I look up at him with a frown. "Is this necessary?"

"Yes," he replies and cups my cheek in his hand. "It's a packed house, and I won't take any chances with your safety."

Jesus, it's then it occurs to me that I'm out with Leo Nash. Lead singer and founder of the worldwide sensation *Nash.* I'm not out with Leo, my boyfriend.

Oh boy.

"Okay." I smile at him reassuringly and pat his chest with my free hand. "Lead the way."

He nods at his security guys, and one leads us in and the other walks in behind us. The band has just begun playing a cover of a Nirvana song. It's still early in the set. The music hits us like a wall as we walk into the large club. The stage is big and in the far back. Most of the patrons are gathered around the stage, drinks in the air, dancing and enjoying the music.

Leo leads me to a booth in the main bar area with a full view of the stage, motions for me to slide in and then joins me, sitting beside me rather than across from me. The security guys sit at an empty table right next to us.

124

"What can I get you?" A waitress yells above the music.

Leo raises an eyebrow at me. "I'll take a dirty martini."

He smirks and gives the waitress my order, along with a beer for himself and all of the bar food I want. He grips my hand in his and kisses my knuckles and smiles down at me. "Do you like Nirvana?"

"Do I live in Seattle?" I respond and wrinkle my nose at him. "Duh."

He laughs and we settle in and watch the band, the people milling about. No one is paying us any attention, and I can't help but think that hiring security was a bit over the top.

No one even cares that we're here.

Our drinks and food arrive and Leo leans in to yell into the waitress's ear. She smiles and nods and turns away.

"What did you say to her?" I ask loudly and shove a delicious potato skin piled with sour cream into my mouth.

"You're so classy." He laughs and wipes a glob of sour cream from my lip.

"I know." I shrug and keep eating.

"I told her to let the band's people know I'm here."

"Oh, cool." We eat and listen, people watch. Glancing at Leo, I see a trail of sweat drip down his neck.

"You're sweating." I frown. "Take your beanie off, babe."

He shakes his head and looks around the room. "Not yet."

He's completely over-reacting. "No one here has even looked at you twice," I remind him.

"Not yet," he says again and reaches for a cheese stick.

"We should offer Thing One and Thing Two some food." There is still a ton of food that we'll never be able to finish.

He smiles down at me and wraps an arm around my shoulders. "They're about to earn their paychecks."

Just then the band ends a song and starts talking to the audience. "Hey, Seattle, are you having a fuckin' good time yet?"

The crowd goes crazy, screaming and whooping, and I grin. I love live shows.

"What would you say if I told you I have a surprise for you?" The lead singer asks and takes a long swig of water. More cheers.

"An old friend of mine is here."

"That's our cue," Leo murmurs to me and nods to security. "Come on."

"I'm not going on stage," I protest, and he laughs.

"No, you're going to be in the wings. I don't want you in this crowd." We join our burly security. "I want you guys to escort her to the wings. They're expecting you and will show you where to go."

They nod and off we go through the crowd.

"Have you guys heard of a little band called *Nash?*" The crowd explodes in applause and cheers. "How about the ugly front guy they have, Leo?"

We are led to the right side of the stage and through a door and to an immediate left, and I'm told to stay right here, behind a black curtain. I'm looking onto the stage, and can see the whole band.

"Well," the singer continues, "I knew Leo back in the day when he was just singing around Seattle, and it just so happens that he's in town and has dropped by to see us!"

He has to stop speaking because the cheers are deafening. I can't help but bounce on the balls of my feet in excitement, my throat clenches in joy and I grasp my hands together, holding them against my chest.

Suddenly, from the other side of the stage, Leo hops up and joins the singer, giving him a real hug and whispering in his ear. He's pulled his beanie off, showing his messy light brown hair and piercings. He's still in his blazer, but he takes it off and throws it off stage to someone in the wings.

The girls scream some more as he stands there in just his Levi's tee, the sleeves hugging his muscular, tattooed arms. Dear Lord, he's beautiful.

And completely in his element.

He's grinning widely, waving and nodding at the crowd, and he takes a mic when it's offered to him.

"Hey, Seattle!"

More screams, and I clap along with the crowd. Leo turns his head and finds me behind the black curtain and winks.

"So bro, what do you want to do?" His friend asks him.

"Well… I don't know." He frowns and looks out at the fans. "Do you guys want to hear something?"

Well, that's a stupid question. The girls go mad, and Leo laughs.

"You're welcome to borrow my guitar, man."

"Nah." Leo shakes his head and motions to the piano. "Can I jack your piano?"

"Anything you want."

The pianist stands and bows to Leo and the whole band exits the stage, saying hi to me as they pass, and Leo is alone on stage. Whoever is running the lights points a spotlight on him, dimming the rest of the stage.

I can't look away. I can't blink.

"So, this is a new song," he begins, adjusting the mic on the stand and settling behind the piano. "Would you like to hear it?"

"I love you Leo!" a girl screams drunkenly from the front row.

"Thank you, sugar," he winks at her, chuckles and begins to noodle the keys, warming his hands. "I'm gonna slow things down a bit. This song is called *Sunshine*."

He plays the lead in. It's soft and sweet and glaringly familiar to me.

And then he starts to sing.

I don't wanna be your friend
'Cause I've already let you in
Every time I see your sweet blue eyes
I know I need to make you mine
My walls crumble… And crumble
So all you see is the real me

I'm stunned. It's me. He's singing about me. And the music is the music he wrote when I was sick, when we were at the piano together.

He hits the hook, and my heart swells to almost bursting.

I wrote that music.

I had no idea he was writing a song about me. Or that it would turn into a song at all. I thought he was just playing around while he was bored and taking care of me.

He wrote a fucking song for me.

When you smile
Your sunshine hits me
And the shadows in my soul
They are gone

Oh how many times
Have I stared at your lips
Wishing I could feel them on me
When you're so close
Baby, I forget how to breathe

He looks up at me and pins me with those deep gray eyes, his look is fierce and possessive, and then one side of his mouth tips up as he leads back into the chorus.

When you smile
Your sunshine hits me
And the shadows in my soul
They are gone

When I run my hand
Over your perfect skin
I know you see me
And not what I'm covered in
My walls crumble… And crumble
So all you see is the me I need you to see

I feel the tears tumble over onto my cheeks, but can't move to brush them away. His voice is surrounding me, cocooning me in its warmth, in the tenderness of the words, in the sweet music from the piano.

Can't play well my ass. I bet he does everything well.

Finally the song comes to an end and he takes a deep breath and grins at the audience. He stands and waves, gives a small bow, and runs off the stage to me, scooping me up into his arms.

"Oh my God!" I exclaim and wrap my arms around his neck.

"Did you like it?" He asks and leans back to look into my eyes.

"It's fantastic," I respond and kiss him soundly.

"It's yours."

"I hope so, or I'd have to cut a bitch." I immediately respond and he lets out a belly laugh, holding me tightly against him. "It's the best gift I've ever been given, thank you." I murmur in his ear and he grins widely. Proudly.

"Let's go back stage." He pulls me behind him as the band resumes their place on stage to finish out their set. I didn't even notice that the security twins had been standing behind me the whole time, and they follow us now. One of them hands Leo his jacket.

There is a decent-sized group of people back stage waiting for the band. Some in business attire, who I assume are industry people. Some look like family members or friends of the band.

And there are more than a few groupies.

Leo leads me in, my hand gripped firmly in his, and begins introducing me to people he knows. I'll never remember their names or even their faces, but the fact that he keeps me next to him and includes me in every conversation says a lot about this man.

He cares about me.

The band comes barreling in the room, reaching for beers and high-fiving each other, obviously happy with their show.

The room is electric with energy.

"Dude!" The lead singer charges for us and tackles Leo in a hug. "Nice song, bro." He winks at Leo and smiles down at me. "I'm Lance."

"Sam," I respond and shake his hand.

"How long are you in town?" He asks Leo.

"A while. We're recording the next album here," Leo responds. "I'd like you to come in and help out on a few tracks."

Lance's eyes spark with interest and he grins. "Done."

"Cool."

"Great show, babe." A pretty redhead hugs Lance from behind and he turns to pull her in his arms.

"Thanks, my love. Tash, this is Leo and Sam. Leo, you remember my wife."

"Of course, hey Tash." Leo leans in and kisses her cheek.

"Hey, so great to see you!" I immediately like her. She's someone I would hang out with, down to earth and nice and not fawning all over *the* Leo Nash.

The happy couple turns to mingle with the other after-show guests and Leo grins down at me. "Having fun?"

"I am." I nod and glance around the room. "It's more laid back than I expected."

"Security will start letting some fans back in a few minutes for photos and autographs." He shrugs. "It'll get louder."

"Well, hello." A busty brunette, in a black halter-top, tight enough to showcase her paid-for tits and a black skirt that barely covers her ass is suddenly pressed against Leo's other side. "Looking for a good time, Mr. Nash?"

Leo frowns down at her and I feel my eyebrows climb into my hairline. The bitch has balls; I'll give her that.

She's also repulsive.

Yuck.

These groupies are so not like the over-zealous fan-girls that I'm used to. They're clearly not here just because of their love of the music or the work. They're here to fuck a band member.

That's it.

I think I just threw up a little in my mouth.

"Do you not see me holding my girlfriend's hand?" Leo asks, his voice cold.

"I can do a threesome, if that's what you're into," she grins and rubs her tits against his arm.

I can't help it, the laugh bursts out of me, and I double over. I have to release Leo's hand so I can hold my stomach; I'm laughing so hard.

She's so pathetic she's hilarious.

I look up into Leo's laughing eyes. He has a wide grin and is ignoring the offended woman still plastered to his side. She's scowling at me, and that makes me laugh harder.

"Are you okay, sunshine?" Leo asks with a chuckle as I straighten and finally take a deep breath. I wipe the tears from under my eyes, thanking God for waterproof mascara, and nod.

"Is this what you were talking about earlier? Girls like this?"

He just shrugs and nods.

"Yeah, I'm so not worried." Now the bimbo's eyes narrow on me and I chuckle again.

"Fuck you," she flings at me and props her hand on her hip, still pressing herself to Leo's side.

"You're touching something that's not yours," I tell her with a wide smile.

"I don't see a ring on his finger." She smirks.

"Wouldn't matter to you if you did," I remind her and she nods thoughtfully.

"True."

Leo is watching the exchange like it's a tennis match, his head bouncing back and forth. Finally, he raises an eyebrow at the slut and pulls away from her.

"I won't be requiring your services, but I'm sure one of the other unattached guys will take you up on it."

"But I want to say I fucked Leo Nash," she pouts. "Come on. I'll let the bitch join in."

I laugh again and then clasp my hand over my mouth as Leo glares daggers at the less-than-intelligent woman.

"I didn't fuck trash like you when I was single. Why would I start now?" He turns his back on her and tips my chin up with his finger. "Wanna get out of here?"

"We don't have to leave just because of that," I assure him, my voice light. "I told you earlier, I don't care."

He leans in until his mouth is pressed to my ear and whispers, "I don't give a fuck about her either, sweetheart. I'm ready to take you home, get you naked and have you beneath me."

My breath catches in my lungs. "Well, when you put it like that, yeah, let's go."

Leo waves at Lance, who nods in acknowledgement, and calls out goodbyes to the rest of the band. Security escorts us out through the back door into the refreshing cool winter air and to his Camaro.

He starts the car and pulls away from the curb.

"That was fun." I turn in my seat so I can see him, watching the street lights flash over his face and reflect off the metal in his ear and lip.

"Yeah, it was," he agrees. "You weren't kidding. The groupies don't bother you."

"They're gross." I wrinkle my forehead. "Why would anyone fuck that? Who knows where her pussy has been, not to mention her mouth. Ew." I shudder and make gagging noises. "Seriously, that's just not sanitary."

Leo throws his head back and laughs.

"How many groupies did you fuck in your day? And don't tell me you can't count that high. You're smart."

"So not answering that question." He shakes his head.

"No, really."

"Sam, there are some questions a woman should never ask. Asking a famous musician how many women he's banged is one of them."

"Just give me an estimate."

"How many men have you fucked?" He asks, frowning at me.

"I asked you first." I grin, enjoying his discomfort.

"I fucked the groupies back in the day. It's been a while." He shrugs. "Who knows how many."

"But no kissing and no oral?" I ask, remembering what Meg said at dinner the other night.

"No, too personal."

"Just a quick fuck then."

"Samantha…" And I know this is as far as he's willing to take his side of the conversation, so I let him off the hook.

"Six," I state.

"Six what?" He asks.

"I've had sex with six guys, including you." I smile smugly at him and wait for his reaction.

"You've only had sex with six guys?"

"Hey, that's a decent number. Enough to know what I like, but not so many that I'm like a fast-food drive through."

Leo laughs again and smiles over at me. "I've had sex with more than six women."

"I figured."

"But I'm only having sex with one at the present time."

"If it were any different, I'd have cut off your dick by now." I nod. "Most guys had a lot of sex when they were young. You're a musician. All you have to do is open your mouth and women take off their underwear. What man can resist that?"

"I didn't have sex with thousands or anything, you know. I'm no Gene Simmons."

I laugh. "I really don't care, it's just fun to torment you."

His eyes narrow on me. "I think I might need to spank you."

I sober and watch his strong hands on the steering wheel. "Sing me my song again and you can do anything you want."

His face turns to mine in surprise, and then he smiles softly. "You really like it?"

I nod happily and reach for his hand as he begins to sing quietly.

I don't wanna be your friend
Cause I've already let you in
Everytime I see your sweet blue eyes
I know I need to make you mine
My walls crumble... And crumble
So all you see is the real me

He sings the whole song, from start to finish, and I trace the ink on his hands as I listen, soaking in the words.

When I run my hand
Over your perfect skin
I know you see me
And not what I'm covered in
My walls crumble... And crumble
So all you see is the me I need you to see

My pretty red panties are wet by the time the song ends, I'm panting.

I want him. Now.

He pulls up at his townhouse and cuts the engine. "I can't wait long enough to drive to your place."

"Good call."

Chapter Thirteen

We barely make it through his front door before we're attacking each other. His alarm system beeps with a warning, reminding him to put the code in before they call for the police.

I so don't need the police to break this up.

He's working on my jeans, not paying attention as I slam the door behind us.

"The code, Leo."

"Huh?" He buries his face in my neck and bites the tender flesh below my ear, sending tingles down my arms.

"What's the code? I don't want to stop for the cops."

"One two three four."

I stop and frown up at him. "Seriously?"

"Yep," He's pulling my tight jeans down my thighs and I struggle to turn to the keypad to enter in the code before the thirty-second window is up. I punch in the numbers and turn back to him.

"Step out of your pants." He's squatting by my feet, and I lean on his shoulders, bunching the material of the t-shirt in my fingers, while he peels the denim off my legs.

"Shirt off," I mutter and he complies and assaults my mouth with hard, demanding kisses.

He pulls me to the stairs as we continue to tug and pull at our clothes, inching our way up toward the bedroom.

"Can't wait." He props me on the landing, my feet planted on the stairs and he leans in and buries his face in my still-covered pussy.

"Holy shit!" I jackknife into a sitting position, watching Leo pull the lace to the side with his forefinger and lap at my labia, through my folds and up to my clit. "Fuck," I whisper.

"Lie back," he instructs me, his voice hard and leaving no room for argument.

I love it when he gets demanding.

He rips my underwear in two and throws them over his shoulder.

"You keep destroying perfectly good underwear." I pant and feel him grin against my pussy.

"I'll buy you more."

"You don't have to. I like it." I hear him chuckle and then his tongue is inside me and my hips raise up off of the stairs, pushing me harder against his mouth. He cups my ass in his hands and holds me tightly against him.

"Fuck you're good at that." And I remember: I'm one of the few who knows that.

He sinks a single finger inside me, and I clench around him, my muscles ready to clench around his thick cock.

I need him inside me.

"Leo," I breathe.

"Yes, baby."

I look down to find him watching me, watching my nipples pucker in arousal, my breath coming fast, my teeth biting into my lip over and over again while he finger-fucks me and licks at my clit.

"God, I need you."

"You have me, Sam." His eyes are happy and full of mischief as he sinks a second finger into me and sucks on my clit, hard.

I explode, screaming his name and grinding against his face, clutching his hair in my fists. I hear him laugh as he rises over me and pulls my nipples into his mouth, sucking hard and running his tongue over them each in turn, which sparks new contractions around his fingers.

"So responsive," he murmurs against my mouth. I can smell myself on him, and damn if it doesn't turn me on even more. "I think I need you in my bed."

Before I can protest, or even respond, he lifts me and carries me quickly to the bedroom, and lays me, face down, on the bed. Just when I think he's going to take me hard and fast, he begins kissing me, lightly biting me, from my ass up my spine and to my neck. He straddles my thighs and I feel his hard cock resting on my buttocks. He's bent over me, caressing and kissing my back, whispering words that I barely understand through the thick sexual haze I'm caught up in, and I can't help but lift my hips in invitation.

"In a minute, baby," he whispers and pulls his large hand down my back to my ass. "You are beautiful, Sam. I love your soft skin. You don't have any scars or marks on you."

"Well, just the ink from your marker," I remind him with a smirk and he bites my shoulder playfully.

"You didn't mind," he mutters and continues to lightly rub me, raising goosebumps on my flesh.

"It was sexy," I whisper.

"You're sexy," he whispers back and kisses my shoulder where he just bit it. "I love your raspy voice." He kisses my spine, right between my shoulder blades. "I love your soft blonde hair." He kisses my other shoulder. "I love the noise you make when I do this." He bites my earlobe and I moan.

"Fucking sexy," he murmurs and slides down my body leaving open-mouthed kisses in his wake. He grips my hips and raises my ass off the bed. Finally!

But instead of fucking me, he buries his face in my pussy again, and sends me straight into another mind-numbing orgasm.

"Holy fuck!" I scream as he drags his tongue up and down my labia, from my anus to my clit. "Leo, please!"

"Please what, baby?" He asks, and I hear him tear open a condom. *Thank Moses.*

"Fuck me!"

"Okay," he agrees and slams inside me, hard. I cry out again and push my ass back on him, meeting his thrusts. He suddenly smacks my right cheek with his palm and I shudder. He smacks the left cheek just before he slams into me again, and I feel like I'm going to simply die from the pleasure.

He continues to alternate lightly spanking me while fucking me, and when I hear his breath catch, and know that he's almost there, I reach down between my legs and fondle his scrotum.

"Fuck!" He cries out and grips my hips roughly, pulling me rhythmically against him as he succumbs to his orgasm.

He pulls out of me and I fall onto my chest, ass still in the air. I can't move.

I don't care.

"Well, that's a gorgeous sight," Leo murmurs with a grin as he walks back into the room from discarding the condom. I open one eye and stare at him.

"You broke me."

He laughs as he settles next to me, rolling me onto my side and into his arms. "I don't think so."

"Mmm."

"Look at me." I pull my eyes open to find him frowning down at me. "Are you okay?"

I nod and yawn and shimmy closer to him. He runs his knuckles down my face and his expression softens.

"Thank you for my song," I whisper.

"You're welcome."

"Are you going to record it?" I ask, blinking lazily up at him.

"Yes, if you don't mind."

I shrug. "I don't mind. You just don't usually do many ballads."

"It's a badass ballad, not a pussy ballad," he mutters defensively and I smile widely.

"Definitely badass," I agree.

"Go to sleep, baby." He kisses my forehead.

"Not tired," I mutter and smile when his chuckle rumbles against my cheek.

"Sure you're not." He kisses my forehead again and sighs deeply, contentedly, and the sound of his steady heartbeat and the warmth of his arms around me lull me into sleep.

* * *

"No, no, no!"

I wake abruptly, eyes wide, to find Leo thrashing in his sleep, soaked in sweat. The covers have all been kicked onto the floor, along with his pillow. He's not touching me at all, and the sounds coming from him are tortured, strained.

"Leo?" I ask carefully, not knowing if I should touch him, or even wake him. He thrashes again and grimaces, as if in pain.

"No, you motherfucker!" Tears begin to fall from his eyes.

What the fuck is this?

"Leo, wake up," I state firmly, and touch his arm gently. He recoils from my touch and his eyes spring open. He sits straight up and shoves himself against the headboard, pulling away from me as if I'm going to hurt him.

"Hey, sweetie, it's me," I croon quietly. "You're okay."

He blinks at me for a minute, looks around the room, and then exhales deeply.

"Fuck," he whispers and clenches his eyes closed before pressing the heels of his hands against them.

"Leo." I reach out for him, but he recoils again.

"Don't touch me." His voice is harsh. Angry.

Not Leo.

"Okay." I hold my hands up and back away. "Okay."

Suddenly, his eyes go wide and he grips his hands over his mouth, flees the bed for the bathroom and throws up violently.

Oh my God. My poor Leo.

What should I do? I sit still for a minute, and when it sounds like the retching is over, I stand and wet a washcloth and press it to his neck, like he did for me when I was sick. Before I can pull my hand away, he grips it in his and holds on tight, pressing it against his cheek.

"Don't go. I'm sorry."

"Hey, I'm not going anywhere." I sink to my knees beside him and stroke his hair, his cheek, his back. "I'm here."

His eyes are clenched shut and he's concentrating on breathing. Whatever it was that he was dreaming about is still repeating in his mind, and it's terrifying him.

"Stop," I murmur and kiss his temple. "You're safe, Leo. It was just a dream." I continue to reassure him and murmur softly, comforting him, until the shudders stop and he's breathing normally again. He turns suddenly and grips onto me, buries his face in my neck, wraps his arms around my middle, and just clings.

Finally, after a few long minutes he backs away and I wipe his face with the cloth, trying to soothe him.

"I'm okay." He takes the cloth from me and scrubs it across the back of his neck and looks at me, square-on. His eyes are sad, still a little haunted.

"Want to talk about it?" I ask.

He shakes his head and stands, crosses to the sink and rinses his mouth, splashes his face with cold water and then just braces his hands on the counter top and hangs his head while the water runs.

It occurs to me that we're both still naked as the day we were born.

I stand and turn off the water and take Leo's hand to lead him back to the bed. He climbs on and I pull the covers up, spreading them over us and hand him his pillow.

"I can't go back to sleep," he murmurs.

"The nightmares won't bother you," I tell him confidently and wrap myself around him, as if I'm protecting him.

"How do you know?"

"Because I'm here, and I said so." I shrug, like that should be the end of it and flinch when he runs a hand down my back.

"You haven't flinched in a while." I hear the sadness in his voice and I prop myself up on my forearms on his chest so I can watch his face as I talk.

"I just didn't expect you to try to comfort me right now, Leo. I'm comforting you, and for the first time in my life, it doesn't scare the fuck out of me." His eyes widen and he pulls his fingertips down my cheeks. "I enjoy having your hands on me. Please don't start thinking that I'm afraid of you or some bullshit like that because you'll just piss me off."

"So, this is you comforting me?" He asks with a grin.

I exhale and rest my forehead against his sternum. "Big jerk," I mutter.

"Thank you," he whispers and kisses my hair, his hands roaming up and down my back.

"You're welcome. Will you ever tell me?" I ask softly as he starts to relax beneath my cheek.

"Yeah, but not tonight."

"Okay."

* * *

~Leo~

Sam is draped over me, her arms holding me tightly, as though she's going to single-handedly protect me from whatever might try to hurt me.

And damned if she wouldn't. She's the strongest woman I've ever known.

I stroke her back, push my fingers through her hair, and grin when she purrs like a kitten and leans into my touch.

Yes, she's grown used to me touching her.

The nightmare still sits like dead weight in the pit of my stomach, the images flitting in and out of my mind. I don't have them nearly as often as I did about ten years ago, but they do still come. I can't figure out what triggers them. There's no way in hell that making love to Sam, singing for her, watching her eyes light up with joy and excitement, should trigger the fucked up mess that lives in my subconscious.

I need to talk to her, to tell her about what happened when I was too young to protect myself. She deserves to know. But I'll be goddamned if I want it to touch her. To see the pity in her eyes, or even worse, revulsion, would destroy me.

I'm just not ready.

"Leo," she murmurs, surprising me. I would have sworn she was asleep.

"Yes, sunshine," I whisper and gently caress her soft cheek. Damn she's soft. She's soft everywhere, and I can't stop touching her.

"Go to sleep."

She's so damn stubborn.

"You sleep," I mutter and kiss her head.

"Not unless you do."

Yep, fucking stubborn.

"Okay, I'll sleep."

"Liar." She sits up and offers me a sweet grin. "It's almost dawn anyway. We could go for a run."

I pull her back to me and roll her so she's tucked beneath me, cradling my pelvis in hers and her hands immediately find my ass.

I brace my elbows beside her head and bury my hands in her hair, nuzzle her nose with mine, and then sink into a long, slow, wet kiss. She makes me forget the shitty past, and is the first person I've been with that makes me feel as alive as I feel when I'm playing music.

I'm never letting her go.

My cock is painfully hard again, and rubbing against the wetness from her pussy. Each time I hit her clit with the tip, she moans and bites her lip. I reach over for a condom, but she stops me, links her fingers in mine and pulls them to her face, rubbing the back of my hand on her cheek.

"We don't need the condom," she whispers, her gorgeous blue eyes watching mine intently.

"Sam." I kiss her tenderly. "I'm fine with the condoms."

She shakes her head and cups my face with her free hand. "We don't need them," she repeats. "I have an IUD."

"But…" I begin, but she interrupts me again, kissing me with those pouty lips of hers, pulling on the hoop in my lip.

"I trust you," she states firmly, eyes still on me and happy, and I know that statement is possibly the most profound Samantha Williams could have made to me.

"I trust you, too." My lips find hers again, sweeping back and forth, teasing her sweet tongue with my own, and I pull my hips back to slowly sink into her tight, wet warmth.

She gasps and smiles. "So much better this way."

"Jesus H. Christ, Samantha I've never not used protection," I admit and watch her closely.

"Me neither." She grins. "I think I prefer it."

If I move, I'll come. It's that simple. God, she feels amazing, her tight muscles gripping my bare cock, legs hitched up around my hips, cradling me. I've never felt so complete.

So whole.

"You have to move," she murmurs.

"I don't want to," I shake my head and rest my forehead on hers.

"Why?"

"I don't want it to be over."

"Leo," she wiggles her hips, forcing me to move within her. It takes my breath away. "This is just the first time."

The first time of many.

My hips begin to move, thrusting softly at first and then gaining momentum, pushing harder, faster. I feel the build-up rush down my spine as the first tiny contractions grip my cock.

"Fuck, baby, you feel so good." Reaching between us, I graze her clit with my thumb, and push her over the edge into oblivion. She bucks and cries out, her pussy squeezing around me even more. My balls tighten and lift, and the world stops spinning as I come inside her, truly inside her, for the first time.

It's the most incredible moment of my life.

"Amazing," I murmur and kiss her softly.

"You're not so bad yourself."

Chapter Fourteen

~Samantha~

"My name starts with a 'c', and ends in a 't'. I'm hairy and round and squishy inside. What am I?" Jules folds over in laughter, the card with the question gripped in her hand.

"I need another beer," Caleb mutters and stomps into Luke and Nat's kitchen for another round.

"A carrot?" Brynna asks, squishing up her face in concentration.

"What kind of carrots have you been eating?" Leo asks with a laugh.

"Ew. Yeah, never mind."

"This is so fucking funny," Jules chuckles.

What the hell could it be? I stare at Jules, as if she can send me the answer by osmosis. We're playing *Dirty Minds* for family game night, all our siblings and better halves are here, and we've turned it into a drinking game.

Of course.

"I know what it is." Will grins at Meg and runs his hand down her back to her hip. "Although yours isn't hairy."

"Yuck. Stop it," I scold him and grin when he laughs out loud.

"Dude, really?" Leo scowls.

"What?" Will asks innocently.

"For the love of all that's holy, Nat, stop fraternizing with the enemy!" Luke has Nat in a firm lip-lock, as usual.

"I'm married to him, Jules. He's hardly the enemy."

"Tonight he is. Girls against guys. Get your sexy ass over here with me."

"Are you going to kiss me?" Nat asks with a raised brow.

"After one more drink, yes."

"Definitely go over there with her," Nate quickly jumps in

and is met with frowns from all the guys, except Leo who continues to laugh next to me.

"Uh, they're our sisters, man." Matt reminds him with a frown on his handsome face, his blue eyes sparkling with humor.

"They're not my sisters," Nate responds.

"It's a coconut, you nasty people!" Jules yells and hands the cards to me. "You go next."

"Okay," I respond and pull a card out of the deck. This game is effing hilarious. "I go in pink and hard and come out soft and sticky. What am I?"

"That's disgusting." Stacey laughs and takes a drink of her margarita.

"That's not what you said last night." Isaac leans in and nuzzles her neck, making her squirm and giggle.

"You are all over-sexed." I announce to the room at large.

"Not all of us," Brynna pouts, sticks her lower lip out and scowls at Caleb.

"Don't start," he warns her.

My eyebrows climb into my hairline. "What the fuck?"

"Caleb's staying with Brynna and the girls for a while," Luke fills me in. "It's a safety issue."

I frown over at the unlikely couple, Brynna with her long dark hair and generously curvy body – God, I wish I had her boobs – and Caleb, the big, muscular Navy SEAL.

"Is something going on there?" I ask Luke softly.

"I have no idea." He shrugs. "But they keep looking at each other. None of my business."

"What is it, Sam?" Nat asks with a grin.

"It's gum."

"Oh! Here's one!" Will exclaims after he takes the box from me. "You stick your poles inside me, you tie me down to get me up and I get wet before you do."

"I like the tie me down talk, you know," I remind the boys and make the room laugh, including the quiet Matt, who chokes on his beer and grins at me.

"Seriously." Leo glances down at me with renewed interest and I feel my cheeks heat.

"Sure." I shrug.

Leo wraps his arm around me, pulls me to his side and kisses my temple, and I immediately stiffen.

I've never, ever shown public displays of affection in front of my family before.

"I'm not a touchy feely person, remember?" I whisper to him. He leans in and lays his lips against my ear.

"Get over it, sunshine. You're mine, I'm yours, and I will touch you." He lightly kisses me again and straightens, his face completely neutral and I feel like I've been hit by a Mack truck.

Luke is watching us thoughtfully while he runs his fingertips up and down Natalie's arm. The rest of the room, including Mark and Meg, are oblivious. I offer Luke a shrug and a slight smile and focus on the game.

"It's a tent, people!" Will laughs and passes the box along.

"I haven't been wet in a while." Brynna announces and I spit out my margarita.

"How many drinks have you had?" I ask her.

"Too many," Caleb responds. "Excuse us, we need to talk." He grips Brynna by the arm and leads her back to Luke's office and we hear the door slam.

I look back and forth between the girls, Jules, Nat, Meg and Stacy, and we all erupt in laughter.

"No orgasm talk tonight." Matt announces in warning.

"Who talks about orgasms?" Mark asks with interest. My baby brother is adorable, and all grown up. He looks so much like Luke and our dad, tall and fair and strong.

And he's a man-whore.

"The girls have a habit of talking about orgasms when alcohol is involved." Nate fills him in and shakes his dark head.

"More drinks, ladies?" Mark asks with his charming, melt-your-panties grin.

"More drinks!" Stacy agrees.

"Orgasms are a perfectly fine thing to talk about." Jules takes a long sip of her drink and offers Nate a goofy grin. "They're better when they're apagasms."

"Julianne!" Nate growls.

"What? Meg called them that first." She points at Meg, who widens her eyes innocently.

"I did?" She asks.

"Yeah, remember? In the van."

"I was completely wasted in the van, Jules." Meg laughs. "But apagasms sound good to me."

"You fucking told them?" Nate turns on Jules in shock and she clasps her lips shut and looks almost embarrassed for a minute but then wraps her arms around his neck and kisses him square on the mouth.

"If you've got it, flaunt it, ace."

"Uh, sweetheart, you don't got it," he reminds her, but she holds up her left hand and wiggles her ring finger at him.

"Yeah, I do."

"I'm surprised you don't have one." I turn to Leo to find his eyes wide in surprise and his mouth gaping. "You're pierced everywhere else."

"I'm not getting my dick pierced!" He gapes at me like I've just told him he should get it cut off.

I snort. Yes, snort. He's adorable.

"Oh, don't be a pussy, I've heard really, really good things about the apa. And speaking of pussies," I gesture at Meg with a wide grin, "Even your sister has her clit pierced."

"What the fuck?" Leo exclaims, scowling between me and Meg and back again. "I raised you better than that!"

"Way to go!" Mark offers her a high-five.

"Can we see it?" Nate asks and wiggles his eyebrows, earning a punch in the arm by Will.

"It's really pretty." Jules smiles sweetly and Natalie nods in agreement.

"You guys have seen it?" Stacy asks.

"Yeah, we went with her when she got it."

"I wanna see it!" Stacy bounces in her seat, her margarita gripped tightly in her hands.

"What do you want to see?" Brynna asks as she and Caleb come back into the room, calmer than when they left, but Brynna's pretty face is flushed.

Interesting.

Meg shrugs and climbs into Will's lap. He wraps his big arms around her and kisses her head. "I wanted a piercing." She informs Leo and winks at me.

"Eyebrow, ear, nose, belly button." He points passionately with his finger with each suggestion. "Are all acceptable piercings."

"That's not what I wanted."

"Jesus." He pulls his tattooed hand down his face and laughs. "I don't ever, *ever* need to know stuff like this about you."

"Hey." Will interrupts. "Don't knock it till you try it."

"So back to orgasms," Stacy begins and Caleb jumps up, waving his arms about.

"No! No, no, no! No orgasm talk tonight."

"I could talk about orgasms," Mark offers.

"No! I'm serious." Caleb glares at all of us and I decide to put him out of his misery.

"Okay, guys… we'll discuss the O during girls night."

"Good plan," Leo whispers under his breath. "I don't need to hear my sister talk about getting off, and," his voice drops further, "every time I make you come, is between you and me, sugar. No one else."

Well, now I'd be happy to discuss orgasms. My purple panties are soaked.

"How are the living arrangements working out?" Matt asks Caleb and Brynna.

"Fine." Caleb shrugs.

"He's nice to the girls," Brynna comments with soft deep brown eyes.

Dear God, she's fallen for him! What the hell has been going on in that house?

We all exchange glances, but no one pushes the subject.

Caleb's face softens into a smile and he rests his big hand on Brynna's jean-covered knee. "They're easy to be nice to."

"No kid talk," Stacy scolds them. "We agreed. We're pretending we're young, with no responsibilities."

"I am young with no responsibilities." Mark reminds us all with a satisfied smile. "I recommend it."

"Right, 'cause you hate kids." I smirk. "You can't stand holding Livie."

"I love her. And then she goes home and I go find a warm body for the night." He winks and I scowl back at him.

"Gross."

"I'm not sure Sam should be having babies any time soon." Meg announces with a laugh.

"Why not?" Luke asks.

"Well, there was a diaper…" Leo reaches over and covers her mouth with his hand, muffling the rest of the words and making them sound like the teacher on the *Peanuts.*

"I'm just definitely not ready." I tell him quickly. "Not terribly maternal. You know." I shrug and glance over at Nat to find her laughing, holding her stomach.

"Did Liv blow out her diaper when you watched her?" She asks and wipes tears from her eyes.

"What the hell do you feed her?" Leo demands.

"Stop talking about kids!" Jules interrupts. "And definitely stop talking about poop."

"She said poop." Will laughs.

"What are you, twelve?" Matt asks him.

"Like you didn't snicker."

"Shit, now I want chocolate," Brynna bites her lip.

"Do you have chocolate?" Jules asks Natalie.

"I live here, girls, and I'm pregnant. Of course there's chocolate! Follow me!" Nat jumps up and we all eagerly follow behind, taking our drinks with us, to the kitchen.

Natalie disappears into a pantry and then opens her fridge and begins piling goodies on the countertop. "We have chocolate ice-cream, kisses, brownies, and whipped cream."

"I am so in love with you right now, I want to lay you out on this countertop and eat this shit off of you," Jules hugs Nat tight and pulls down bowls, passes them around.

"Don't mind us, we'll just watch." Nate calls from the living area.

"Oh my God, so good." Brynna moans as she chews a chunk of brownie. I love Brynna's body. Like Nat, she's curvy, but more so. "I wish I had your boobs," I tell her, not able to keep the envy out of my voice.

She smirks. "Right."

"Dude, I do!" I take a sip of my drink, already happily fuzzy in the brain, and walk over to her and cup her size C cup boob in my palm. "See? You have the perfect boobs. Stace, have you felt her boobs?"

"Oh yeah." Stacy waves me off. "She has great tits."

"I wanna feel!" Jules bounces over to us.

"Give me more chocolate and you can touch all you want." Brynna laughs. "This is the most action I've had in months," she glares at Caleb and he swears long and loud.

"Your boobs are fine the way they are, sunshine." Leo reminds me from the living room, and I blow him a kiss.

"I'm glad you approve, sexy man."

We continue to gorge ourselves on junk, the guys are laughing and arguing about football and cars and other things that I just frankly don't give a shit about.

"So, how's the sex?" Jules asks me and glances over toward the other room.

"I don't want to know." Meg frowns. "Wait. Yeah, I do. Spill."

I so want to tell them. I really, really do.

"And after you tell us about the sex, tell us how you are." Natalie adds.

They're all looking at me with a mixture of curiosity, sympathy and pure pride.

God, I love these girls.

"Sex is… amazing," I admit and bite my lip. "I'm good. We're still figuring it out."

"Sounds about right." Nat nods with approval. "He's sexy, that's for sure."

"God, he's sex on a stick," Stacy agrees.

"I want to lick his stars," Brynna adds and we all giggle.

"Dude, I do that all the time. They're so lickable."

"I hate you." Brynna laughs. "I really hate you."

"Yeah, 'cause living with a hot Navy SEAL is so difficult."

"Asshole won't touch me, no matter how hard I try," she whispers. Jules' eyes go wide in surprise.

"Oh my God!" She gasps.

"Talk about sex on a stick," Meg agrees. "Look at them. Goddam, we're in the same room with what looks like an issue of *People Magazines* sexiest men alive."

"I need an orgasm." I sigh just as Leo looks in my direction and catches my eye. A slow, smug smile spreads across his handsome face, as if he can read my mind.

Probably because he can, damn him.

"I don't know what else you guys are trying to figure out," Meg comments and unwraps a kiss.

"It's only been a few weeks," I remind her.

"True." She shrugs and pops the chocolate in her mouth.

My favorite Sara Bareilles song, *King of Anything* begins to play over the sound system. "God, I love this song."

"I do too!" Jules toasts me and all of us girls begin to sing and dance around the kitchen, using forks for microphones, laughing and shaking what our mamas gave us.

Who cares if you disagree
You are not me
Who made you king of anything

The song ends and we high-five and spin around the to the sound of applause coming from our laughing men.

I don't remember the last time I had this much fun and felt so... content.

We bow for the men.

"Encore!" Mark yells. "With less clothes. Except you, Sam, keep your shit on."

"We're a one-song show, guys. Sorry."

"I think it's time we head out anyway." Isaac responds as the guys wander into the kitchen to join us. He wraps his arms around his wife and kisses her cheek.

"It's late," Nate murmurs to Jules.

"Killjoys," Meg grumbles but laughs when Will plants his hands on her ass and lifts her up to his more than six-feet height to plant a kiss on her. "Okay, I could go home."

Leo slides up behind me and wraps his arms around my middle, pulling me firmly against his flat abdomen, and after stiffening for just a moment, I relax against him.

"That's better," he whispers in my ear. "I'm ready to have you to myself."

"Okay." I grin up at him. "Let's go."

Will has already carried Meg to the door, and the rest of us grab our jackets and say our goodbyes.

Leo escorts me to the car and holds my door open for me. He's a gentleman rock star; I'll give him that.

We're about halfway home when I just can't stand it anymore. I unclasp my seatbelt and turn in the seat, startling him.

"What are you doing?"

"Can you scoot that seat back a little more and still drive comfortably?" I ask.

He pushes a button on the side of the seat that moves him back a few inches. I unbuckle his belt and unfasten his loose jeans, pull his growing cock out of his tight black boxer-briefs, and lower my face down to him, suck him into my mouth firmly and groan as he hardens instantly.

"Holy fuck!" He exclaims and buries one hand in my hair. I don't give him a chance to get used to my mouth, I assault him, in the best way possible, sucking and running my teeth gently along his skin, licking and gripping him with my lips, jacking him with my hand. "Sam, Jesus, what the hell, baby?"

I prop my ass in the air, my knees on the seat, and grin around his cock when I feel him slap my ass.

I suck harder, and feel the tension grip his thighs just before he comes hard, squirting into the back of my mouth. I swallow quickly and continue to gently caress his dick with my lips until he relaxes in the seat again.

He grips my chin between his thumb and forefinger and lifts my face to his, kisses me deeply and quickly and then smiles with lust in his gray eyes. "Not that I'm complaining because that was fan-fucking-tastic, but what was that for?"

"I love your cock." I shrug and sit back in my seat. "I wanted to suck it. So I did."

"Can't argue with that." He laughs. "But you're lucky I didn't drive us off the road."

"You're a good driver." I wave him off and laugh. "I wasn't worried."

He links his fingers with mine and rubs his thumb over my knuckles. "What color is your underwear?"

"Purple."

"Are they favorites of yours?" He asks casually.

"I do like them, yes."

"Then I suggest you take them off before I get my hands on you when we get home unless you want another pair of ripped panties, sunshine, because I'm taking you against the front door."

"Well, can't argue with that."

Chapter Fifteen

Leo shuts my front door behind us, catches my hand in his before I can walk farther into the room, spins me and pushes me up against the door, his mouth on mine and hands yanking and tugging on my clothes.

"You weren't kidding."

"Hell, no," he mutters and pulls my shirt over my head, unclasps and slips my bra off, and cups my breasts in his hands. "Your tits are perfect, you know."

"They're not very big." I wrinkle my nose at him and pull his tee over his head.

"They're perfect for your small body, baby." My back arches as his lips claim my right breast, and he tugs my jeans down and off my legs.

"Don't rip those," I mutter when his hands close around my panties. He growls and peels them down my legs as well, plants his hands on my ass and lifts me, wrapping my legs around his waist, pinning me against the door.

"You make me fucking crazy," he murmurs against my lips. "You are so damn hot." He slips inside me, to the root, and holds me there, between his hard body and the hard door to my back. "I wanted to pull my car over and fuck you there at the side of the road."

"Next time." I grin at him and bite his lower lip, pull on his piercing, and gasp as he thrusts hard, in long, smooth strokes. He's so strong, his arms are flexed and bracing me firmly.

He buries his face in my neck and bites me lightly, then soothes the skin with his lips. "You feel amazing. God, I love being inside you bare."

"Mmm," I agree and bury my hands in his soft hair, pull his head back and kiss him hard, our tongues sliding over each other, noses nuzzling, until I feel my legs start to shake. "Oh, God, Leo."

"That's it, baby," he whispers and increases his speed, "Give it to me."

"Fuck, fuck, fuck," I chant and suddenly, the orgasm washes over me, clenching every muscle of my body. I cling to him and ride it out, and as I come down, he pivots and carries me across the room, down the hall to the bedroom.

Without pulling out of me, he lays me back on the bed, braces his hands on the mattress at my shoulders, and moves even faster, chasing his own climax.

I reach down between us and circle my clit with my fingers, the zing of electricity spurring my pussy muscles to tighten around him even more. His eyes are pinned to my fingers, to the place where our bodies are joined.

"So beautiful," he whispers. "Keep touching yourself."

"You're bossy," I mutter with a grin. His hot gray eyes shoot up to mine and he grins at me, wolfishly, possessively.

He leans down to his elbows, trapping my hand between us, buries his hands in my hair and grins against my lips. "Are you complaining?"

"Nope." I nibble his lips.

"I didn't think so," he whispers and brushes my lips, back and forth, lightly kisses down my jawline to my ear and bites my earlobe. "So beautiful," he whispers.

With the pressure of my fingers against my nub, Leo's hips moving quickly and his hard cock moving rhythmically inside me, I'm a goner. My body clenches and I can't help but cry out as my climax moves through me like an earthquake.

Leo's body stiffens and he cries out as he comes, his hips jerking, his hands tightening against my scalp. He shudders and gasps for air, kisses my cheek and my lips softly and sighs deeply as his gaze catches my own.

"See what you started?" He asks.

"You're welcome," I respond with a laugh.

He grins widely. "Let's take a shower."

"You'll get me dirty again," I pout, teasing him.

"I'll clean you up too. C'mon, sunshine, let's get slippery."

* * *

"You're going to need more than that," Leo tells me with a frown from the bed. After another round in the shower, finally getting clean, and the water running cold, we pulled on some clothes and I am busy packing my bag for the L.A. trip.

"I'm only going for one night," I remind him.

"No, we're going to be gone for a few days." He glances back down at his iPad, missing my scowl.

"*We* aren't going anywhere." I plant my hands on my hips and glare at him.

"I'm coming with you." He still doesn't look up from his dumb iPad.

"Why?"

"Makes sense." He shrugs. "My house is there. We'll stay there, and I've scheduled meetings that I needed to have anyway for while we're there."

"When, exactly, were you going to share these plans with me?"

I don't know why I'm so pissed, but I am. We've been together for a few weeks. It's not his place to make arrangements around me, for me, without talking to me. I'm not his possession.

"I'm telling you now."

"Look." I begin but he throws the iPad down on the bed, pulls his long, lean body off the bed and cups my face in his hands.

"I don't want to be away from you for a few days. I'm not ready for that. I want to have you in my bed. I want to see you in my house. I want to show you my beach. It's only for a few days, and I didn't say anything before because I know how fucking stubborn you are and I knew you'd say no."

"It's only over night." I frown at him, part of me completely giddy that he wants to be with me, but wary that neither of us can stand the thought of being apart for just a few hours.

He closes his eyes for a brief second, shakes his head and clenches his jaw as he looks at me again. *I've hurt his feelings.*

"But I'd like to see your house." I amend thoughtfully. "You live on the beach?"

His body relaxes and his face calms. "I do."

"Have you ever had sex on the beach?" I ask him. He smirks and his thumbs rub my cheeks softly.

"No."

"I have." I shrug and smirk when he narrows his eyes on me. "We'll need a blanket 'cause I do not need sand in my bits and pieces."

"So, you're assuming we'll have sex on my beach?"

"I'm pretty sure." I kiss him quickly and pull out of his embrace, getting back to packing. "Shit, I need more stuff."

As he laughs, I stomp out of the room to my closet room to choose more clothes for our trip to sunny California. When I return, he's sitting on the bed again, examining his iPad.

"What are you doing?" I ask.

"Reading email, setting up appointments."

"No one is working at this time of night," I remind him.

"No, but when they get my messages tomorrow, they'll make it happen."

"So, you say jump and all of your little followers say 'how high'?" I ask with a raised brow, fold some khaki capris and lay them in my suitcase.

"Pretty much." He shrugs.

"Must be rough," I mutter sarcastically.

"I pay their salaries," he reminds me. "They can make time to meet with me."

He has a point. I nod and finish packing my bag as a thought occurs to me. "Holy shit, you're going to ride in coach with me on the plane tomorrow?"

He snickers and then breaks out into a full on belly laugh. "No, sweetheart. We'll take *Arista's* jet."

"What?" I sputter.

"Well, one of their jets." He frowns deeply. "If I get on that plane with you, we'll have a mess on our hands."

I nod slowly. "Fans."

"Yeah."

I take a deep breath and meet his eyes with my own. "I hate that part." He scowls, and I feel the need to clarify. "I'm so proud of you, babe." I climb on the bed and straddle his hips and wrap my arms around his neck. "I love your music, and I am proud that you do what you love."

"But." He prompts me, his large hands gliding up and down my back.

"But." I frown, trying to gather my thoughts. "The fame part makes me nervous."

"Hell, it makes me nervous."

"Been there, done that," I remind him. "Have the baggage to prove it."

"Look, Sam, I don't expect you to be a part of the celebrity side of my life. That's just work. If I worked in an office, I wouldn't take you there with me. If you want things to be on the down-low, fine, but I won't lie. You're mine." He kisses me and pulls his fingers down my cheek. "But we don't have to take out a spread in a magazine either."

"Okay," I agree.

"The reality is, we'll be photographed at some point. The press will catch on. After a while, it'll be old news."

I nod, knowing he's right. This is the shitty part. If I don't want to deal with his celebrity status, I'll have to choose to lose him. Because he is who he is. He can't change it.

And I don't want him to.

"Okay," I say again and smile at him. "No biggie."

"You're not a good liar," he murmurs, his eyes serious. "It's not as intense as what Luke when through, babe. His fans were obsessive. Mine are just… persistent."

I shake my head and chuckle. "Okay."

"Do you know any other words than 'okay'?" He asks.

"Yes," I respond simply.

"Brat." He laughs and hugs me to him. "Don't sweat it, sweetheart. We'll be fine."

I rest my head against his chest, listening to his steady heartbeat.

God, he makes me nervous.

* * *

"What time is your interview?" Leo asks. He's sitting next to me in the limo as we leave the airport.

I'm still squirming in my seat, wet and swollen. Who knew private airplane sex could be so fun?

Leo's smile is smug. "You okay?"

"I'm fine." I lift my chin and smooth my skirt over my legs. "Um, interview is at two this afternoon."

"Good, we have time to go to my place first."

"Where do you live?" I ask, curious to see where he calls home, and nervous as hell, and not about the interview.

Why does it make me nervous to be going to Leo's house?

"Malibu," he responds and kisses my knuckles.

"But my interview is in Burbank," I remind him.

"Don't worry, you'll be there on time." The limo pulls onto the freeway and Leo pulls me to him, wraps his arm around me, and my eyes drift closed. I'm so damn tired. I didn't sleep well last night, afraid that I'd sleep through the alarm.

"Sleep," he whispers to me and kisses my hair. "I'll wake you when we get there."

I try to sleep, but I just can't seem to shut my brain down. I'm too nervous to see Leo's house, about today's interview, about the possibility of being recognized with him.

Yeah, that's the part that makes me the most nervous. It's been a long time since I saw my photo in a magazine, and I'd rather not start now. Not to mention, I turn into a raging bitch when I'm nervous.

Not good.

"What are you thinking?" He asks softly. My eyes find his in surprise and he smiles softly. "I know you're not sleeping."

"Just thinking about the interview." It's only a half-lie.

"You'll do great." His voice is flat.

"What's wrong?" I ask with a frown.

"I just know you don't want to move down here." He shrugs.

"I'm not going over this again." I roll my eyes and lean my cheek against his chest again.

"You'll do great," he repeats. "Here we are."

The limo pulls through a gate and parks before a large, modern, white home. There are shrubs lining the driveway, and flower gardens here and there. "You must have a gardener."

"I do." He smiles and offers me his hand to help me out of the car. The driver pulls our bags out of the trunk and sets them on the front steps.

"We're good from here, thanks." Leo nods at him.

"Very good, sir." The driver tips his hat and drives away.

"Welcome." Leo grins and kisses me softly, unlocks the door and motions for me to go in ahead of him.

I feel like I've walked into the twilight zone.

I'm completely confused.

I hate it.

"This is… nice." I mutter, my eyes trying to take everything in. It's ultra modern. There is a white baby grand piano resting over a polar bear rug in one corner of the room. The three-piece furniture arrangement around a gas fireplace is also stark white. There are splashes of red and black pillows, throws and end tables scattered about.

The floors are cold marble.

The living area opens up to the state of the art kitchen and a small eating space. The cabinets are black, but again, the countertops are white marble. All of the appliances are stainless steel.

There is a spiral staircase that leads up to the second floor.

My eyes immediately find a gorgeous porch off the kitchen with an outdoor kitchen, fireplace, and steps down to an infinity pool.

"Let's take our bags upstairs," Leo murmurs and leads me to the stairs.

The upstairs is more of the same. Everything is crisply white with weird, modern art on the walls. We pass doors that I assume are to offices or spare bedrooms, and he leads me to a large, sparsely furnished master bedroom. The bed is the size of Alabama, soft and all the linens are white. There are black throw rugs covering the marble floor.

"Bathroom is through there." He motions to the door to the left. "You can hang your things in the closet there, and the balcony is there."

The balcony is the best thing I've seen so far. I wander over, open the glass door and step out onto the covered space. There are two oversized rocking chairs, and the view is breathtaking.

The ocean is bright blue, reflecting the sun. There is a slight breeze.

I would spend every minute of every day out here if I could.

"You haven't said a word," Leo says from behind me. I turn around and lean against the railing, watching him. His hair moves with the breeze. His tattooed hands are tucked in the pockets on his ass, pulling his red tee tightly over his hard chest. "What are you thinking?"

"I would spend every day out on this balcony."

He chuckles and nods. "I usually do when I'm here."

"How often are you here?"

He frowns. "Not often. Maybe about two days every two to three months."

"So, you spend roughly one to two weeks here each year?" I ask, surprised.

"Lately, yeah."

"Damn, no wonder you needed a break." I cross my arms over my chest. *When will he leave again?*

He tilts his head to the side, watching me closely. "What was that thought you just had?"

"Just thinking about your busy schedule," I respond.

"That's the second time you've lied to me today," he murmurs softly, his eyes hard.

"It's not a lie."

He moves toward me and brushes my lower lip with his thumb. "Talk to me."

"You're busy," I state simply.

His eyes narrow, watching me, and then he sighs. "I've slowed down."

"For now." I shrug. "Did you decorate this place?" I ask before he can drill me further on the subject.

"No." He laughs. "This is pretty much what it looked like when I moved in."

"It's not you," I tell him honestly. "It's cold and impersonal."

"What am I?" He asks and moves a little closer.

"You're not this ultra modern, sterile place."

"Maybe I should have it redecorated?" He asks with a grin.

"Maybe." I shrug.

I don't like it that he lives here. That's what it boils down to. I hate it that he owns a house in L.A. and not in Seattle. This isn't where he belongs.

"Okay, your brain is moving past the speed of light, and as much as I'd love to torture you until you talk to me, we need to get you to Burbank." He leans in to kiss me softly, tenderly, and I'm shocked to feel tears trying to form in my eyes. "We'll talk later."

"I'm fine."

"We'll talk later."

* * *

"Thanks for coming all this way for this interview, Ms. Williams." Mr. Foss smiles and shakes my hand. He's shown me around the offices, introduced me to a few people, and now we're settled in his office, ready to get down to business.

"Thanks for having me." I smile brightly.

"Your resume is certainly impressive, and there are about three other people who will join us shortly to proceed through the interview. But before they do, I have a couple of questions."

"Of course."

"I called your former employer at *Seattle Magazine*."

Fuck.

"Yes?"

"I've known Bob for quite some time. As you know, the world of journalism is a small one." He smiles kindly, but I feel my stomach clench.

"That it is." I nod. *Get to the point.*

"Bob wasn't terribly complimentary." He begins and I feel my cheeks heat. That sonofabitch! "But I know, being in the business we are, that there are always two sides to a story." He raises an eyebrow.

"Mr. Foss." I begin and clear my throat. "I love what I do. I think you'll see from my resume and other references that I'm dedicated and that I'm good at my job. But I'm fiercely loyal to my family, and I would hope that any employer who takes me on would respect that."

He watches me for a moment, leaned back in his chair, his fingers laced over his round belly. Finally, he purses his lips and nods. "Fair enough."

Chapter Sixteen

"Why am I going to this again?" I ask Leo as he drives up the freeway the next morning.

"Why not?" He asks.

"I could have just stayed at your place and sent out resumes until you got home."

"That's boring." He grins over at me. "Besides, I thought I'd take you over to the pier in Santa Monica on the way back home."

"Sight seeing?" I ask with a grin.

"Sure." He shrugs. "I'll take you on the Ferris wheel."

"I'm afraid of heights."

"I'll keep you safe." He kisses my hand and pulls into a parking lot.

"We're at Arista records." I tilt my head back and stare at the tall building.

"Oh good, 'cause that's where I wanted to go." He laughs at me as he climbs out of the car.

"You're a smart ass." I smack his arm and then laugh when he swings me back into a deep dip and kisses me silly.

"I'm sorry," he whispers, his eyes happy.

"You're forgiven," I whisper back.

"You're easy." He laughs and hugs me to him as we enter the building and he leads me to the bank of elevators.

"What are we doing here?" I ask.

"The other guys are already here."

"Nash is here? Why?"

"We're doing an interview and some photos for a spread in *People* for when the next album releases. It's not for a few months, but this way we don't have to do it later."

"Okay, so again, why am I here?"

"I thought it would be fun." He frowns down at me. "Are you seriously uncomfortable with this?"

"I don't know."

"We won't be long." He kisses my forehead as the doors open to a lobby that wraps around to a photo studio already set up with lights and a white backdrop.

"Hey, man." A shorter guy with a tall Mohawk grips Leo in a hug. "How you been?"

"Good, man. Hey, this is Sam." Leo turns to me with a grin. "Sam, this is DJ, our bassist. You've met Eric and Jake. That over there is Gary."

Everyone smiles and waves.

"Good to see you again." Eric smiles, his voice friendly and void of the flirtation from before.

"Were you testing me when I met you back in Seattle?" I ask him and plant my hands on my hips.

"You passed." He shrugs and grins widely. Jesus, no wonder the women throw their underwear at him.

"You're too cute for your own good." I offer him a mock glare. "Don't flirt with me or I'll have to hurt you."

"I like her." Gary calls out from where he's sitting in a director's chair having his makeup done.

"Gee, you look pretty." Leo taunts him.

"Shut up."

"Mr. Nash, if you'll sit here, we'll get you ready. Everyone else is good to go."

"You are not touching me with makeup," Leo growls and I slap my hand over my mouth before I laugh out loud.

"But, the lights…" The pour gay-as-can-be makeup artist stops talking when Leo raises his hand at him.

"It's called Photoshop."

"You're an ass." Jake smirks and scrolls through his phone.

"But I'm makeup-free," Leo agrees. "Where's Lori?" He asks Gary.

"Right here!" We all turn as a very pregnant, very tall brunette woman glides into the room.

Good God, she's gorgeous.

"Hey, pretty face." Leo grins and hugs Lori gently, lays his hand on her belly and kisses her cheek.

I might have to kill her.

"How are you feeling?" He asks her.

"Fat, tired and pregnant." She laughs. "But Gary's taking care of me."

"Get your hands off my wife, asshole." Gary calls out, his eyes closed. This must be usual behavior.

"I want you to meet someone." Leo backs away and gestures toward me. "This is Sam."

Lori's mouth drops in surprise and her wide eyes meet Leo's. "You're introducing me to a woman?"

"Shut up," he mutters and laughs.

"Holy shit. Hi." She moves as quickly as she can toward me and instead of shaking my hand, she pulls me into a tight hug. "It's so great to meet you."

"Hi." I smile and pull out of her embrace. "Shouldn't I know you from somewhere?"

"Oh." She waves me off and rubs her belly. "I used to do some modeling back in the day, but these days I'm a stay at home mom."

And then it hits me. "You're Lori Fitzgerald!"

"Yeah." She smiles shyly.

"'Some modeling, huh?" I ask with my tongue in my cheek. "That's like saying I do 'some breathing'."

Lori laughs. "Well, I guess that's true."

"Hey, guys." Another woman enters the room, consulting an iPad gripped in her arm, not looking up. She's clearly used to being around famous people.

Thank God.

"I'm glad you're all here." She scowls at Leo, but he just stares her down, unflinching.

Leo Nash doesn't apologize for being late.

A photographer joins her and begins snapping photos of the guys where they are, getting ready for the shoot, talking to each other.

Me, standing next to Leo and Lori.

"Why is that man taking my picture?" I ask, my bitch voice on full-throttle.

"He's taking candids for the spread." The woman answers me.

"I'm Melissa, the publicist for Nash."

She eyes me for a moment, and then her blue eyes go wide. "Oh my God, you're Luke Williams' sister!"

And just like that, my walls go up and I school my features, pull away from Leo and clench my hands into fists. *Luke Williams' sister.* No name of my own.

"I haven't given anyone my permission to take my photo."

Melissa looks to Leo for guidance, but he just shrugs. "She's right. It's her call."

"Are you two an item?"

"No!"

"Yes." We answer at the same moment. Leo scowls down at me. "We are."

"Holy shit, this is a scoop!" Melissa moves in and I bare my teeth.

"I am not answering questions. I do not want my photo in this spread. Not one goddamn word, do you understand me?"

She comes to an abrupt stop and frowns. "You dated Scott Parker, didn't you?"

"You did?" Lori asks, her voice impressed.

"No comment," I reply and wish with all my might that I wasn't here. What was I thinking taking an interview in L.A.? I can't move here.

"Hey." Leo turns me around and hugs me, but I stay stiff as a board. "Sam, stop this."

"Do your interview, take your pictures, and get me the fuck out of here." I glare at him for a moment and then soften. He didn't do this on purpose. He just wanted me with him.

I take a deep breath, my back to the rest of the room, facing Leo. He's frowning, but his eyes are full of worry, not anger. I shake my head and grip his hands tightly in mine.

"I'm sorry," I whisper. "I just don't want my picture in this spread."

"Done," he replies and kisses my forehead. "Her photo does not appear in this spread." Melissa bristles.

"But this is a major scoop, Leo."

"I don't give a fuck. Unless you want to lose your job, you'll leave her out of it."

"Or we leave," Eric agrees quietly. For the first time since Melissa walked in the room, I glance around at the other guys. They're all glaring at her.

"You're not TMZ," Lori reminds her.

"Fine," Melissa snaps, glaring daggers into me. "Let's do this." She turns her back and her heels click across the floor as she walks into the studio.

"She's a bitch," Lori whispers and winks at me.

"I'm not a fan of the press."

"Yet you work in the industry." Leo shakes his head and laughs at me.

"I am an editor for lifestyle magazines, not rags," I clarify.

"So, you dated Scott?" Lori asks, catching my attention again.

"Briefly, a long time ago," I murmur so Melissa and the interviewer she's speaking with can't hear me.

"He's hot."

"He's an asshole." I grin sweetly. "No matter how wholesome and sweet he wants everyone to think he is."

"I knew it!" Lori laughs. "No one is that put together."

"You have no idea."

Leo is watching us quietly and catches my eye. I shrug.

"Let's go guys!" Melissa calls. "We'll be out of here in thirty."

"Famous last words," Lori mutters and lowers herself down into a chair as the guys move into the studio for photos and to answer questions. "Sit with me."

"Okay." I join her and watch the flashes go off in the other room.

"How long?" She asks, her eyes also on the studio.

"A few weeks."

She nods. "These guys aren't easy. Sexy as all get-out, but not easy."

"Are guys ever easy?" I ask with a laugh.

"Good point," she agrees.

"Do you two have a past?" I ask calmly. She glances down at me and back over to the men.

"No. It's always been Gary for me. We're good friends." She

sobers again. "He's different you know."

"Yeah, I know."

"Well, then." She exhales and smiles down at me while she rubs her belly. "Welcome to the clan."

* * *

"When are we heading back to Seattle?" I ask Leo when we are in his car, heading back toward the freeway.

"Thursday morning, why?"

"Do you have your heart set on going to the pier?" I turn in my seat to watch his face. I just enjoy watching him. He glances over at me and then back to the street.

"Do you have something else in mind?"

"I'd love to spend time at the beach, but I'd rather it was more private." I smile over at him and run my fingertips up and down his thigh.

"Hmm, private, huh?" He grins and slips his sunglasses on. "I know a spot."

"Great."

He guides the car onto the freeway, and less than twenty minutes later, we're in his driveway.

"Well, this would be private," I murmur and grin up at him as he helps me out of the car.

"As private as it gets around here."

"Do you actually own a piece of the beach?" I ask, excited to get down to the water.

"Yeah, I could have bought a small third world country for what it cost me, but it's pretty great."

I start to walk around the house, but he stops me. "Let's go through the house."

"I want to go down to the water."

"So impatient." He smiles down at me and leads me inside. "We need a few things."

"Such as?"

"A blanket." He winks and my stomach clenches and the cute little pink thong I wore with these khakis is immediately soaked.

One look from this man, and I'm a puddle.

God, I love it.

"Let's go." I'm practically jumping up and down with excitement.

"You don't get to the beach often do you, sunshine?"

"It's January, Leo. I believe it was forty degrees and raining when we left Seattle. It's seventy-five and gorgeous here. Hell yes, I want to go walk on the beach."

"You can leave your shoes up here. The sand is soft." He takes my hand in his and leads me down a wooden staircase to the soft white sand below. The water here is so different from the north coast.

"You'd never imagine this is the same ocean," I murmur and happily breathe in the ocean air.

"Pretty different." He nods, watching the waves crash on the shore. It's a picturesque day, sunny and warm, the water fairly calm. The beach is empty.

"Let's go."

Leo drops a thick blanket onto the sand and leads me down to the shoreline.

"It's gonna be cold!" I squeal and step into the warm water. "Oh, it's like bath water."

I jog in place, enjoying the feel of the water on my feet, ankles and legs and kick and splash around, until I realize I'm frolicking like a loony toon all alone. I stop and look around and find Leo about twenty feet behind me, his arms crossed over his bare chest, sunglasses down over his eyes, and a wide smile across his face.

"Aren't you coming in?" I ask.

"I don't think you play very often," he comments and joins me in the warm water.

"You do?" I ask with a raised eyebrow.

"Not as often as I should," he agrees and pulls me to him. "I love watching you like this, happy and smiling."

He lifts me into his arms, and he doesn't just kiss me, he possesses me. Consumes me.

Finally he allows me to slide down his body, my feet splashing back in the water.

"Let's walk." I grab his hand and pull him down the shoreline, splashing my feet in the water as we walk.

"Talk to me about Parker." His voice is quiet, but strong. He's not going to allow me to evade or give him half-answers.

Hell, I wouldn't either.

"He was in the *Nightwalker* movies with Luke. He played the older brother." I begin and watch the white foam on the waves.

"Yes, I remember who he is. How did you become involved with him?" He asks.

"Are you going to get all jealous and stupid?" I ask him, only half joking.

"No, but I have a feeling this might explain quite a bit."

It'll explain some of my baggage, but not all of it. I'll tell him this. I'm not ready for the rest yet.

"I went on location for about a week with Luke when they were filming. He was cute. I was stupid." I shrug. "You know how it is."

"And then?" He asks.

Damn him.

"And then we dated for a while. The movies were ridiculously popular. Well, you remember." I roll my eyes at him. "Scott just loved the attention. He couldn't be any more different from Luke if he tried. He also hated it that Luke was the one that got most of the attention because he was the lead, and the one all the stupid teeny boppers were hot after."

I shake my head and hop over a piece of driftwood.

"Anyway, I knew relatively quickly that he and I weren't going to last long. He's way too egotistical for me, way too self-centered. But I was suddenly caught up in the whole media storm that came with those guys at the time. Poor Luke." I stop and face the water, staring out at the sun beginning to sink into the horizon, the sky is turning pink and orange, but all I see is my poor young brother in my head.

"Women would chase him. Literally, chase him down the street. They'd find ways to sneak into his hotel rooms. Give blow jobs for phone numbers."

"Sounds like groupies." Leo smirks and I nod.

"Yeah, except these groupies were thirteen, fourteen years old."

"Fuck," Leo murmurs.

"Exactly." I rub my face with my hands and push them through my hair. "Leo, I don't know how many young girls claimed they were pregnant and that Luke was the father."

"Are you kidding me?"

"Nope." I shake my head and laugh ruefully. "He, of course, never touched one of them, but that didn't stop the accusations. Anyway, we were all chased all over the place during filming, and during the whole five years or so that the movies were popular. Well," I amend and offer him a small smile. "Not me so much because after about six months, I broke it off with Scott and went home. But, in those six months, we were hounded every day. Paparazzi in our faces, whether we were out in public or not."

I shrug and we start walking again.

"That's not really what my life is like, Sam." Leo's voice is calm and his hands are in his pockets as he walks beside me.

"I know it's not quite the same, but you're still recognized all the time. We couldn't even take a regular plane to get here."

He frowns. "What are you saying?"

"I'm just telling the story. You asked," I remind him and he nods. "Let's turn back. So while we were still together, Scott and I were out for lunch one day, and the paparazzi found us, as usual. They wouldn't stop asking questions, taking pictures, you know. And it pissed us both off, but Scott didn't want to cause a scene and ruin his squeaky clean reputation. I didn't give a fuck."

"Sounds like you," he murmurs with a smile.

"Well, I should have kept my mouth shut. They hounded us the rest of the day. Ended up causing a small car accident."

"Hold it." He pulls me to a stop, his hand on my arm. "Did you get hurt?"

"No." I shake my head. "But it scared me. And it pissed Scott off."

"It should have." He's so angry on my behalf and I just want to kiss him.

"No, he was pissed at me," I clarify.

"For what?"

"For not keeping my mouth shut. According to him, it was my fault."

"Mother fucker sonofabitch!"

God, he's hot when he's pissed.

"Yeah, that's why I broke it off. And then a few years later was the incident in Luke's house not too far from here."

He sighs deeply and pulls me into his arms, rocking me back and forth, his hands rubbing up and down my back.

I feel so safe with him.

"Let's sit on our blanket and watch the sunset," he murmurs into my ear and pulls away to lead me over to the blanket in the sand.

We spread it out and plop down in the middle, leaning on each other, not saying anything as we watch the sun begin to sink into the water.

"I love the water here," I comment.

"Me too, but honestly, I'll take Seattle over this any day of the week."

"Really?" My startled gaze finds his.

"Yeah, I guess I didn't realize until I'd spent the past few months there how homesick I've been."

"I like it when you're in Seattle, too," I whisper, tracing the tats on his hand with my fingertip.

"Do you?" He kisses my head.

"Yeah."

He tips my head back with his fingertip, his gorgeous gray eyes the color of the ocean in the setting sun, and I'm completely caught up in him.

I fucking love this man.

Chapter Seventeen

My eyes drop to the piercing in his lip and he leans in and gently sweeps his lips over mine.

"You are so sweet," he whispers and sinks into me, his hands pushing into my hair, holding me to him.

I moan softly as he pushes me onto my back in the soft sand, protected by the blanket. He lays over me completely, we're still in our clothes, and he just kisses me, brushes my hair from my face, and then pulls up, just a few inches, and smiles down at me.

"You're going to get cold," I whisper and rub his warm back with my hands. I love the way his smooth skin feels.

"I'm fine," he murmurs and shakes his head. "You smell so good."

"So do you." I smile shyly and nuzzle his nose with mine. "You're still wearing pants."

"Do they offend you?" He asks with a chuckle.

"Yes, I'm horribly offended," I give him a mock-glare and shove my hands between his underwear and the skin of his ass. "I love your ass."

"I love your ass too. And it's still covered."

"You're on me."

"Yep." He agrees and doesn't move so I can remove my clothes.

"Well, then it looks like we're at an impasse."

"What if I just want to lie here and kiss you all night?" He asks, his face sober, his gaze wandering over my face, his fingers still gently skimming my skin.

"Do you?" I ask.

"Hell no, I want to be inside you, but that wasn't the question." He laughs.

"Well, you can kiss me whenever you want."

"Good to know."

He kisses me again, and then rises up to his knees, pulls my pants down over my hips and raises his eyebrows when he sees my thong.

"Nice underwear."

"Please don't tear them." I laugh.

"No, they're staying on." He unfastens his pants, pushes them down around his thighs, and lowers himself over me again, cradled between my thighs. I can't believe I never had sex in this position before him. I love the way he feels over me.

Although, I never would have trusted anyone before him to put me in this vulnerable position.

"What are you thinking?" He whispers.

"That I love how you feel when you're on me like this."

He pulls his hips back, reaches between us to pull my thong to the side with his finger tip, and slowly, so damn slowly, sinks inside me. "Oh, baby."

"Okay, I like this, too." I smile against his mouth.

"Oh, sunshine, you are incredible." He kisses my nose and my cheeks. He's so not fucking me right now. He's making love to me, and I can't get enough of it.

"Why do you call me sunshine?" I ask, and wonder if he'll tell me. My hands are roaming all over his back, arms, ass. I can't stop touching him.

"I told you before, because of your hair."

"I don't think that's true." I pull my fingers down his face and kiss his lips softly.

He takes a deep breath and moves very slightly inside me, making me gasp.

"I call you sunshine," he whispers and brushes his knuckles down my face, "because when you smile, you light me up inside."

"Oh, baby," I whisper and pull his face down to mine and kiss him fiercely, rocking my hips. He begins to slide in and out of me, still slowly, but more firmly, rocking his pubic bone against my clit each time he's buried as far as he can go.

Night has descended completely around us, and I can hear crickets blending in with the rush of the waves down the beach. I am wrapped in Leo's warmth, literally as well as emotionally. He pulls one of his hands down from my hair, along my face, and farther still to rest over my breast. His thumb and forefinger worry the nipple through my shirt, sending electricity straight to my center, and I pulse around his hardness.

He kisses down to my neck and bites my shoulder. "Come."

And I do, softly, but no less intensely than when he fucks me stupid. I'm shattering beneath him, gripping onto his back with my nails.

"Ah, damn, baby," he groans and follows me over the edge into bliss.

* * *

"We really should get up," I mumble and turn my face to kiss his chest.

"Why?"

"It's almost noon." I laugh. Leo chuckles and kisses my head.

"We don't have anywhere to be until this evening." He turns on his side to face me.

"What are we doing this evening?" I ask and trace the tattoo on his shoulder.

"We have been invited to Gary and Lori's for a barbeque with the whole crew."

"Oh, okay." I sigh and snuggle deeper into my pillow, watching him. "What are we gonna do today?"

"What do you want to do?" He asks and brushes a piece of my hair behind my ear.

"We could go for a run," I suggest and chuckle when he frowns.

"Take a day off, sweetheart."

"Well, we could at least start by getting out of this huge bed of yours and getting some food. I'm hungry."

He grins wolfishly. "Worked up an appetite, did you?"

"Come on." I hop up onto my knees and nudge his leg. Leo's eyes travel up and down my nakedness and I laugh. "No more sex until I've been fed, Mr. Insatiable."

"But you're irresistible." He grabs my hand and pulls me back down on top of him.

176

"No way, I can't do anymore of the sex stuff until I've had food." I kiss him and playfully tug on his piercing.

"Fine." He sighs deeply, pretending to be put out.

"Do you have food here?" I ask. We've grabbed food out since we've been here.

"There should be some basic supplies here. I had my house-keeper bring in a few things the day we arrived."

"Cool. Come on." I jump up and throw a Train tee over my head, grab a pair of black lacy panties out of my bag and pull them on and walk out the door of his bedroom without looking back. "Get your lazy ass up, Nash!" I yell over my shoulder.

"Are you always such a nag?" He yells back.

"Yes!"

I hear him laughing as I reach the kitchen and pull out what I need for French toast and bacon.

He pads into the kitchen, barefoot and bare chested, in just jeans with the top button left undone.

My God, he's delicious.

He smiles smugly as I look him up and down. "Like what you see, sugar?"

"You're okay." I shrug, smirk, and pull four slices of bread from the loaf.

"Don't stroke my ego or anything." He laughs and pulls the orange juice from the fridge, pours us each a glass, and leans against the countertop, watching me bustle about his kitchen.

"Your ego doesn't need more stroking. You know you're hot."

He just shrugs and sips his juice. "It means something when you say it."

When breakfast is finished, we carry our plates and juice outside onto the patio. There are more clouds in the sky today and the air is not quite as warm.

"I think it's going to rain today," Leo comments and takes a big bite of his toast. "God, this is good. Where did you learn to cook?"

"Mom and dad both cook really well." I shrug and take a bite of bacon. "They made us all learn. Earning our keep, I believe mom called it."

He stops eating and frowns for a moment before taking another bite of toast.

"What?" I ask.

"What what?"

"What made you frown?"

He swallows and lowers his fork to his plate, a crease between his eyebrows. "My mom used to say that too."

He's quiet for a while, staring at his food.

"Do you want to talk about them?" I ask quietly.

He shrugs and then exhales hard. "It's weird, the things that trigger a memory."

"How old were you when you lost them?" I ask.

"Twelve. Fucking car accident."

I nod. I knew that from Meg. "What was your mom like?"

"She was so funny." He laughs and smiles at me. "Seriously funny. I remember laughing with her a lot, the way you and I do."

"And your dad?" I ask with a grin.

"Dad was fun too. He was the musician. He taught me to play the guitar and piano by the time I was six."

"Wow, that's amazing."

"I preferred the guitar. Still do." He shrugs and his eyes sober. "We listened to Bob Dylan for hours on end. Dad had good taste in music."

"What about your mom? What kind of music did she like?" I love that he's talking about his family. I have a feeling it doesn't happen often.

"She liked pop music. We listened to a lot of radio in the car. She had a beautiful voice." He frowns again and I just want to scoop him up and hold him close. It breaks my heart that he lost those wonderful people.

"I'm sorry you lost them," I whisper.

"Me too."

"Do you have photos?"

"Yeah, in one of the bedrooms. When they died, all of their belongings went into a storage unit until I turned eighteen. I also got their insurance money at eighteen. So, I packed up all of their personal stuff, sold or gave the furniture away, and I've just kept all of their things in the boxes."

"You've never gone through them?" I ask, surprised.

"No."

"Not even to find some photos or birth certificates or something?"

"No," he shakes his head and his sad gaze finds mine. "It always felt like an invasion of their privacy."

Poor man. "They would want you to do that." I tell him with confidence.

"Some day, maybe." He shrugs and then stands. "Come on, you've eaten. Let's shower."

I know the subject is closed. My heart is full and warm knowing that he shared something so personal and sacred with me. We've come a long way in the past few days.

We work together cleaning up from breakfast and he takes my hand and leads me up the stairs toward the master suite.

"Is your favorite color white?" I ask.

"No, why?"

"It's really white in here."

He laughs and shakes his head. "You're dying to redecorate the place, aren't you?"

"Something needs to be done with it."

"I like your place," he comments and turns the water on in the walk-in shower, adjusting the temperature.

"You do?" I'm surprised. "You don't think it's too girly?"

"At first I did," he admits with a grin. "But it's really homey. Comfortable."

That's the best compliment anyone could pay me about my home. That's exactly how I want it to feel.

I'm smiling widely at him, still fully dressed, as he shucks his jeans and pulls towels out for us. He turns to find me watching him and offers me a half-smile.

"What is going through that gorgeous brain of yours?"

"Nothing." I shrug, the smile still firmly on my face.

"No, that smile is not nothing. What are you so happy about?" He asks, wrapping his arms around me.

"You," I tell him simply and kiss his chin. "You make me

happy."

"Good, that's the goal." He pulls my shirt over my head and slips my panties down my legs. "Now let's make you clean."

He leads me into the shower, wets a rag and lathers it up with my body wash and begins to wash me, massaging my muscles.

Pampering me.

"God, that feels good. You have good hands." I lean into him and close my eyes.

"They like touching you," he murmurs and spins me so my back is to him and he can wash and rub my back side.

"Seriously, if this music thing doesn't work out for you, I'll hire you to be my massage therapist."

"Good to know I have something to fall back on." He chuckles and leads me into the water to rinse me off. "Lean your head back."

He methodically washes and conditions my hair, rubbing my scalp and thoroughly rinsing it clean. When he's done, I turn to him, take another cloth and lather it up with his cedar-scented body wash and return the favor, washing him.

"I love your tats." I watch my hands as they soap him up. "Mine are gone." I wink at him and glance down at my body, the black lines all gone.

"Mine won't wash off." He chuckles.

"Good, I don't want them to." I spin him around so I can wash his back and his ass. "Okay, now your hair."

"You don't have to wash my hair."

"Why?"

"I'm a little tall." He smirks.

Hmm. True. He's so tall, and I'm so short, that washing his hair will be a stretch.

"Lift me." I back up against the wall and hold my arms out to him.

"Happily, sweetheart." He plants his big hands on my ass and pulls me up to him. I wrap my legs around his waist, loving how he braces me against the wall, pinned by his lean hips. His happy eyes watch me as I soap up his hair and massage his scalp, making the soapy strands stand on end.

"This is a good look for you," I tease him. "You could start a new trend.

"Smart ass," he whispers.

"Okay, you need to rinse."

Without releasing me, he leans back into the stream of hot water, letting it wash the soap away, then straightens and kisses me, the water from his head running in streams down our bodies.

"I think we're clean," I murmur against his lips and roll my hips against his erection. He gasps and bites his bottom lip.

"Let's fix that."

"I thought the point was to get clean." I raise an eyebrow.

Without answering, he lifts me higher and slides inside me. "You're so wet, babe."

"Yeah, well, that seems to happen a lot when I'm around you."

He leans his forehead against mine, our hips moving in a perfect rhythm. He leans back and presses his calloused thumb against my clit, sending me over, my legs clamping around his hips, my pussy clenching around his cock.

"Fuck, you feel so damn good," he growls as he comes, his hips jerking and thrusting hard. "So damn good," he repeats while he catches his breath.

He kisses me hard and long and lowers me to my feet.

"I spend a lot of time off the ground with you," I comment as we rinse and towel off.

"Complaining?" He asks with a grin.

"Nope, an observation."

I comb my wet hair and blow it dry, throw on some mascara and lip-gloss and follow him into his bedroom. He's pulled on his jeans and a t-shirt, and I can't help but be disappointed that he's covered his tats.

"What's wrong?" He asks with a grin.

"I wanted to lick your stars," I pout, making him laugh.

"What is it with you and the stars?"

"They're fucking hot. I'm not the only one. Brynna said she wants to lick them too and claims that she hates me because I get to lick them whenever I want."

"Women are weird." He smirks.

Just then my phone rings on the bedside table. "That's Mr. Foss." My stomach clenches as I look down at the caller I.D.

"Answer it. I'll be on the balcony."

He kisses my forehead and lets himself out the glass door to his covered balcony as I reach for the phone.

"Hello?"

"Ms. Williams?"

"This is she," I respond and pace around the room, my feet cold on the marble.

"This is Foss calling regarding our interview from the other day."

"Yes, hello, thanks for calling."

"I'm afraid I don't have great news, Ms. Williams. We've decided to go with a different candidate."

"I see." Why am I relieved?

"I am certain you'll find the position that suits you soon. Best of luck to you, Samantha."

"Thank you, Mr. Foss. Have a good day."

I disconnect the call and sit at the side of the bed.

Now what?

* * *

~Leo~

Sam is pacing in my bedroom, her phone pressed to her ear. It's started to rain. Not a light, soft rain, but a pounding, all-consuming rain that seems to have a life of its own. It sounds like drums on my roof and almost obscures the view of the water.

I rock in my chair, in time with the music of the rain, and think about the small woman with the enormous personality in my bedroom. She's bloody amazing. Her strength, her big heart, her loyalty, all bring me to my knees.

I can't get enough of her.

The glass door opens and Sam slips out onto the balcony.

"Well?" I ask.

"They turned me down." She shrugs, her gorgeous face sad

182

and maybe a little scared.

If you'll let me, I'll take care of you and you'll never have to work again.

"Come here, baby." I take her hand in mine and pull her into my lap. She settles her cheek against my chest, and I wrap my arms around her, rocking her gently. "Just rock with me for a while."

She smiles up at me softly, remembering the last time I said those words to her and we made love in my chair.

"I don't know why I'm sad. I don't think I wanted that job anyway. You were right, I don't want to move to L.A."

"Rejection sucks," I mutter and kiss her soft blonde hair.

"Yeah," she agrees.

"I'm kind of glad you didn't get it," I admit. "I don't want you to move out of Seattle either. I think I'm going to sell this place and move up there." I frown and watch the rain around us, my mind wandering. "This place has never felt like home. You said it yourself, it's not exactly 'me.'"

"Hmm…" she agrees and snuggles down closer to me. God, she feels perfect in my arms.

"I'm tired of traveling so much. I can probably arrange it so we only tour about three months out of the year. They would be three solid months, with no breaks, but then the rest of the time I'd be able to be home. The guys would like that too. Especially Gary and DJ, since they have families."

"When is Lori due?" she asks quietly.

"Next month. We're all getting too old for touring all year long anyway. It's not like we need the money."

"It's good that you can be choosy," she agrees.

I nod and kiss her again. I can't stop kissing her sweet honey-scented hair.

Fuck, I have it bad.

"It'll be good to be near Meg too. Keep an eye on her."

"Wait." She sits up and frowns at me. "Why all these big life changes?"

"Oh, sunshine," I whisper and smile gently. "Haven't you figured out that I'm completely in love with you?"

Her eyes go wide and her hands grip onto my shirt and for the first time since I met her, I think she's speechless.

"You had to know that, baby." I kiss her forehead and cup her face in my hands. "I don't bring women around my band. I don't write songs for girls. I don't bring them here. I certainly don't talk about my family with just anyone. I love you, Samantha."

"Oh, wow," she whispers and drags her fingers down my face, watching my eyes with her beautiful, bright blue ones. "I'm afraid to fall."

"I'll catch you, baby."

She blinks and swallows hard, her brain in overdrive. We sit quietly, listening to the rain, as she processes her thoughts. I expected this from her. She's not a girl who would squeal and throw herself at me, screaming her love for me.

That's not how she works, and that's just one of the many things I love about her.

"I love you too," she whispers so quietly, I can barely hear her through the rain.

I tip her chin up with my finger, forcing her to look me in the eye. "What was that?"

"I love you too," she repeats, louder this time. "You scare me."

"Good, 'cause you terrify the hell out of me." I laugh and pull her in. "But being without you scares me more."

"Are you really moving to Seattle permanently?" She asks, her face hopeful and happy.

"Yeah."

"You're not living with me." She scowls suddenly, making me bust out laughing. "We're not ready for that."

"Last time I checked, I have my own place," I remind her.

"I guess this means I'd better find a job in Seattle," she murmurs and kisses my cheek sweetly.

"It would be convenient," I agree.

"What about when you're on tour?" Her brows are pulled together in a frown, and I rub the soft skin with my thumb.

"If you're not busy, you can come with me. If you can't come along, we'll survive it."

She nods and smiles. "No more ugly Malibu house?"

184

"No." I laugh and hug her close. "I'm selling the ugly Malibu house."

"Thank Christ."

Chapter Eighteen

~Samantha~

"You're here!" A pretty blonde jumps out of an Adirondack chair on the patio by the pool and runs for Leo and I. "You are Sam," she informs me and throws her arms around me, hugging me tight.

"Yes, I am." I look around the pool area of Gary and Lori's gorgeous home. It's amazing to me how quickly the weather changes down here. Just a few hours ago we were listening to the rain on Leo's porch, and now it's sunny and warm again.

Lori's laughing eyes meet mine and I mouth "Help!" to her but she just laughs harder.

Traitor.

"I'm Cher." She pulls back and grins. "Lori was right, you're hot. She's hot," she says to Leo who is laughing his ass off next to me.

"Yep, she is," he agrees.

DJ, with his tall Mohawk, joins us and wraps his arm around Cher's shoulders. "Cher is my wife." He grins lovingly down at her. "She's been excited to meet you."

"Leo never brings women around to meet us."

"Really?" Leo asks loudly. "Are we going to go through this every damn time?"

"Well, now she's met everyone." Jake snickers.

"Come sit with us," Cher grabs my hand and pulls me over to the shaded patio where Lori is resting, her hands rubbing her belly, and motions for me to sit. I look back over my shoulder, and Leo is watching me, his eyes happy.

He loves me.

He shrugs and takes the beer DJ offers him and wanders over to hang out with the other guys standing near the grill.

186

There are a few things I know for certain in this life, and one of them is men can always be found near the grill.

Gary is grilling, the other guys are in chairs or standing around, sipping beers from the bottle and laughing. Eric is holding a sweet little boy, around two years old, making faces at him and grinning.

The world-famous rock band Nash is just a bunch of normal people.

"I'm glad you're here." Lori smiles.

"Thanks for having me," I respond and glance around her lush back yard. "You have a lovely home."

It's true. The pool is kidney shaped and large, with an attached hot tub at one end. The entire space is covered in cobblestone, with a huge outdoor fireplace at one end, surrounded with plush furniture. A large child's play area with swings, a slide, and a tree house take up another corner. The patio we're sitting on has twice the square footage of my apartment, is covered, and also furnished with comfortable and colorful chairs and tables. The guys and the grill are about twenty feet away, also on the patio.

"Thank you," Lori responds with a smile. "We don't get to spend much time here, so when we're home, we enjoy having everyone over."

"I can't believe how big Maddox has gotten," Cher comments, pointing to the little boy on Eric's lap.

"I know, he's growing like a weed," Lori agrees. "That's our son, Maddox," she tells me.

"He's adorable."

"I want to talk to you guys about something," Leo begins and everyone frowns at him.

"Don't tell me you're thinking of taking on another leg of tour dates right now." Lori scowls, her voice hard. "In case you didn't notice, I'm about to give birth."

"No." Leo shakes his head and glances at me, then at his guys. "In fact, I'd like to talk to you guys about cutting back on touring."

"Thank God," Gary mutters and runs his fingers through his hair.

"Why?' Jake asks and takes a swig of his beer.

"I don't want to quit," Leo clarifies. "I'm thinking about just cutting our touring down to a few months a year, and the rest of the year working on albums, writing, working with other artists, stuff like that."

The guys all exchange glances. Cher and Lori are literally holding their breath, tightly holding hands.

"That's not a bad idea," DJ responds. "We're not twenty-two anymore."

"We can do special appearances now and then, awards shows, shit like that," Eric agrees.

"I can play with my kids," Gary adds and exhales. "Honestly, I'm ready to slow it down a bit."

"I need all of us to be on the same page." Leo stuffs his hands in his pockets, his face worried. "You guys are my family. We do this together or not at all."

I didn't think I could love him any more than I already did, and then he goes and says stuff like that. I understand family.

All eyes turn to Jake and he shrugs. "Yeah, slowing down might be good. We'd be able to record more often."

"Maybe you'll settle down," Gary suggests, but Jake smirks. "Let's not go crazy."

"One more thing," Leo adds as Gary flips steaks on the grill. "I'm relocating to Seattle permanently. I don't expect DJ and Gary to follow, but I want to let you know."

Silence. After a few seconds everyone starts to laugh, including Lori and Cher.

"What the fuck is so funny?" Leo demands.

"We had bets on how long you'd last in that horrible house of yours," Cher informs him as she wipes tears from the corners of her eyes. "I lost the bet a year ago."

"Everyone hates your house?" I ask in surprise.

"Oh honey, it's awful." Lori rolls her eyes, and I smile at her. "I know. I'm thankful he's selling it."

"I bought it for the view," Leo reminds us all and then laughs with everyone else. "Yeah, it's horrible."

"I wouldn't mind moving to Seattle," Cher murmurs, her big

brown eyes watching DJ.

"We can look into it," he agrees.

"I hate L.A. Please, God, tell me we can move too." Lori begs her handsome husband.

"You hate L.A.?" He asks, surprised.

"Yes! Let's move before Maddox starts school and we don't want to uproot him."

"I guess we're all moving to Seattle and becoming boring suburbanites," Gary mutters.

"Speak for yourself, man. I'm no suburbanite." Eric holds his hands up and shakes his head.

"Says the man with a baby on his knee," DJ quips.

"You're a dick," Eric throws back at him.

"Dick!" Maddox yells with a wide smile.

"Ah, hell," Lori mutters. "Stop teaching my kid all the swear words."

"His uncles are all musicians," Leo reminds her. "It's inevitable that he has a potty mouth."

"But does it have to be as a toddler?"

"Dick!" Maddox yells again and claps his chubby little hands.

"My kid is going to be the one who has detention every day after school because he cusses in class," Lori complains, earning smirks from the guys.

"How long have you been married?" I ask Cher.

"Ten years," she replies and laughs at my surprised look. "Or, in rock band years, fifty."

"Good for you guys." I feel hope spring. These women have made their relationships work with their famous husbands. Maybe it won't be that hard.

Maybe I'll be twenty-five again tomorrow.

"Not easy," Cher concedes and watches her husband with happy eyes. "But worth it. It'll be so nice to have him home more. Maybe we'll actually have a baby."

"No kids?" I ask. She shakes her head no and her eyes soften.

"I can't have kids," she confides, her voice low. "But we want to adopt."

"I've told you before, I'll be a surrogate for you," Lori reminds her. "I seem to be a baby making machine."

"You're crazy." Cher laughs.

"Better yet," Lori takes a crying Maddox from Eric. "You can have this one. He's slightly used, but he has his cute moments."

"How about you, Sam? Do you want kids?" Cher asks and it suddenly feels like everyone, including the guys and little baby Maddox, have gone quiet, waiting for my response.

"Uh, no, I don't really want kids of my own. My brother and his wife have one and another on the way, and I have extended family with kids. I like being the fabulous aunt, and then sending them back home hopped up on sugar and rated R movies."

Leo's eyes are trained on mine, his face calm and relaxed, but I can't read him. Finally he smiles softly and me.

"Sam is a really great aunt," he murmurs. "But we're on the same page when it comes to kids."

"Well then, there's no need to have sex," Lori comments, and bites her lip as she tries not to laugh.

"True," I agree and nod thoughtfully. "It's a good thing he's horrible in bed."

Leo's eyebrows climb into his messy hairline and all the guys laugh, doubled over.

"Oh, man, I knew it!" Eric points at him and then slaps his knee.

"Is that so?" Leo asks me, sets his beer down on a table, and saunters over to me.

I shrug and clench my lips together, fighting laughter.

"I think," he grips my hand and pulls me to my feet, then bends and lifts me onto his shoulders. "You deserve to be punished for that."

"Oh, shit, Leo do *not* throw me in the pool! I don't have any other clothes with me!"

"Too late!"

And suddenly I'm flying through the air and into the warm water with a loud splash. I kick my way to the surface of the water, sputtering and pushing my hair out of my face, glaring up at the impossibly handsome man laughing down at me.

"You're an ass!" I hiss at him.

"Ass!" Maddox repeats, earning more laughter.

"Here, I'll pull you out." Leo squats by the side of the pool and offers me his hand. I reach up and take it, plant my foot on the side of the pool, and yank him into the water with me, much to the delight of our audience.

Before I can turn around, I'm yanked under the water, and then tugged back to the surface so I can catch my breath. Leo's face is inches from my own, his hair wet and pressed to his scalp. Water is dripping down his face, off the piercings in his ear and eyebrow, his plain black tee is clinging to his shoulders.

"God, you're sexy," I whisper and his eyes grow hot with lust. He yanks me to him and kisses me hard, thoroughly, his arms holding me to him tightly and his hands pressed to my sides. He pushes me against the side of the pool and devours me with his lips and all I can do is hold on for dear life.

Finally, he pulls back and grins down at me, panting. "You're gonna pay for that remark."

"Gladly," I agree and laugh as he splashes me.

"Food's ready, moron," Gary calls down to Leo. "Lori do you have clothes for Sam?"

"Uh, probably not, Gary," I respond as Lori laughs and I pull myself out of the pool. "I don't know if you noticed, but Lori and I couldn't be more different."

"You could go naked," Eric offers with a grin. Leo smacks him upside the head.

"Shut the fuck up."

"Fuck up!" Maddox agrees.

"I'm gonna kill all of you," Lori growls.

* * *

"You know, I have to tell you." Lori leads me through the house to the master bedroom so I can borrow a tee shirt and pair of yoga pants. "I was so proud of the way you handled Melissa the other day."

"I heard about that!" Cher nods. "Most people don't stand up to her."

"How do you guys deal with always being in the tabloids?" I ask them without thinking.

"You know about being in the tabloids," Lori remarks.

"Yeah, but I'm getting the feeling it's different with rock stars than actors."

"The guys told Melissa that we are never to be included in publicity stuff." Cher confides as Lori tosses me clothes to change into.

"Really?"

"Yep," Lori agrees. "No family photos are to be released. Melissa knows better."

"She just wanted the scoop on getting the first photos out there of Leo and his new flame."

"First flame," Lori adds. "I don't think that Leo's ever been photographed with a woman."

"Never?" I frown in disbelief. "That's hard to believe. I'm sure he's had girlfriends."

"I don't know." Cher shrugs. "But if he did, he never took them out. He's a really private guy."

"We're lucky." Lori nods. "Our guys are all about the music and the fans. The rest of it is all frills, and they don't really play into it too much. They play the publicity game when they have to, but…" She shrugs.

"I like that," I mutter thoughtfully.

"I thought you might." Lori grins. "Leo's the best. He'll have your back."

We join the guys back on the patio, already eating and talking about music and bands and who has what single coming out when.

I sit quietly, nibbling on salad and steak soaking it all in. These guys are just so… normal. And kind.

"What are you thinking?" Leo whispers into my ear and offers me a bite of his steak.

"I like them," I whisper back and he smiles widely.

"I'm glad." He kisses my forehead and goes back to eating his dinner and chatting with his band, and it occurs to me, I just made friends who don't give a shit who my brother is or what family I come from.

192

Imagine that.

* * *

"So tired," I yawn and lean back in the seat of Leo's car as we drive back to the ugly Malibu house from Lori and Gary's late that night. We stayed much later than I expected we would, chatting and laughing. The guys also got a little work done, talking song selection for the next album.

"I think you've won over the band." He links his fingers and mine and I trace the ink on his hand.

"It was the sex remark." I smirk.

"They'll never forget that," he agrees and glares at me. "You'll be punished for that."

"You already punished me, babe. Hence, the clothes that don't belong to me." I point to Lori's purple tee and smirk.

"Are you wearing her underwear too?" he asks.

"I'm not wearing any underwear at all," I respond and yawn again.

Leo pulls into his driveway and parks in the garage, and before I can open my door, he's pulling me to my feet and lifting me in his arms.

"I can walk," I murmur and link my arms around his neck, bury my face next to his skin and breathe him in. "But this is nice."

"You're tired."

"I don't know why," I murmur and enjoy the way he effortlessly carries me through his horrible house to the staircase. "Uh, I might need to walk up this weird staircase."

"You're fine." He kisses my forehead and carries me to the bedroom. "Do you need to use the restroom?"

I nod and he takes me into the master bath, sets me gently on my feet and leaves me alone to do my thing. When I return to the bedroom, he's turned the bed down and is standing on the balcony, stripped down to just his short, black boxer-briefs.

I stand and watch him, his back to me, leaning on the railing and staring into the blackness, most likely listening to the ocean.

Even his back is gorgeous, smooth and bare of tattoos, except the very tops of his shoulders where his sleeves end.

I wonder why he never got any ink on his back?

As if he can sense me, he turns and grins and comes in through the glass door.

"You okay?" I ask and tilt my head to the side. There's something in his eyes that looks sad.

He nods and crosses to me, lifts me back into his arms and kisses me softly.

"The bed is only a few feet away," I remind him.

"I like having you in my arms."

I brush his hair back with my fingers as he moves us to the bed and lays next to me, pulling me to him.

"You're not trying to seduce me." It's not a question.

"I want to hold you."

"I was just kidding when I said you were bad in bed," I remind him and pull myself up onto my elbows. He smirks and pushes my hair back behind my ear and then laughs, a full, belly laugh.

"I can't believe you said that."

I grin and shrug. "It was funny."

"You're funny." He kisses me and tucks me to his side, my head on his chest. "You should sleep."

"Okay," I agree but just lie quietly and listen to him breathe. I can almost hear the wheels turning in his head. "Are you going to tell me?" I ask quietly.

He stiffens beneath me. "Tell you what?"

"What's on your mind?" I frown but don't look up at him.

He sighs and relaxes. "It was a busy day."

"True. Full of job rejections and being thrown in pools."

He pushes me to my back and gazes down at me while running his knuckles down my cheek. "And you telling me you love me," he whispers.

I take his face in my hands and kiss him softly. "I do love you," I whisper.

"I'll never get tired of hearing you say that you know."

"Good," I smile. "I'll remind you often, in case you forget."

"I don't think that's something I'll forget." He kisses my forehead and pulls me against him again as I yawn. "Sleep now, sunshine."

"Will you sleep too?" I ask as my eyes fall.

"Soon," he whispers and I feel him smile against my forehead as he kisses me there. "I'll sleep soon."

Chapter Nineteen

~Leo~

"What do you have going on today?" I ask Sam as I pour her some juice and dump some sugar in my coffee in her kitchen.

"I have an interview today and two early next week. I didn't hear anything from anyone for weeks, and now I have a bunch of interviews." She shrugs and purses her pretty pink lips. "Weird."

"You'll be great." She smiles softly and my gut clenches, the way it always does when she looks at me like that; like she trusts me. Like she loves me. We've been back in Seattle for a few days, and I still can't believe she's mine.

She's mine.

"What are you doing today?" She asks and I do my best to keep my face totally straight. She has an uncanny ability to read me, and this is a secret.

"I have some errands to run." I take a sip of coffee and swallow it over the jumble of nerves in my stomach. "I might meet with a real estate agent."

"Fun." She grins. "So you're gonna move out of Meg's place?"

"Yeah, she might as well sell it. Her neighbors figured out who I am and the guy next door always wants to chit chat with me when I get home." I frown and then laugh. "I don't think I'm a townhouse kind of guy."

"Probably not," she agrees and chuckles. "At least it's a guy who appreciates music and not some annoying young girl."

"Oh, there are those too. Thank God Will installed the alarm system."

"Seriously?" Her eyes go round and then she starts to laugh. "That's hilarious!"

"Sure it is." I scowl at her.

"It is," she insists and shakes her head. "Well, then you need a house."

"Yeah," I agree and rinse out my mug, set it in the dishwasher and grab my wallet and keys. "I better go."

"Okay." She smiles and stands to hug me, wraps her strong arms around my middle and presses a kiss to my sternum. "Have a good day."

"You too, baby." I tip her head back and kiss her slowly, rubbing my lips over hers and nibbling the side of her mouth until she smiles. "I'd better go before I pull you back to your bed and fuck you raw," I growl, smiling smugly when her bright blue eyes dilate with lust.

"I'm up for that."

"Later." I kiss her again, grin at the way she sways when I let go of her, and head out of her building.

Half way down to my car, my phone rings. I expect it to be one of the guys, and frown at the caller ID in surprise.

"Nash."

"Hey, it's Will," he clears his throat and I'm immediately put on guard.

"Has something happened to Meg?" I ask and climb into my car.

"No, she's fine. She's sleeping. Listen." I hear him start his car and tap my fingers impatiently on my steering wheel. "Do you have time to meet with me today?"

"About what?" I ask. "I'm kind of booked up today."

"I just need about ten minutes. I'd rather talk with you in private."

I check my watch and grimace. "Can you meet me in about ten minutes in Seattle?" I ask him.

"Sure, no problem. Where?"

I rattle off the address and work my way through mid-morning traffic. There is a lot to do today, and not nearly enough time.

I pull up outside the small recording studio near Sam's apartment and cut the engine. Will pulls up behind me less than five minutes later.

"Hey, man, thanks for meeting with me." He shakes my hand and glances at the building. "Where are we?"

"Studio." I grin at him. "I'm working today."

"Cool, I won't keep you."

"We can talk inside." I lead him inside to find Skip near the entrance. "Can I use your office for a minute, man?"

"Sure, you know the way. This time, don't wrinkle my papers." He smirks as I flip him the bird and lead Will to the office, close the door behind us, and lean back against the desk.

"What's up?"

For the first time since I met him, Will looks nervous.

Ah, hell, this can't be good.

"So, Meg and I have been together for a while."

"Not a long while," I remind him and purse my lips so I don't smile. He frowns and begins to pace.

"She is just..." He stops and pushes his hand through his hair and I cross my arms over my chest, enjoying his discomfort.

The man is fucking my sister. He should be damn uncomfortable.

"She's everything," he finally says. "She makes me happy and stupid and so fucking angry I could just smack her ass."

"Dude," I interrupt and he smiles over at me.

"Sorry. Anyway." He paces some more. "I love her. I refuse to ever live a day without her. She is the best part of my life."

"I figured this out already, man, what are you getting at?"

"I want to marry her." He exhales deeply and scrubs his hands over his face.

"So ask her."

"No, you don't get it." He shakes his head and faces me. "That's why I'm here. I'm asking for your permission to ask her."

I'm stunned. "Why do you need my permission?"

"Because she's yours," he answers simply. "You're her family. You're the one she's depended on the majority of her life, and she loves you. Your opinion matters. I may be an arrogant ass a lot of the time, but I was raised right." He swallows and shoves his hands in his pockets. "It's right that I ask you for your blessing before I propose to her. I give you my word, Leo, I will protect her, respect her and love her until the day I die."

"I know," I respond automatically.

"You do?"

"Of course I do. Meg isn't stupid. She wouldn't be with you if it were any other way." I stay here, leaning and watching Will for a moment and remember Meg as a young girl, wide-eyed and freckled and all red-hair and long limbs, and then I think of her when we were all together for game night and how vibrant and happy, how secure and lovely she is.

Will is to thank for some of that.

"You can marry her on one condition," I tell him, my voice low and steady, eyes on his.

"Name it," he immediately responds.

"You have to name your first kid after me." He sighs, his shoulders slump like he's been carrying the weight of the world, and he grins from ear to ear.

"What if it's a girl?" He asks.

"I don't give a fuck."

"Done." He agrees and offers me his hand, which I take and pull him in for a guy hug, slapping him hard on the back.

"She deserves to me happy." His face sobers.

"More than anyone I know."

"How are you going to do it?"

"Well, that's the other thing I wanted to talk to you about. Are you guys still doing the show at *Key Arena* in a few weeks?"

"That's the plan." I nod.

"So, here's my idea…"

* * *

~Samantha~

"This is gonna be fun!" I'm practically bouncing in the front seat of Leo's hot Camaro, excited that he asked me to go house shopping with him. He was gone all day yesterday, taking care of whatever business he had on his plate, and today has been laid back, enjoying each others company.

"You're like a kid." He grins over at me and chuckles.

"I like to shop." I shrug. "Where are we going first?"

"Well, we're only going to see one today."

"Okay, where?" I ask again.

"It's not too far from Luke and Nat's place."

"I love that neighborhood," I smile happily at the hot tattooed man next to me.

"Well, let's see what we think of the house." He drives through a gate and down a short driveway to a beautiful, white and blue traditional-style home. The view of the Sound is breathtaking. There is a red Toyota parked in the driveway and a short, round young woman with dishwater-blonde hair is standing on the porch consulting her phone.

"I like the outside," I comment, taking in the rose bushes and cherry-blossom trees that will be blooming in a couple of months.

"Okay, let's go in," he grins at me and we both hop out of the car and walk toward the front porch.

"Hi there! I'm Melody Jenkins, the agent sent out to help you today." Melody has a pretty, friendly smile and oozes youth. She's clearly still new to the real estate business.

"Didn't you tell them who you were when you called?" I whisper to him.

"Hell, no." He frowns down at me and offers Melody a hand to shake. "Thanks for meeting us."

"Holy shit, you're Leo Nash!" She exclaims and almost falls down the front steps. I turn my back to her so she can't see the hilarity written on my face.

"Guilty," Leo offers her a charming smile. "Nice to meet you."

I school my features and turn back around to see Melody's mouth opening and closing like a fish, her eyes wide and pinned to Leo, completely struck dumb.

"Oh for the love of... Melody?" I wave my hand before her face, catching her attention. "Hi. I'm Sam. We'd love to see the house."

"Oh, of course." Her hands are shaking as she consults her phone for the code to the door and leads us inside.

I turn back to Leo and mock the fan-girl, holding my hands over my mouth like I'm shocked to meet him, and he narrows his eyes at me and whispers, "Be nice."

"This is hilarious," I mutter just as Melody turns back to us.

"So, this is the house, of course. It's really nice. It has a state-of-the-art kitchen, a sun-room, a hot-tub." Her eyes wander down Leo's body to his hips and then she coughs and turns away.

"It's the stars," I mutter to him, earning another glare.

"I just have to tell you," Melody says in a rush, turning to face Leo, "I am such a huge fan. I have all your albums, even the really old ones."

More laughter from me. *The really old ones are roughly four years old.* Of course, she would have been in high school.

"Uh, thanks," Leo mutters, clearly uncomfortable and looks around for a means of escape.

"What is so funny?" Melody asks me, her hands propped on her round hips. She really is cute.

"Absolutely nothing. Nash is great," I agree with her and smile up at Leo who continues to glare at me.

"You know what, Melody, I think we'll just look around on our own, if that's okay with you."

"Oh." She pouts and glares at me before turning big hazel eyes on Leo in what I'm sure she thinks is her flirty look. "Are you sure? I don't mind showing you around."

"I'm sure, thanks." Leo grabs my hand and pulls me toward the stairs. "You are not helping," he growls.

"I'm sorry, but that's hilarious, and your own fault."

"My fault?" He asks incredulously.

"Well, yeah. One, you should have told the agency who you are so they could send someone more appropriate, and two, you're the one who always walks around shirtless in all your videos and photo shoots. I know for a fact she wants to lick your stars."

"Shut up," he mutters and pulls me down a hallway, looking in each of the rooms.

"You can't get tattoos on your sexy V, the one spot on a man's body that makes a woman sit up and beg, and not expect to get attention." I inform him smugly and giggle some more when he continues to glare at me.

As we pass the top of the staircase on our way to what I assume is the master suite, we hear Melody's voice downstairs.

"You will *not* believe who I'm showing a house to right now! Leo freaking Nash! I'm not lying. No, he's wearing a shirt."

I bust out laughing some more as Leo growls and pulls me into the master bedroom. "Told you."

"I just wanted to look at some houses," he mutters and wanders around the large, empty space.

"I think you should have your assistant call the agencies from now on."

"Probably. Do you like this room?" He asks me.

"It's big." I wander to the window and look out at the Sound, the water reflecting the mid-afternoon sunshine. "The view is great."

"Yeah, I like the view too."

"The floors aren't giving my feet frostbite, and the walls are a light mocha color, which is warm and nice."

"You're wearing shoes," he reminds me with a grin.

"Your floors in Malibu would still give me frostbite through my shoes."

"Smart ass." He grins and opens a door to an enormous walk-in closet with built-ins for shoes and bags, and even a center island for other accessories.

"I might have just died and gone to heaven," I breathe, feeling my eyes widen and my heartbeat increase. "This is just... Oh my God."

"Closet is a yes." Leo laughs.

"This is your house," I remind him and consciously make my face go blank. "Not mine."

"Yet."

"Not mine," I repeat and shake my head.

"Okay, let's just say there's space in here for you to have a drawer of your very own for when you stay over."

"Are you mocking me?"

"Yes. Let's look at the bathroom."

The bathroom is even better. "I could swim in that tub," I mutter and wander through the space. The shower is the size of Manhattan. We could host parties in there. Full concerts.

Oh my God, the sex we could have in that shower.

"Are you okay?" Leo asks, his voice light and full of laughter.

"Yep," I respond and trail my hand over the light granite countertop. There are two sinks, roughly four feet apart, with a plethora of counter space and drawers beneath. I turn around and lean against the granite, watching Leo across the room. "I think I want to lick your stars too," I murmur and look him up and down.

His eyes narrow on me and he slowly moves to the door, latches it shut and locks it, then walks to me, leans on his hands on either side of my hips and stops, his face just inches from my own.

"You don't get to lick anything right now."

"Really?" I raise an eyebrow and watch his eyes as they roam down my body.

"No. But I do." He grips my sides and boosts me up onto the countertop so my feet are dangling and my pussy is close to the edge.

"Leo, that girl is right downstairs." He moves between my knees and leans in close, his lips against my temple and hands unfastening my jeans.

"I don't give a shit. It wouldn't matter to me if Jesus and JFK were right downstairs. Even they couldn't stop me from tasting you right now. Lift your ass."

I comply and he peels my jeans and panties over my butt and down my legs and discards them on the floor. He cups my hips in his firm hands and kisses my cheek, down to the soft spot below my ear and along my jawline to my lips.

"I can smell how turned on your are," he whispers against my lips and one of his hands roams between my legs and cup my center. "God, you're warm and already wet, baby."

"It was the closet that turned me on," I whisper and then moan when he pushes a finger inside me.

"Then I'd better buy the house," he murmurs with a smile.

"Just kidding," I breathe.

"What made you this wet?" He asks and bites my lower lip, then soothes it with is tongue.

"You."

"What about me?"

"Thinking about the fun we could have in that shower." My

breath catches as he gently brushes my clit with his thumb.

"Mmm, yeah, that could be fun," he agrees and kisses me softly. "Samantha?"

"Yes." Oh, God, just push a little harder. Just a little harder. I move my hips, trying to increase the pressure against my sensitive nub, knowing I'm so damn close.

"I'm going to eat you out here on this counter."

I didn't think I could get more turned on, but that did it.

"And then I'm going to take you home and lose myself in you."

"We have to go to dinner with the family," I remind him and gasp when he pushes another finger in with the first.

"We have time." He sinks to a squat, spreads my legs wide, pulls his fingers out of me and licks between my folds and up to my clit twice, making me gasp, and then settles on my folds, pulling them into his mouth, hollowing his cheeks and sucking them firmly. He rubs his nose against my clit and my hips push up off the counter top.

"Easy," he whispers and pulls back, his eyes glued to my pussy. "God, you're so beautiful, my love."

My muscles contract at his words and he grins up at me as he pushes those talented fingers back inside me, finds my sweet spot and latches onto my clit with his lips, pulling and sucking, pushing and biting, rubbing that fucking awesome metal against me, until I come apart against his mouth, my heels digging into his back, shuddering and bucking and biting my lip until it bleeds so I don't cry out.

He kisses and soothes, caresses my thighs and stands to kiss my lips. "Love the way I taste on you," I murmur.

"Me too." He smiles and kisses me deeply, and then pulls back, his hands on my shoulders to keep me steady.

"Well, that was fun." I hop off the sink and pull my jeans on.

"Leave the panties off. You won't need them."

"Pretty sure of yourself, aren't you?"

He just raises an eyebrow and a wide smile spreads slowly across his lips. "I think I just proved that I'll take you anytime, anywhere, sunshine."

"Point taken."

Chapter Twenty

"How often do you all get together for these family dinners?" Leo asks me as we drive to Will and Meg's house.

"About once a month," I shrug.

"That's a lot of people in one house." He chuckles and shakes his head.

"Yeah, but otherwise we don't see each other much. Everyone is busy." He pulls into the driveway behind Luke's Mercedes SUV and takes a deep breath. "Ready?" I ask.

"As I'll ever be," he mutters as he helps me out of the car. He takes my hand in his and leads me to the door.

"We don't knock on family dinner days. No one would hear us." I smirk and open the door to chaos. Babies are running, or toddling, around, adults laughing and arguing and bustling around in the kitchen.

"Hey!" Jules exclaims when she sees us and pulls me into a big hug. "Will's a douche bag and ordered pizza."

"Everyone likes pizza." He scowls at her from his couch and then smiles over at us. "There are thirty pizzas in the kitchen along with beer, soda and I think Matt is mixing drinks too."

"Are my parents here?" I ask Jules.

"Yep, all the parents, and I do mean all the parents, including Brynna's, are upstairs in the loft enjoying some quiet away from the chaos. Although, they took Olivia with them, so they're living in their own special chaos."

"Yes, we're aware." Leo nods and opens pizza boxes on the kitchen counter. "She's adorable, but a handful." He takes a big bite of pepperoni as he snags a beer in the bottle and walks into the living room to sit by Meg and chat.

"That's my offspring you're talking about." Luke informs us and gives me a big hug. "How are you?" He whispers in my ear.

I nod happily up at him and his deep blue eyes soften. "Good."

He grabs his own beer and follows Leo into the living room, scoops Natalie up into his lap and kisses her hair.

"What would you like to drink?" Matt asks me from across the kitchen island.

"What do you have, handsome bartender?" I ask and climb up onto a barstool.

"Pretty much anything you want. I raided Will's liquor cabinet."

"I heard that!" Will calls from the living room.

"I don't care!" Matt yells back. "So, what'll it be?"

"Do you have olives?" I ask with a grin.

"Uh, no." He shakes his head and laughs.

"Damn. Okay, I'll have a fuzzy navel." Matt sets to work. "Where are Brynna and the girls?"

"I'm not sure. Caleb called earlier and said he was taking them somewhere this weekend and they wouldn't be here."

"Mysterious." I wiggle my eyebrows. "How did you get the bartending job?"

"Might as well, I don't drink." He shrugs and pours orange juice over my peach schnapps and ice and passes me the glass. "Pizza?"

"I'll get some in a few." I take a sip of the drink and smile in surprise. "This is really good."

"Don't be so surprised. I tended bar in college."

"A jack of all trades." I tease him with a grin.

"Hey, friend! When did you get here?" Stacey appears at my side and stares longingly at my drink and then up at Matt, who laughs.

"You want one of those?"

"Yes, please." She grins and winks.

"Leo and I got here a few minutes ago. Where's Isaac?"

"He's playing xBox with Nate and Mark. Nate's kicking ass." She smirks and finds a box of pizza mostly full, tucks a couple beers under her arm, lifts the box and takes her drink from Matt to wander back into the game room.

"Do you need help?" I ask.

"No, I'm a mom. This is nothing." She winks.

I lean back against the island and observe the family around me. Matt is wiping down the counter, deep in thought. I can hear Nate and Isaac yelling at each other in the other room, and Jules and Stacey laughing. Leo and Meg have their heads together, plotting something. Will and Luke and Nat are in deep conversation.

"We need to find you a girlfriend." I mention to Matt who stops and frowns at me.

"Why?"

"You're not getting any younger." I laugh when he scowls. "You're not gay."

He throws his head back and laughs, shoves his hands through his dark blonde hair and smiles at me. "No, I'm not."

"Well, then."

"I have particular tastes," he murmurs.

"I know."

His eyes shoot up to mine. "You do?"

I raise an eyebrow at him, a half-smile on my lips and he sighs and nods.

"You're damn observant."

I smile sweetly and sip my drink, waiting for him to talk.

"It'll happen eventually." He finally concedes. "But I have a feeling she won't be easy to find."

"She'll be worth it." I assure him and pat his broad shoulder.

"What's up with you and Leo?" He asks quietly.

My eyes turn to the man in the living room, still in deep conversation with Meg. I'm always aware of him, what he's doing and where he is. I can't help it.

"I went and fell in love with him." I smirk and glance back at Matt who has taken a seat next to me. "What do you think of him?"

"I like him." He nods. "Looks to me like he fell in love with you, too." He gestures over and I turn my head to find Leo watching us. I wink at him and he smiles softly before returning to his conversation.

"It's kind of disgusting." I choose a piece of pizza and take a bite. "But it's fun. We'll see how it goes."

"You're so not into the mushy stuff, are you?" Matt asks with a chuckle.

"Not really." I shrug, and then realize that's a lie. I love the mushy stuff with Leo.

"I get it." He nods.

"You're not either," I remind him.

"There's a time and a place for romance." He disagrees. "But *I* decide when and where that is."

"God, you're bossy."

He just laughs at me and clinks his glass with mine in cheers.

"Uh, Sam?" Stacey is moving through the room, her phone in her hands and she's frowning down at it.

"Yeah?"

"Have you seen this?"

"What?" I ask as she pushes her phone in my hands. Matt leans close to look over my shoulder and swears under his breath as my world stops moving.

It's a photo on an on-line gossip page of Leo and me from the photo shoot last week in L.A. Lori has been cropped out of the photo.

Of course.

The caption below is, *Leo Nash with his new girlfriend, actor/ producer Luke Williams' sister.*

No name.

"What is it?" I hear Leo ask, his voice closer than before and I feel my cheeks heat in anger and embarrassment and pure betrayal.

"Fuck."

* * *

~Leo~

Sam's face has turned bright red as she stares blankly down at Stacy's phone, her hands are shaking and Matt is glaring at the phone as if it's going to bite.

"What the fuck is wrong?" I ask as I approach her. She wakes the screen back up and shoves it at me.

"That's what the fuck is wrong."

The photo is from last week in L.A., the exact photo Sam said she didn't want leaked.

Melissa just lost her motherfucking job.

"What the hell, Leo?"

"What's going on?" Luke asks as he joins us.

"A photo got leaked," I murmur and pass it to him. He scowls down at the phone and back to Sam.

"Sam, this isn't new. You were in L.A. with Leo. What did you expect to happen?"

"I specifically told that bitch of a publicist that she didn't have my permission to use my photo."

Luke turns his accusing eyes to me, his face hard and eyes narrowed.

"Hey, man, I backed her up. I'll fire the bitch who leaked it."

"Are you going to fire everyone who leaks this shit?" Luke demands and shoves Stacy's phone back to her. "Sam's worked hard to stay out of the tabloids."

"I'm aware." I stand strong and cross my arms over my chest.

"I told you." Luke points his finger in my face. "I told you this would happen. This," he points a the phone, "is why I warned you to stay the fuck away!"

"Don't talk to him like that!" Meg steps between Luke and me, her hazel eyes glaring at Luke. "He already said he backed Sam."

"Stay out of this," Luke mutters to her but she stands her ground.

"I will not. This shit happens. You should know that. Hell, *she* knows that. She works for a magazine." Meg plants her fists on her hips, and I want to tell her to back off, but I know it'll be futile.

She's in protective sister mode.

"Meg." I begin but she holds her hand up to me to stop talking and my eyebrows rise in surprise. Matt grins at her. Isaac, Nate and the others have come out of the game room to see what all the commotion is about.

"He's put my sister in a position he doesn't even understand."

He points his finger at me again, his voice rising as Mark moves up beside him.

"How in the bloody hell can you say he doesn't understand it?" Meg roars. "He lives in that world every goddamned day! You're no more of a celebrity than he is, you know. If anything, he's even more submerged in it."

"This is not about who is more famous," Luke interrupts.

"Leo would never hurt Sam."

"He's not good enough for my sister!" Luke exclaims and a cold sweat breaks out on my face.

He's right. I'm not.

But I'll be goddamned if I'll let her go.

"Luke," Sam softly interjects but he shakes his head.

"No, you told him you didn't want this kind of publicity, and what happens? That bullshit," he points to Stacy's phone. "This is bullshit." He turns to me. "You're supposed to fucking protect her, not feed her to the fucking wolves! You promised!"

"Are you kidding me?" I grip Meg by the shoulders and move her to the side toward Will, knowing he'll keep her out of the way. "You think I don't know what fame, *your fame* has done to your sister?"

"Leo." Sam's voice is full of warning, but I ignore her. I've had enough of this bullshit.

"Your fame, all of your fame," I point to Will and then turn back to Luke, my heart hammering in my chest, "lost Sam her motherfucking job. She's been unemployed for over a month because she wouldn't sell her family out."

Luke's jaw drops and his eyes fly to Sam's, who now has tears in her eyes. "Is this true?"

"Fuck this," she whispers and shakes her head. "I'm out of here." She pushes through the bodies that have gathered around us and slams through the front door, Natalie close behind.

"What the fuck are you talking about?" Mark asks, his hands on his hips.

"Her boss wanted her to do a story on Luke and Nat last year after they got married. She refused."

"But you just said she's only been unemployed for a month.

We've been married for over a year."

"I wasn't finished." I push my hand through my hair. "About a month ago, the bastard bitched her out for not telling him sooner that she was connected to the Montgomerys. More specifically, Will Montgomery."

"Sonofabitch," Will whispers. "I would have done an interview for her."

"She wouldn't have asked you to, man. She loves you. All of you." I look around the room, at Sam's family. Jules has tears in her eyes, the men's mouths are clenched, fists balled. "She would never put her family in any magazine, especially knowing how fiercely private you all are."

If she had just confided in them sooner, they would have fought for her.

"So, they fired her because they said she wasn't a team player for not being willing to sell out her family. She went to L.A. for a job interview."

"She's not moving to L.A." Sam's dad insists from his stance on the stairway. The parents have come out to listen.

"No, she's not." I confirm and shake my head. "She's had interviews here in town this week."

"Why didn't she say anything?" Luke asks.

"This is Sam we're talking about." I remind him with a rueful laugh. "She's stubborn as hell. She also didn't want anyone to worry." I turn back to Luke and get in his face. "So if you think I'd let a rag get their hands on something like that." I point at the phone clenched tightly in Stacy's fingers. "You're sorely mistaken. The bitch will be fired. I know about Scott." The last sentence is whispered, for Luke and Mark's ears only.

His surprised gaze finds mine and then he sighs deeply. "Fuck."

* * *

~Samantha~

What the fuck just happened? I run out the front door toward Leo's car and realize that not only didn't I drive, but I don't have any keys.

I can't leave.

Damn it!

"Sam." Natalie's soft voice comes from behind me and I turn to find her standing on the porch, her green eyes worried and wet.

"Go back inside, Nat," I just want to be alone. God, my heart hurts. He fucking told them.

He told them after I told him not to. And what in the name of all that's holy is up with that photo?

"Sam, talk to me." Nat insists, and walks to me, her arms wrapped tightly around her middle.

"Nothing to say." I plant my hands on my hips and stare off down the driveway.

"Spill it, Williams." Nat's voice is hard. I glance over at my gorgeous sister-in-law, so thankful for her.

"I told Leo not to tell the family about my job." I finally admit.

"Why?" She asks with a frown. "We would have helped you."

"That's why." I kick at a rock on the pavement. "Luke would have tried to fix it, or pay off my mortgage, or something stupid like that."

"I'm pretty sure your mortgage will be paid for by tomorrow afternoon," Nat agrees with a grin.

"He better not." I warn her and then feel tears start to fall from my eyes, which pisses me off more. "Damn it."

"You know, we all love you." Nat smirks when I start to cry harder. The bitch. "You distance yourself from us, from everyone really, but we love you so much. Your brothers would do anything for you."

"I know," I whisper.

"I have a feeling Leo feels the same way." I shake my head but she just laughs at me. "Sam, did you take a second to see his face when he saw that picture?"

No. I shake my head.

"It devastated him. He'll make it right," she states confidently and smiles gently.

"Why are you so nice to me?" I ask her. "I was horrible to you."

"Because I know why you were, and because I love you for wanting to protect my husband."

I shake my head and wipe the tears off my cheeks.

"Are you crying because of that photo?" She asks softly.

"No." I shake my head and wipe my nose on the back of my hand. "I feel betrayed by that tattooed asshole in there, and embarrassed that everyone heard that I'd lost my job."

Nat nods and then frowns. "You'll get another job you know."

I shrug. "They're not knocking down my door."

"You will. What does Leo say?"

"He's moving up here to be near Meg more and the band is going to record the next album here."

"That's not what I meant and you know it." She narrows her eyes at me, making me laugh.

"God, you're such a gold digger." I fling at her with a laugh. She chuckles and nods her head.

"Yeah, don't tell Luke. He thinks I love him for his good looks."

I wipe the rest of the tears from my cheeks and sigh. "Leo says he'll take care of me."

"I bet that pissed you off, too," she correctly observes.

"Hell yes, it did. I don't need him to take care of me."

"Nope," she agrees with a grin.

"What is it with men thinking they can just take care of everything? I'm not a damsel in distress. I got this shit."

"I hear you." She shrugs. "But it is kind of nice to know you don't have to do it all on your own. I like it that Luke has my back."

"I think he prefers your front." I smirk.

"No, he loves my ass." She laughs.

"You have a good ass." I confirm with a nod and then frown. "I'm still really, really pissed at him. He shouldn't have told the family."

"No, that was yours to tell." Natalie puts her arm around my shoulders. "I'm sorry you're hurt."

The front door opens and I expect to see Luke, or my parents, come outside, but instead it's Leo, moving quickly, a scowl on his face.

"Get in the fucking car."

"Excuse me?"

"I'll see you later," Nat whispers and kisses my cheek before letting herself back inside.

"You heard me."

"I'm not going anywhere with you." I stand my ground; my arms crossed and glare defiantly at him.

"The fuck you're not. Get in."

"No."

He stops and turns to me, his gray eyes angrier than I've ever seen them. He gets in my face, his voice low and deceptively calm. "Get in the motherfucking car before I put you there myself."

"Leo…"

"Get in the fucking car!"

Jesus, Mary and Joseph he's pissed.

Chapter Twenty-One

~Leo~

"Damn, you piss me off," I mutter and grip the steering wheel tightly, enjoying the rumble of the engine as I stomp on the gas and tear out of Will's drive way.

"You're going to kill us both," she mutters and glares at me.

"No, if I decide to kill you, I'll choke the shit out of you." She has the audacity to laugh.

"Do you think that's the first time I've been threatened with a choking?"

"No, sweetheart, I'm sure that happens on a regular basis. You're so fucking stubborn."

She glares again and looks out the passenger window.

I'm so angry with her, I dare not touch her. I'm pissed on so many levels; I don't even know where it starts and how to dig through to the root of it.

I just know that I haven't been this angry since I was sixteen years old.

"Leo," she begins, but I cut her off.

"Stop talking."

Her startled gaze whips to mine, and I glare at her, seething.

"You're really upset," she whispers and sits quietly while I navigate through downtown Seattle to her building. I park, and take the car out of gear so her door unlocks and she can get out.

"I'll talk to you later."

"You're not coming in?" She asks, surprised.

"No."

"Leo, come inside and talk to me." I glance over at her, and her eyes are scared, and a piece of me softens. She's worried I won't be back.

"Fine." I turn off the ignition, round the hood of the car and pull her out of her seat, walk briskly into her building and press the elevator button. When the doors close, she tries to speak, but I cut her off.

"No, you want me to talk, fine, I'll talk. When we get into your place."

She frowns up at me, about to argue, but she shuts her lips and looks straight ahead. At her floor, I stomp ahead to her door and wait for her to unlock it and walk inside.

"Sit."

"No, I'm not a fucking dog, Leo. If you're pissed, talk. If you're just going to be an asshole, go home. I'm sick of you bullying me."

"Bullying you?" I round on her, the rage rising anew. "Bullying you. I fucking stuck up for you, Samantha."

"No, my brothers did that." She responds, her eyes on fire. "You betrayed me."

I stumble backward, as if she'd physically struck me.

"You know, for a smart woman, you can be unbelievably stupid." Her eyes flash but I glare at her, shutting her up. "You want to talk this out? Fine, I'll talk, and you're going to listen to every motherfucking word I say."

~Samantha~

If he swears at me like that one more time, I swear to God I'm going to throw him out on his ass.

"Who the hell do you think you are to treat your family like that?" He plants his hands on his hips and pins me in a glare. "You have a family who adores you. Your brothers would do anything for you. Jesus, Sam, even the Montgomerys would kill for you." He stomps away and begins pacing about my living room, his face tight with anger.

"Do you know what I would have given for just a moment of that when I was growing up?" He turns to face me and I feel all the blood drain from my head. "I would have crawled through fire to have such a big family that loved me. To have siblings to fight with and defend when someone else tried to fuck with them.

But do you know what I got instead?"

Oh, God, I don't know if I want to know this. He begins to pace again, his eyes distant, and I realize that it's not really me that he's angry with.

He's just angry.

"My folks died when I was twelve, and they didn't have siblings, so there was no one to take me. Instead I was thrown into foster care. The first place wasn't too bad, but they couldn't keep me for long, so I kept getting shuffled about, from home to home, until I was about sixteen. Most of the homes were okay. Some of the dads liked to hit, which I learned to deal with." He shrugs and goes to look out my window to the busy street below.

"What happened when you were sixteen?" I whisper, my stomach roiling in anger and pain and sheer horror.

"I woke up one night." His voice is so low I can barely hear it, so I quietly inch closer. "And the man I lived with was on top of me, trying to get my pants off."

Holy fucking shit.

"I was always a tall kid, but by the time I was sixteen, I was strong too, and I fought the fat fucker off of me. Blackened his eye." He braces his forehead against the glass, lost in the horrific memories running through his head. "I woke up like that, almost every night for a week. He just wouldn't give up. It got to where I would fight sleep, doing everything in my power to stay awake and sleep during class in the day time, but I would inevitably fall asleep."

He takes a deep breath and closes his eyes. "Then they brought in this other kid, a few years younger than me, named Tom. He was weaker than me. He had the bed next to mine."

"Oh, God," I whisper, my hand over my mouth.

"Yeah, he wasn't as lucky," he whispers. "But worse than that, Meg came along."

"Don't tell me…"

"No, the bastard preferred young boys, but I made it my mission in life to protect her and make sure that no one ever touched her like that." He turns to me, his face carefully void of any emotion at all. His balled hands are at his sides, and every muscle in his body is clenched. "That's what family does, Samantha. They protect each other. Instead of you giving your brothers, your parents, your friends the opportunity to help you, you shut them out."

"I don't need their charity," I begin but his face hardens once again and I cringe. "That's not what I mean. I don't want them to feel obligated to help me."

"They don't feel obligated. They feel love, damn it!"

"I don't deserve it!" I yell back at him. "I've never done anything to deserve to be in this family, with all of these wonderful, beautiful people."

"What are you talking about?" He asks, his face completely confused.

"I'm not anyone special. I don't have any amazing talents, I don't make a ton of money, I'm not even a very nice person. The only thing I have is famous family members." I shake my head and move across the room, my back to him. "Do you know that aside from family and people I'm related to by marriage I don't have one person that I consider my friend? Not one. And that's not a coincidence." I turn back to him. He's watching me like I've gone crazy.

He could be right.

"Why?" He asks.

"Because someone always wants something from me, Leo. In high school, they wanted to get close to Luke or Mark, so they'd pretend to be my friend so they could hang out at our house and try to get glimpses of them. When Luke got famous, it intensified by a thousand. Hell, a million." I laugh ruefully. "I finally got smart and separated myself from it, found a career I like and am good at, and even that fucked me over."

I brace my head in my hands, rubbing my forehead with my fingertips. "I learned a long time ago to look out for myself, and not depend on others to take care of me. Fame is fleeting and honestly, it's just a lie." I find his eyes and shrug. "Being famous doesn't make anyone happy. It's just… scary."

"Sam, you deserve your family. They love you."

"Yes, they do." I nod and then shake my head. "And I love them more than anything. But I don't deserve to have them pick up the pieces when my life falls apart. I'm in my thirties, for the love of Christ, Leo, I need to pick up my own pieces."

"I notice you're not including me anywhere in this equation," he murmurs and shoves his hands in his pockets.

"I don't need you to fix anything either," I tell him firmly.

"No, you don't need me to fix anything, but supporting you and being there for you is not fixing."

"I don't need your fame," I mutter and turn my back on him, shuffling back and forth across my small living room.

"What do you need?" He asks, his voice tight with frustration, but I don't answer. I just continue to pace.

"I don't need your money," I mutter again and push my hands through my hair.

"Okay." He's right behind me now, and I can feel the frustration rolling off him in waves, but he places his hands gently on my shoulders and his touch is my undoing. "What do you need, sunshine?"

"You!" I spin and clasp my arms around his middle, press my face to his chest so I don't have to look him in the eye and let the tears come. "I just need you," I whisper.

"Sam," he whispers and wraps those warm, strong arms around my shoulders, hugging me close. "You have me, baby."

"It pisses me off." I lean my forehead against his chest. "I don't like this feeling. In the car, I thought you were dropping me off and not coming back, and it killed me. I don't want to depend on you."

"Hey." He tips my chin up so I have to look him in the eye. "You make me so angry, I just didn't think I could talk with you without wanting to throttle you. Sam, you have to work on this whole not feeling worthy thing. Your family adores you, and you feel the same. You need to trust them."

"I know." I drop my gaze to his mouth and frown.

"And another thing." He kisses my forehead. "You *are* a nice person, whether you like it or not. You are the most amazing woman I've ever met. If you keep talking shit about my woman, I'll have to punish you."

"No more tosses into pools." I smile.

KRISTEN PROBY

"I'm sorry you feel like I betrayed you." His face sobers, his eyes are sad. "That's the very last thing I would ever do."

"I know, but I told you…"

"You know, one of the things that you'll learn about me," he kisses my forehead softly, "Is that I will always have your best interests at heart. Your family deserved to know."

"And I deserved to tell them." I stand strong. "I need you beside me, not fighting my battles for me."

A slow grin spreads across his face and he cups my face in his hands before lowering his lips to mine. "Well put. As long as I'm in the picture."

"Leo, you *are* the picture."

He stills, his eyes searching mine, and then he kisses me, softly at first, and then demandingly. He bends and scoops me into his arms and carries me to my bedroom.

"I need to get you naked and lose myself in you. Is that okay?" He asks, his gray eyes have softened.

"Yeah, that's okay." I pull his shirt up over his head when he sets me on my feet. We quickly undress each other and tumble onto the bed. Leo rises over me, his leg resting between my own, and pulls his fingertips down my face.

"I love you, Samantha Williams. Every damn day, I love you." His lips capture mine again before I can answer, and he contentedly kisses me, brushing his mouth over mine, letting me bite and pull on his piercing, his thumb tracing circles on my cheek.

His erection is pressing against my hip, but when I try to reach down for it, he captures my hand in his and kisses my fingers. "Not yet," he whispers.

"What's wrong?"

"We have all night. This isn't a quick fuck, sunshine." He nibbles the corner of my mouth and down to my jaw line. "I wasn't kidding when I said I'm going to lose myself in you. I'm going to make love to you, baby."

"I don't know…"

"Yes, you do." He interrupts, and eyes on mine, and kisses me again. "You do know."

I glide my fingertips down his side to his ass and my hands

clench when his fingertip circles around my nipple, tightening the sensitive skin.

"I love your breasts," he whispers and pulls the nipple into his mouth, suckling gently. "So responsive."

"I love your mouth." I squirm beneath him as he gently bites the tight nipple. "Can't get enough of it."

"Good." He chuckles and kisses my jawline again and up to my lips. He continues to kiss my mouth, his tongue teasing mine, as his hand glides down my torso, over my stomach, to my core, and pushes two fingers over my clit and into my folds.

"Oh, God." My back automatically arches, pushing me against his hand. "God, you have good hands."

"I love how wet you get," he whispers. "You're so fucking sexy, baby."

He nibbles down to my collarbones and farther still to my breasts, paying them both close attention. His fingers are moving rhythmically through the lips of my labia, almost tickling me.

"Haven't we already decided that I'm not a guitar?" I ask.

"You're better." He licks my navel, pulls my piercing gently with his teeth and then kisses it sweetly. "This piercing will be my undoing."

"All those piercings you have." I gasp as one of his fingers dives inside me and brushes my sweet spot. "And my little navel piercing turns you on?"

"It's hot as hell on you, baby."

"I like yours too, even the eyebrow."

"Yeah?" His lips move lower down my abdomen to my pussy and then he leans back and just stares at my core.

"What are you looking at?"

"I love how pink you are." He grins wickedly and then leans in and licks me, from my anus to my clit and back down again. "God, you taste good."

"Holy fuck," I whisper as my hips begin to move like they have a life of their own. He spreads my legs wide and pins them down to the mattress with his forearms, and uses his hands to spread my pussy wide and buries his face in my core, thrusts his tongue inside me, then closes his mouth and moves that glorious piercing all over my lips and up to my clit.

"Dear God, that lip is awesome," I mutter and feel him smile against me. "Is that why you got it?" I ask, panting.

"No, side benefit." He does it again.

"Leo." God, I can't breathe. I can't even open my eyes. He's turning me inside out.

"Mmm…"

"Need you, Leo," I whisper, not even sure if the words are actually coming out of me, or if they're simply in my head.

"I'm right here, sweetheart." Okay, so I spoke them aloud.

"I need you inside me." I shake my head against the pillow, going out of my mind with lust. If he turns me on any further, I'll die.

Or burst into flames.

"I'll get there," he mutters and continues to assault my pussy with his mouth.

"Please," I whisper and then whimper when he latches those amazing lips onto my clit and sinks two fingers inside me.

He's trying to kill me.

I come like crazy around his fingers, my hips bucking and pushing against him, and finally he kisses and licks his way back up my body, rests his lower body against mine, and braces himself on his elbows on either side of my head, his hands in my hair and his face only centimeters from mine. My hands drift up and down his back and up over his shoulders so I can trace the tattoos on his arms.

"I love your ink," I whisper and watch my fingers on his skin. "What does this one mean?"

"It represents the first song that I wrote that we recorded on our first album," he replies, watching me intently.

"And this one?" I ask, tracing the other shoulder.

"That was the original artwork from the third album, but the studio chose to go with something different." He brushes a piece of hair off my forehead and kisses me gently there.

"What about this?" I ask, touching his forearm.

"That one reminds me of Meg."

"Really?" I ask with a smile.

He nods and nuzzles my nose with his. "If we keep this up, we'll be here all night."

"We have all night," I remind him with a smile.

"Let's continue the tattoo talk in a little while," he suggests.

"Okay, what would you like to do in the mean time?" I continue to trace his ink with my finger.

"I can think of a few things." He slowly sinks inside me. "Jesus, sunshine, I never get used to being inside you without a cover."

"Mmm..." I agree and sigh as he keeps his hips still, seated completely inside me. "You feel so good."

He links my hand with his, kisses my fingers, and lifts my hand over my head to rest against the bed. He clenches his hand firmly as he begins to move in and out of me, slow, but steady. He rests his forehead on mine.

"I've never in my life felt like this," he murmurs and continues to make love to me. "You are everything I've ever wanted, Sam. More than music. More than anything."

Tears pool in my eyes at his sweet words and I bite my lip.

"Don't cry," he whispers.

"I'm not," I respond as a tear falls down into my hairline.

"Sure you're not." He grins and kisses me gently as he begins to move more swiftly, hitting that amazing spot with each thrust, until I feel the orgasm move through me, and I clench around him, pulling him under with me.

Chapter Twenty-Two

"Where are we going?" I ask and frown out the window of Leo's car. We're in the middle of nowhere.

"I have to show you something."

"Another house?" I ask, unable to keep the excitement from my voice.

"Sure." He shakes his head and smiles over at me.

"I hope it's a different real estate agent. That chick was not the one for you." I laugh at him and run my fingers through his messy, soft light brown hair.

"Definitely a different agent." He catches my hand to kiss my palm.

We continue to drive on side roads, and I've completely lost track of where we are. Leo flips on the radio, turns to a popular local rock station and sings along with Pink.

"You're a Pink fan?" I ask, surprised.

"Isn't everyone? That chick is badass." He laughs and shakes his head. "And she can fucking party like no one I've ever seen."

"I've heard she's slowed down since she had a kid." I sing along with the radio. This song is currently one of my favorites. *You've got to get up and try...*

"I think that's true, but I haven't seen her in a while."

"Where is this house we're going to see?" I ask and examine our surroundings. "We're in the middle of nowhere."

"Be patient." He laughs.

"I'm not patient. Have you not learned this by now?"

"That blue scarf looks beautiful on you." He grins over at me, changing the subject. "Makes your eyes look even bluer."

"You're a charmer." I wave him off and scowl at all the trees along the road. "And you're going to be a single charmer if you buy a house I can't find."

He laughs and shakes his head at me, and I stop trying to figure out where we're going and sit back to look at him. He's in his black leather jacket today with his trademark faded blue jeans. No beanie, which I prefer, so I run my fingers through his hair again and sigh contentedly.

He keeps checking his watch as he continues to drive.

"Are we going to be late?"

He just shakes his head and grips the wheel a little tighter.

Why is he nervous?

"I think this is it," he murmurs and pulls up to a cliff area that looks out over the Sound. I didn't even realize we were this close to the water. There is a grassy bluff to my right with trees behind it. The view is spectacular.

But there is no house.

I frown over at Leo, but he's already climbed out of the car and opens my door for me.

"Uh, Leo, there's no house here."

"Give me a minute."

After he's pulled me away from the car, he leans into the open passenger door and cranks the volume of the radio up so high that I'm pretty sure my brother over in Alki can hear it.

He checks his watch again, nods and pins me in his gaze.

"What are you doing?" I ask and laugh. "This is not like you."

"Listen," he murmurs.

The song on the radio ends and the DJ comes on.

"Hey there, Seattle, that was *Life After You* by Daughtry here on KLPR, Seattle's best rock radio station. I have a special treat for our listeners. I got a call from Seattle's own Leo Nash of the mega band, Nash, yesterday asking me to play their newest single from their upcoming album, *Sunshine*. The album doesn't release for another month, but we have a sneak peak of the title track for you today. Leo tells me this song is dedicated to someone special. I hope you enjoy it."

"Are you kidding me?" I ask, my eyes wide. Leo's smiling softly and he grips the ends of my scarf in his fists and pulls me against him.

"Dance with me."

He wraps me in his arms and as the piano begins, he moves us back and forth along the cliff, the wind blowing through our hair and stinging my cheeks. He pulls back briefly, so I can slip my arms under his jacket, and tightens his arms around me again, holding me close, looking down into my eyes.

I don't wanna be your friend
'Cause I've already let you in
Every time I see your sweet blue eyes
I know I need to make you mine
My walls crumble… and crumble
So all you see is the real me

When you smile
Your sunshine hits me
And the shadows in my soul
They are gone

He softly sings along, his eyes dropping to my lips and then back to mine. He kisses my forehead softly.

"I love this song," I whisper.

"I love you," he whispers back, bends me back into a deep dip, and then circles me more vigorously around the car. The song is swirling around us, the rest of the world has stilled, and it even seems like the crashing waves beneath the cliff have quieted.

Oh how many times
Did I stare at your lips
Wishing I could feel
Them on me
When you're so close
Baby, I forget how to breathe

When you smile
Your sunshine hits me
And the shadows in my soul
They are gone

When I run my hand
Over your perfect skin
I know you see me
And not what I'm covered in
My walls crumble… And crumble
So all you see is the me I need you to see

I can't look away from his eyes. This is how he sees me. What did I do to deserve him?

He cups my face in his hands and brushes my lips with his, gently nibbling and caressing my mouth, and then sinks into me, kissing me with all he has as our song comes to an end.

He pulls back, his stormy gray eyes happy and shining with lust, kisses my cheek and then releases me to lean in the car and turn the radio off.

When he turns back to me, his face is uncertain.

"When did you record the song?" I ask, a little out of breath.

"Last week." He shrugs and pulls me back into him, my arms under his jacket again to keep me warm. "DJ and Gary came up from L.A. and we spent some time in the studio."

"Was that your mysterious errand?" I ask and give him a mock-frown.

"Yes." He chuckles and kisses my nose.

"I love it." I kiss his chin and grin. "I really, really love it. Are you seriously naming the whole album *Sunshine*?"

"Yeah, we are." He rubs my cheek with his thumb. "It's appropriate."

I grin and then look around us at the water, the trees, the cliffs. "So, no house, unless it's wearing the invisibility cloak."

"I didn't know you're a *Harry Potter* fan."

"Sure." I shrug.

"No house yet." He nods and follows my gaze.

"What do you mean? Are you going to build a house on stilts?" I smirk and gesture to the Sound. "Do you know how many houses fall into the water every year here?"

"So, here's the deal." He kisses my forehead again and pulls back, takes my hand, and pulls me closer to the cliffs.

"This is as far as I go." I plant my feet and stop. "I'm afraid of heights, remember?"

"Okay, scaredy cat." He laughs and his eyes travel over the water. "Do you know how much I wanted to live on the water when I first moved out here? I'd never seen the ocean until I moved here when I was nineteen."

He turns his eyes down to mine and squeezes my hand.

"You couldn't find a house to buy on the water?" I ask.

"After the interesting afternoon with the last agent the other day, I thought it might be easier to build." He shrugs. "Plus, then you'll get exactly what you want."

"Leo." I swallow and try to keep my panic down. "I told you, I'm not ready to live together."

"Me neither." He laughs and turns to me, taking both my hands in his. "Do you know how long it takes to build a house?"

"Yes, Isaac is a contractor."

"Great, he can build it."

"But…"

"Listen." He kisses me, his smile still in place, and I calm, just a bit. "We don't even need to break ground until we both agree that we're ready to take that step, Sam. The land will be here."

"But it's so far out of town."

"No, it's not." He shakes his head and chuckles almost shyly. "I took the scenic route. I was trying to kill time while waiting for the radio to play your song."

"How far out are we?"

"Only ten minutes from downtown." He runs his fingertips down my cheek. "Think of the closet you can build, baby."

"Oh God, it's not fair to bribe me with a closet."

"I'm not bribing you." He tosses his head back as he laughs. "I want you to have full input on the house. You can have anything you want, whenever you're ready."

"Did you already buy it?" I ask, already knowing the answer. He looks down and frowns nervously and then looks back into my eyes.

"Yes. For us. For when we're ready. It's gonna happen, sunshine. You're mine."

He's right. And I love him for not pressuring us into jumping into it right now, but rather letting things progress as they should.

"So, when we're ready to move in together," I clarify, "we'll draw up plans and have Isaac build us a house here, on a seventy-five foot cliff?"

"Or on the grassy part over there." He agrees.

I look out over the gray water, covered in dark clouds with white seagulls flying over it looking for food. A ferry is carrying people to one of the islands.

"It's a beautiful view."

"Yes, it is." I glance over to find him staring down at me with serious eyes. "I want to look at it for the rest of my life."

Wow.

"Thank you." I hug him tight, bury my face in his chest and breathe him in.

"For what, sweetheart?"

"My song. This place." I lean back and look up into his handsome face. "Being so good to me."

"You're welcome." He kisses my forehead and leads me back to the car. "Wanna get take-out and a movie on the way home?"

"And cupcakes."

* * *

"Seriously, why do men think all this blood is cool?" I cringe as another poor bad guy gets blown away on the big screen TV in Leo's bedroom.

"Ask your brother, he's the expert." Leo laughs and takes another bite of his lemon cupcake. I eye it longingly and he pulls it out of my reach. "Mine."

"But I didn't get lemon." I bat my eyes at him and cup his dick in my hand. "Please?"

"You don't fool me." He smirks and pushes my hand away. "You're a selfish brat when it comes to cupcakes."

"Meanie." I pout and cross my arms over my chest. My cupcake was devoured long ago.

He smirks again as his phone rings.

"Nash." He swallows his cake and frowns. "When?"

I don't like the tone of his voice. He pauses the movie and sits up straight, checking his watch.

"Okay man, don't panic. I'll call the airport and get the jet ready. You just get your shit together and meet us there. Yeah, I'll call the other guys too. Tell Lori we love her."

He hangs up and runs his hand down his face.

"That was Gary."

"What's wrong?" I immediately ask.

"Lori's in labor."

"She's early." I frown.

"Yeah, we thought we had time. Gary's still here. We need to get him down to her." He jumps up off the bed and just looks around, his eyes worried, like he doesn't know what to do first.

"Okay, you make your calls and I'll pack your bag." I reach for his large duffle.

"Are you sure? You should come with me."

I fold his jeans and a few tees and lay them in the bag. "I can't, babe. I have interviews and Luke called today while we were at the cliffs. He wants to chat." I shake my head and smile at him reassuringly. "It'll be okay. Get Gary home; check on Lori. Tell her I'm sorry that I can't be there."

"Okay." His mouth is grim and I can see the internal struggle of taking care of his guy and being here with me. "I don't like it."

"It'll be okay." I repeat and hug him tight. "Make your calls."

"Thanks." He kisses my forehead and gets to work, calling the airline first to make sure the jet will be ready within the hour.

Must be nice to have a plane at your beck and call.

As he paces the bedroom, placing call after call, I gather his things and pack his bag. His toiletries, socks, underwear. He really has great underwear. They're all the really short boxer-briefs, in black. Some say Armani along the elastic waist. Some say Ed Hardy. God, they're hot.

"Why are you staring at my underwear?" He asks with a laugh.

"I was picturing what you look like in them." I smirk and throw them in the bag. "You have hot underwear."

"What's up with your obsession with underwear?"

"I just like it." I shrug.

He shakes his head and makes his next call. I run downstairs to grab his computer and anything else he might need down here when I spot a notepad on the couch. The top sheet is covered in half-finished song lyrics. I read them and grin. This is definitely not a ballad, badass or otherwise.

I flip to a fresh sheet and scribble a note, fold it in half, and carry the rest of his things to the bedroom to add them to his bag.

"I think I'm about ready." He frowns as his eyes move around the room and over to me. "Will you drive me to the airport?"

"Sure, but I don't have my car." I remind him. "I'll have to drive your car."

"I'll drive to the airport, and you can drive it home, if you promise to be careful."

"Are you insinuating that I'm a reckless driver?" I ask and plant my hands on my hips, feigning annoyance.

"No, I just want you to be careful with my car. It's new. And really cool."

"It's okay." I shrug and laugh when his jaw drops in disbelief.

"Did you just disrespect my car?"

"Get over it." I roll my eyes and zip up his bag. "You're packed."

He takes the bag from me and sets it on the floor, cups my face in his hands and kisses me, not gently and softly, but passionately, like the thought of being away from me is killing him.

I wrap my arms around his waist and lean into him, pressing my belly against his erection.

"No time for this," I murmur against his lips and smile as he growls in frustration. He kisses me again, and then pulls me in for a tight hug.

"Be good," he whispers, making me smirk.

"I'm always good. *You* be good." I lean back and push my cheek into his hand, enjoying his warm touch. "Seriously, tell Lori I'm thinking of her. Be safe."

"Let's go."

* * *

"Where is my wife?" Gary demands as we approach the ER desk at Sinai Hospital in L.A.

"Uh, who are you?" The plump brunette asks, her voice bored. She's reading a magazine and gossiping with a co-worker.

"Gary Hovel," he states impatiently, tapping his hand on the countertop. "My wife is Lori and she's having a baby."

"She'll be up on four, in the maternity wing. Are you all together?" She asks with a frown, eyeing all of us.

"Yes," Gary calls to her, already halfway down the hall to the bank of elevators. He's been a mess and a pain in the ass since we left Seattle.

Poor guy.

The elevator delivers us to the fourth floor and Gary charges over to another nurse's station. "Where's my wife?"

"Which one would she be?" A petite blonde asks with a grin. She's way too chipper to be working at this time of night.

"Lori Hovel."

"Room four oh nine, down the hall." She points and Gary is off like a greyhound after a rabbit.

The rest of us aren't far behind him.

"Oh thank God," Gary breathes and rushes to his wife, taking her in his arms and burying his face in her neck, then kissing her face. "Are you okay?"

"Yes, I'm fine. We're both fine."

"Where is Maddox?" He asks.

"With my sister. Everything is okay, babe." She smiles at him and rubs her belly. There's a belt strapped around it with thick wires leading to a monitor.

"Hey, handsome!" Cher leaps from her chair next to Lori and launches herself at DJ. "Welcome home."

"Thanks." He grins at her and kisses her hard. The rest of us plop down in chairs around the room and grin at Lori.

"So, how much longer do we have to wait?" Eric asks.

"Well, my labor stopped," Lori responds with a sigh.

"What?" Gary frowns. "How is that possible?"

"Oh, it's possible. Trust me." She shakes her head and sighs. "They won't let me go home because my water broke, and they don't want to risk infection, so here I am."

"Can't they make it start up again?" I ask with a frown. "I'll make a call."

"Even your contacts can't make the baby come faster than it wants to." Lori laughs at me. "If the labor doesn't start again by tomorrow morning, they'll induce me, but we could be looking at days, I guess. I'm not really sure."

"Jesus," I whisper and swallow. What the fuck am I going to do for a couple days in L.A., besides go crazy from wanting Sam? And then it occurs to me. I grin and pull my phone out of my pocket, find the number I want and dial.

"What's he doing?" Cher asks.

"Hey, Kat, this is Nash." I grin. "I'm in town and need a favor."

"He's doing what Leo always does when he's bored," DJ answers and kisses her cheek. "He's gonna get another tat."

"We should all go and let you guys sleep," Eric mutters as I end my call.

"Thanks, man." Gary hugs me and slaps my shoulder. "I owe you."

"Fuck that." I frown at him like he's nuts. "This is what we do."

"Thanks for getting him to me so quickly." Lori's eyes have tears in them. "I can't do this without you guys."

"You're gonna be fine, pretty face." I kiss her cheek and follow the guys out of the room.

Chapter Twenty-Three

~Samantha~

"It could be *days*?" I ask incredulously and sit up in my bed, scoot back to lean on the headboard, and raise my knees up to my chest, my phone pressed to my ear.

"That's what she said, but I hope she's wrong." Leo sighs. I love his voice.

"Poor woman, I hope she's wrong too, for her sake." He chuckles in my ear and I smile. "What are you doing now?"

"I just got to the house a little while ago. I'm unpacking." His voice sounds flat and unhappy.

"Have your feet frozen off yet?" I ask with a grin. Levine jumps up on the bed, head-butts my hand and begins to purr as I stroke his back.

"No, smart ass, not yet." He chuckles.

"Well, wear socks, or they will. What's on tap for tomorrow?" I lean my head back and close my eyes, listening to him move about his bedroom, trying to picture what he looks like.

"I'll probably be up at the hospital most of the day. Gary…" he stops suddenly and goes quiet.

"What's wrong?" I ask and frown.

"I just found something tucked in my clothes." I hear the smile in his voice.

"What is that?" I try to sound nonchalant, but can't help the grin on my face.

"A note," he murmurs. "I love you too."

"I don't usually do mushy stuff like that, you know," I remind him with a laugh, and my stomach clenches when I hear him chuckle.

"Yes, I know. You're very anti-mush."

"Damn straight."

"You know, I always knew this house was cold and uninviting, but I didn't care because I was hardly here. Now that I'm here without you in it, it's even worse." He whispers the last few words.

"Sounds like you have it bad, Nash."

"I'm having my assistant put it on the market tomorrow. I'll have my personal stuff sent up north. I'm not staying here again. How's my car?"

"Well, the tow truck guy told me that it would be just fine in a few weeks," I slap my hand over my mouth so he can't hear the laughter.

"That's not funny."

"What?"

"I will spank your ass when I see you, Samantha," he warns.

"Promises, promises."

"Tell me it's safe in your parking garage."

"It's safe in someone's parking garage." This time I don't hold back on the laughter.

"Samantha Williams!" He's laughing too and I hear rustling around like he's getting undressed.

"Are you naked?" I ask.

"Yes. Climbing in bed. You?"

"No, I'm not naked, but I'm in bed."

"Which shirt are you wearing?"

"Cyndi Lauper," I lie.

"Liar," he whispers.

"Journey," I lie again.

"Try again, sunshine."

"I might be wearing a signed Nash shirt that my sweet boyfriend gave to me."

"That's better." I hear him yawn and I scoot back down to lie under the covers.

"You should go to sleep. We had a long day."

"You should sleep too."

"We have to hang up." I laugh.

"You hang up," he mumbles.

"Are we sixteen?"

"Get some rest, baby. I love you."

He hangs up and I turn on my back and think back on the day. The song, the dancing, the cliffs where we'll build a house some-day.

If this is a dream, I don't want to ever wake up.

* * *

"I don't know why you wouldn't let me take you out to lunch." I complain to Luke when he opens the door to his house.

"Maybe because you're not making any money, so how would you be able to buy lunch?" He takes my coat and evades when I try to punch him in the arm.

"Don't be a douche." I scowl at him. "I have savings. I'm not about to be homeless or anything."

"Gee, I'm so glad to hear that." He rolls his eyes and walks ahead of me into the kitchen.

"Where are Nat and Liv?" I pull myself up onto a barstool and lean on the breakfast bar. I'm in an oversized sweatshirt and leggings, opting for comfort today.

I have no one to impress.

"They're out with Jules."

"They didn't invite me." I frown.

"They knew you were going to be here with me," he grins and shakes his head as he pours me a glass of iced tea. "Don't get all offended, sis."

"Well, okay then." He passes me the tea, pours his own glass and then leans against the counter and sips his drink, contemplating me over the rim.

"What?"

"You and Leo work things out?"

"Just cut to the chase, Luke." I roll my eyes at him but he just lifts his eyebrow. "That doesn't work with me either. I'm your sister, not your wife."

"Boy, that's the truth. You are definitely not my wife."

"I'm never going to be anyone's wife." I shrug and take a sip of tea.

"Why?" He asks with a frown. "I thought things were going well with Leo."

"They are. That doesn't mean I need a ring on my finger. We're not even moving in together for a while. I know you don't understand that concept given that you and Nat went from a mugging to a baby in about twelve minutes."

"Fuck off." He smirks.

"You don't need a contract to be in a committed relationship."

"Okay." He frowns again and then shrugs. "To each her own."

"Yep." I agree.

"Why didn't you tell me your job was giving you grief because of me?" He asks, his eyes sad.

"Because I didn't want to see that look on your face." I sigh and rub my hands down my face.

"C'mon, Sam, this is always going to be an issue, and I'm sorry for it, but you need to stop being so stubborn and let me help."

"How are you going to help, Luke?" I jump off the stool and pace over to his floor-to-ceiling windows that look out onto the Sound. "There's nothing to do."

"You can at least talk to me about it."

"And then you'll feel guilty and I'll have to kick your ass because it's not your fault." I shrug and turn around to face him. "Luke, it's not your fault. I'm so proud of you and all that you've accomplished. You've earned it."

"I know you are, but I also know that being related to me isn't easy. And now you're romantically connected to someone even more famous than I am, and that makes me worry about you."

"I've already discovered that it's different with thirty-something rock stars than it is with heartthrobs." I grin as he scowls.

"I'm no fucking heartthrob."

"Anymore." I shrug. "We don't have young girls following us around. The groupies are interesting." I concede and then laugh.

"There will be more photos printed," he reminds me. "That didn't seem to thrill you."

"It surprised me that Melissa, the publicist." I clarify at his raised eyebrow. "Let it leak after Leo specifically told her not to.

It pissed me off more that he told you guys about my job."

"You should have told us."

"I know, but I didn't want you to worry. Leo reminded me that that's what family does; they worry."

"Leo's smart." Luke offers me a half-smile.

"But not good enough for me." I remind him and sigh.

"Sam, I said that in anger. You're my sister. No one is good enough for you because I love you." He pushes his hands through his blonde hair and scratches his scalp.

"Just like Natalie wasn't good enough for you either." I smirk. "At least you didn't accuse Leo of being a gold-digging whore."

"There is that." He agrees with a laugh.

"And now I love her. She's perfect for you." I tilt my head to the side and watch as his face softens as he thinks of her; his eyes smile. "You're good for each other."

"You know." He begins and hops up on the counter, his bare feet dangling. "Livie's picture has never appeared in a magazine. And we were offered millions for photos of her after she was born."

"I remember." I nod, wondering what his point is.

"There are ways to make sure that you lead a relatively private life while being with a celebrity." He shrugs.

"I know. I've already spoken with the wives of the other band members. Honestly, I'm not too worried about it."

"You're not?" His eyebrows climb and he's completely surprised.

"No, I'm not. I'm tired of letting my fear of fame dictate whom I love and how I act and who I am. We'll figure it out."

"Wow, you got really smart."

"Don't be a sarcastic ass."

"I paid off your apartment." He casually mentions as he jumps off the counter.

"What the hell? Why would you do that?"

"Because now you don't have to worry about the mortgage and because I can."

"I'm not a charity case."

"If you ever fucking say that again I will kick your ass" His face is red and his eyes are on fire. "You are not a goddamn charity case. You're my sister. I have more money than my children's children can ever spend, Sam. I can afford to buy your apartment."

"Bragger," I mutter and pout.

He laughs and hugs me and then refills my tea.

"Thank you."

"You're welcome." He scowls and sighs. "I'm sorry that I said that, about Leo not being good enough. I like him. He's a good guy, and if he makes you happy, then I'm glad. After all he's done for you, I he's probably the closest you're gonna get to finding someone good enough for you."

"Wow. Did little brother just give me permission to keep dating my boyfriend?"

"God, you're a bitch." He laughs.

"So I've been told," I agree and chuckle with him.

* * *

~Leo~

My shoulder is on fire, but damn if it doesn't look fucking awesome. Kat is the best there is.

I stroll into the hospital waiting room to find the other guys and Cher lounging about, playing on their phones or iPads, reading smut magazines.

Irritating the hell out of each other.

"Hey, guys." I grab a cup of horrible hospital coffee and sit next to Cher. "Any news?"

"Not yet." She shakes her head. "We do know that they started labor back up this morning, but it could be awhile."

"What the hell is the hold up?" Jake asks irritably. "Just make the kid come out."

"Right," Cher rolls her eyes. "All babies come on their own time. This is the baby of a rock star. It'll definitely make an entrance when it's good and ready."

"Why didn't they find out if it's a girl or a boy?" DJ asks.

240

"Lori wanted it to be a surprise," I remind him and text Sam. At the hospital. Still waiting for baby.

I wonder if she got the cupcakes I had delivered to her this morning? I sent both chocolate and lemon, since I'm not there for her to steal a bite from.

"Well, if we knew ahead of time, we could have bought fun gifts," Cher mutters and frowns. "I hope it's a girl."

"Why?" Eric asks, his eyes not moving from his iPad.

Be patient, Sam responds. *And thanks for the cupcakes.*

You're not one to talk about patience, sunshine. YW.

"Because I want to help her decorate the nursery in pink." She claps her hands with excitement, and then her pretty green eyes look sad. DJ leans in and whispers in her ear, making her sweet smile return to her lips. "I know."

I hope they can adopt a baby soon. Cher would be a fantastic mom. Why is it that those who should have kids have such a hard time, and so many people who have no fucking business having kids have twenty?

Time passes slowly. By mid-afternoon, we've ordered pizza and Gary has been in to give us three updates. Lori's fine, but the labor is difficult.

"What tat did you get?" Eric asks, pointing to my plastic-covered shoulder blade.

"I got a sun."

"It's time for that bandage to come off," Cher comments and motions for me to stand in front of her so she can remove it. "Oh, this is so great," she breathes.

"I know."

"Kat?" Jake asks with a grin. He and Kat had a thing for a while.

"Yeah." I nod and grin.

"She's the best." He shrugs. Cher goes to the restroom to wet some paper towels and carefully cleans my shoulder.

"Wear tanks for a few days," she murmurs.

"Thanks, mom." I smirk. "This is not my first tat."

"It's a good thing you're hot, or I'd have to hurt you. Want me to take a picture of it with your phone and you can send it to

Sam? I'm assuming it's for her."

"No, she'll see it later."

Honestly, I'm nervous, not sure how she'll react to it.

Early evening sets in, and I'm sick of sitting in this waiting room.

"I can't stand this anymore," I mutter and stand to pace about the room just as Gary comes rushing in.

"It's a girl! It's a girl! Holy fucking hell, I have a girl."

Cher squeals and we all take turns hugging our friend and each other.

A new member of the band has been born.

"How is Lori?" I ask him.

"Gorgeous, tired, perfect." He grins at me. "We have a girl."

"You know what this means, don't you?" Eric asks him with a grin.

"What?"

"We get to fuck with teenage boys in about fifteen years. Lori's a fucking knockout. Just think what the baby will look like by then."

"Fuck me, I'm going to jail." Gary pulls his hand down his face and then grins.

"What did you name her?" Jake pulls Gary into a headlock, rubbing his knuckles on his head.

"Do not say Apple," Cher warns him and he laughs.

"No, Alexis Mae," he announces proudly. "Come on, you can come see her."

"All of us?" I ask, doubtful.

"Lori wouldn't have it any other way. The nurse can kiss my ass." Gary leads us down the antiseptic-scented corridor to Lori's room and peaks his head in to make sure everyone is decent before waving us into the room.

"Hey guys." Lori grins at us; her face void of makeup and her hair is back in a simple ponytail. She's holding a little tiny bundle in a pink and blue blanket in her arms.

"Hey, pretty face." I lean down and kiss her cheek and peek at the pink face in the blanket. "She's gorgeous, like her mama."

"Thank you," she whispers. I kiss her hair and back away so

everyone else can see the brand new baby. When I turn around, I'm met with dozens of roses in pink and white, balloons, baby clothes and the softest big, brown teddy bear I've ever seen. Next to it is a small toy guitar.

"Read the card," Gary calls over to me.

I'm sorry I can't be there. Congratulations! The guitar is for Maddox. He should have presents too. Best wishes, Samantha Williams

I'm just struck dumb. My eyes roam over all the gifts again. She sent these things because these are people I love. Because she's so fucking amazing.

Not a good person, my ass. She has the biggest heart of anyone I've ever met. She just does a damn good job of keeping it hidden.

I turn back to the guys to find everyone watching me.

"When did these arrive?"

"This morning." Gary grins.

I stride to the bedside and lean over Lori, looking into her happy eyes.

"I'm sorry, I have…"

"Go get her, tiger." She grins. "We're fine."

I smile back at her and kiss her forehead, then hug all my guys, kiss Cher's cheek, and start making calls to get back to Seattle.

Chapter Twenty-Four

~Samantha~

It's only been twenty-four hours since Leo went to L.A. and I'm already going stir crazy.

This is not good.

I'm sick of my own company. I don't want to go to Luke's or my parent's. I want Leo.

So, to clear my head, I decide to go for a run. Leo would most likely spank my ass for running alone this late. The thought makes me smile.

The man gives good spank.

I zip my hoodie, grab my keys and palm the pink vial of bear spray I carry with me when I run alone, and set out. The neighborhood is relatively quiet, and the streetlights are on. Because of the late hour, I'll just run a mile or so. It feels good to be out in the cool air.

I make a big circle and as I approach the entrance to my building, a see a familiar man leaning against the wall. My first thought is Leo, but Leo is taller and leaner than this guy.

"Hey, Samantha."

What the fuck is he doing here?

"Brandon."

"You shouldn't run at night by yourself." He's frowning down at me as I approach him, panting.

"I'm fine. What are you doing in town?"

"I'm here seeing family for a week, thought I'd stop in and see how you are." He shrugs and grins. "For old times sake."

"Old times, right." I smirk and grin at him.

"So, how about it? Gonna invite me up?"

I prop my hands on my hips and tilt my head, eyeing the handsome man interested in getting in my pants. He's not as tall as

Leo, has black hair and blue eyes, a square chin. His body is cut and perfect, and he knows his way around a woman's body.

But the thought of fucking him makes my stomach turn.

"Brandon, we had fun, but I'm seeing someone."

"So, it's true?" He laughs mockingly. "You always told me you were just interested in a hard fuck."

"That's true. That's all I was interested in." My walls immediately go up. Brandon is hot, but he's also an asshole.

"I would have given you anything you wanted, you know." He shakes his head and scowls. "I've been in love with you for years."

My mouth drops. "We were fuck buddies," I counter.

"That was your call," he responds softly.

"Well, I'm sorry that we weren't on the same page, Brandon. Had I known…"

"You would have stopped calling." He interrupts. "I know."

"Well, good luck." I turn toward my building, but he stops me.

"How about you invite me in, and I remind you how good I make you feel?" He steps close to me, and pushes his hand up under my hoodie to cup my breast.

"How about you take your hand off me right now and I don't kick your ass?" My voice is cold and hard, and I shuffle the bear spray in my palm, ready to show him who's boss.

"Come on, baby, don't be like this."

"I believe she said no." A hard voice comes out of the darkness. Brandon immediately releases me and steps away as Leo – *Leo!* – strolls to me and wraps his arm around my shoulders, kisses my temple and glares at Brandon. "Are you deaf?"

"Fuck off," Brandon sneers.

"I believe she pretty much said that to you, too." Leo chuckles. "Cut your losses, dude."

"You don't know anything about us," Brandon begins, but Leo holds up a hand, stopping him.

"Do you want to press charges for sexual assault?" Leo asks.

"No, I want him to go."

"Fine." Brandon's scowl roams my face. "Your loss."

"Okay." I shrug and turn my back on him, buzz Leo and me into the building and into the elevator before I jump on him, wrapping my legs around his waist and arms around his shoulders and kiss him silly, biting his lips, his piercing, soaking in his warmth and his smell.

"I missed you," I whisper against his lips, grinning.

"Me too, and I'm pissed at you."

"Why?" I hop down and frown up at him.

"You went running at midnight."

"How do you know?" I ask and bite my lip.

"Well, you admitted as much to that asshole down there, and you're dressed for a run."

"Wait, you heard our entire conversation?" I ask incredulously. I wrack my brain, trying to remember everything that was said.

"I did." He nods and sighs and runs his fingers down my cheek. "I almost killed him."

The elevator arrives at my floor, and I lead him to my door.

"You seemed very calm."

"I almost killed him." At the sound of his voice, Levine comes running from the bedroom, jumps onto the arm of the couch and cries for attention.

"He missed you too."

He strokes Levine's back and watches me, his eyes steady and warm, but his mouth is set disapprovingly.

"I don't want you running this late."

"I only went a mile," I counter.

He sighs and pulls me into his arms. He doesn't just kiss me. He takes ownership of me.

And damn if I don't love it.

"Please don't do it again," he whispers. "If anything happened to you, it would kill me."

Well, when he puts it like that…

"Okay," I agree.

"Thank you for sending the baby gifts today."

I smile widely and bounce on the balls of my feet. "They got there?"

"Yeah, they're pretty great. Maddox will love that guitar."

"He should have a guitar like his daddy." I nod. "How is the baby?"

"Small." He laughs and shrugs.

"And Lori?"

"She's great." His eyes are happy as he lifts me into his arms and carries me to the bedroom.

"Do you want something to drink?" I push my fingers into his soft brown hair.

"Later," he murmurs and kisses my temple.

"What do you want now?" I ask with a grin.

"I haven't been inside you in too many hours to count, sunshine." He sets me on my feet and strips me naked, his lips kissing my skin as he uncovers it. By the time he pulls my socks off my feet, I'm panting and on fire.

He pulls his shirt over his head, shucks his pants and guides me onto the bed, onto my back.

"Spread your legs, sweetheart."

"Gee, this is awfully fast. I usually ask a guy to buy me dinner before he can just insist I spread my legs." I giggle and he pinches my thigh, then bites it and kisses the hurt away.

He systematically kisses his way up my body; his hands are moving over me, gently caressing my breasts, my nipples.

He nuzzles my belly button and sighs. "Sexy."

He leaves open-mouthed, wet kisses on my skin and climbs up to rest his pelvis against my own. His lips wreck havoc on my neck, making me squirm beneath him, my hips circling and inviting him inside me.

"I missed you," he whispers.

"Me too, but it was only one day."

"Missed you anyway." He kisses his way over to the other side and sucks my earlobe, grazes my jawline with his teeth and settles in to kiss me stupid.

His hand brushes down my ribs and between us to cup my center.

"You're so wet, baby."

A finger slips inside me, his thumb brushes my nub, and I gasp. "Want you."

"Mmm…" He agrees. "Do you know how amazing you are?"

I can't even think at the moment. "If this is a pop-quiz, I'll take the zero 'cause I don't remember my name right now."

He chuckles and bites my lower lip, brushes my hair from my face, and continues to drive me crazy with his fingers. I gasp when he adds another finger, my toes curl and I push my pelvis against him.

"You amaze me," he whispers. "Come." He bites my chin, pushes my clit with his thumb, and I see stars, clenching his fingers tightly, moaning and shaking under him.

And he's not even inside me yet.

He pulls his fingers out of me and sucks them clean, his eyes laughing down at me. "You're delicious, sunshine."

I just grin as he grips both my hands in his, linking our fingers, and pulls them over my head as he rears back and sinks inside me, quick and hard.

"Ah, shit," I mutter and strain against his hands, but he holds me strong, his gray eyes pinning me in his gaze, and pumping into me, over and over, harder and harder. His breath is coming hard and fast, and finally he clenches his eyes shut and lets go, shuddering as he spills himself inside me.

"Love you," he whispers and kisses me softly.

"Love you back."

He kisses me once again and then lifts off me, pulls out and staggers off the bed to walk into the bathroom to clean up.

I watch him leave, happily admiring his tight ass, when his shoulder catches my eye.

"What the hell is that?" I demand and pull myself off the bed. He reappears in the doorway, wiping his hands on a towel.

"A tattoo," he replies.

I roll my eyes. "Clearly. When did you get it? You didn't have it when you left last night."

"I got it this morning. Kat got me in early."

"Kat?" I frown and then my eyes go wide. "*That* Kat?"

"I know people." He turns to walk back into the bathroom and I follow him, inspecting the new ink in the mirror.

It's spectacular in the light. It's a yellow and orange sun, outlined in black. The rays look like they're moving in a riot of color. Surrounding it, and between the rays, is a vibrant blue, like a blue sky.

"It's beautiful," I breathe. "I hope I didn't hurt it when I hugged you."

"I'm fine." He smiles. "She did a great job."

I can't look away from it.

"The blue is your eyes," he murmurs and turns to me, cupping my face in his hands.

"You put permanent ink on you that reminds you of *me*?"

He frowns for a moment and then sighs. "Yes."

"Is it okay if that freaks me out a little?"

"Yes." He laughs and nods.

"Good, 'cause it freaks me out a little." I look at it in the mirror again and warmth spreads through me, knowing that he wants something of me on him, but at the same time, it's a big commitment.

"Tell me why you're freaked out." He's watching me closely.

"It's permanent," I whisper and he just nods, waiting for me to continue. "Shit, Leo, it's more permanent than a ring."

His eyes narrow. "Trust me, when I get a ring on your finger, it'll be there permanently."

When he gets a ring on my finger?!

"Leo." I begin and pull out of his arms. "I thought we were on the same page. I'm not interested in having a ring on my finger."

"What are you talking about?" he scowls.

"You said that marriage doesn't interest you. It doesn't me either." I shake my head and cross my arms over my chest. "We can be committed to each other without rings on our fingers."

"Samantha, I was a different man then." He props his hands on his hips, just over his low-hanging jeans and boxers. "Meeting you, falling for you, has changed that. You're mine."

"Yes, so you keep reminding me. Often."

"Because apparently you need the reminder. You've marked me, and this tat is me showing the world that I'm yours, permanently."

I continue to scowl at him, but holy shit, he's mine. *Permanently*.

"Leo, I am committed to you, but marriage…"

"Jesus Christ," He interrupts. "It's not like I'm down on one knee with a ring."

"Okay." I frown.

He closes the gap between us and pushes his hands into my hair, holding me still. "I'm yours, sunshine. Get used to it. The rest will work itself out."

"You are so mine," I agree and feel my insides loosen.

"God, you're fucking stubborn. Most women would be thrilled that their man inked himself for her."

"At least you didn't have my name tatted on your neck." I shiver as he laughs.

"Not really my thing." He shakes his head and sighs. "What am I going to do with you?"

Just keep loving me. I don't say it aloud. Instead I stand on my toes and press my lips to his.

"Your new tattoo is pretty," I whisper.

Chapter Twenty-Five

One Month Later

"You don't have to walk me to the door. I remember where Jules and Nate live." I smirk at Leo as he walks me down the hallway of Jules and Nate's building to their door.

"I don't mind. So, you are all going to meet us guys at the venue at six thirty, right?"

"Yes." I nod and roll my eyes. This is the third time he's reminded me since we left my place, and I only live four blocks away. "Why are you so worried about us being there on time?"

"Because women have a tendency to be late as it is, six of you getting ready together and getting somewhere on time? Impossible. The show starts at seven."

"Oh ye of little faith." I laugh and ring the doorbell. "We'll be there in time. We have like three hours to get ready."

"Hey! You're here!" Jules opens the door, dressed only in short red cut-off sweats and a tight black tank. "We're doing hair now. I already have an idea for you."

"Thanks for the lift." I turn to follow Jules, but Leo snags my hand and pulls me back to him, kissing me deeply and possessively, before pulling back with a smug grin.

"You're gonna be great tonight, baby," I whisper to him. He smirks, but I know he's a little nervous.

"Wear something sexy for me." He smacks my ass as I walk away.

"Yoga pants it is!" I call over my shoulder and wave as he laughs and closes the door behind him.

"Hey guys!" I call out, set my over night bag on Jules' bed, along with everyone else's it seems, and saunter into the bathroom. "It looks like a beauty supply store has exploded in here."

"You're here!" Natalie kisses my cheek happily. Stacy and

Brynna are hunched over the sink, studiously applying makeup.

"This is a rock concert, you know. You'll sweat a lot of that makeup off."

"No I won't." Stacy laughs. "I don't sweat. I glisten."

Meg laughs. "Just wear waterproof everything, you'll be fine."

She looks awesome. Her hair is a riot of red and blonde curls, and she's added purple streaks around her face.

Jules and Natalie have both gone for the long, sleek straight look with their hair.

"Sit," Jules instructs me.

"I can do my own hair." I scowl. "I've been doing it for a long time."

"Don't be a pussy. I'll do something really awesome."

"Gee, great. Just don't rat it like the hair bands from the 80's."

Jules grins and pushes me into a chair, reaches for her flat iron and gets to work.

"Sam, how do you like your new job?" Stacy asks and smiles over at me.

"I love it." I grin as I think of my new job at *Wine Northwest*, a popular magazine that showcases wines and wineries in the Northwest.

"Do you get to sample the goods?" Jules asks as she rubs some sort of gel shit in my hair.

"Actually, yes. It's awesome."

"Good for you." Nat finishes her lipstick and primps her hair. She doesn't even look pregnant yet. "We're proud of you."

"Thanks, it's just a relief to be employed again."

"Is Leo nervous about tonight?" Brynna asks, catching my eye in the mirror.

"He says he's not, but I think he might be a little. This is their first show in almost six months."

"Plus, it's home turf, so it means more," Meg agrees. "He's probably acting all badass, but his stomach is going crazy."

"Poor guy." Stacy laughs. "God, I hope he goes shirtless tonight."

"Can you arrange that, Sam?" Nat asks with a giggle. "God, those stars." She fans her face with her hand and giggles.

"I'll put in the request," I respond dryly. Of course he'll go shirtless. This is Leo Nash.

I can't wait.

"Brynna, you look hot," Jules comments and continues to tug on my head.

"Thanks." Brynna winks.

Jules is right; Brynna looks great. Her curvy body looks fantastic in her skinny jeans and shiny black, low cut top.

"Sex agrees with her." Stacy smirks and I feel my eyes go wide.

"No way!"

Brynna blushes and lowers her gaze for just a moment and then turns around to face the room with a happy smile.

"You're getting your orgasms!" Natalie exclaims happily.

"Boy am I." Brynna nods. "I can safely say the Montgomery men give some amazing orgasms." Both Stacy and Meg nod in agreement and I laugh, relieved that Jules has let go of my hair so I don't get burned.

"Oh my God! That's so great!" Jules rushes around me to hug Brynna and then scowls. "Wait. Ew. That's my brother. Yuck."

"Jules, I hate to break it to you, but your brothers have sex." I grin and pour myself a flute of champagne from a bottle on the sink.

"They have really, really great sex." Meg applies her lip-gloss and blots her lips. "Really great."

"If he hurts you, I'll fucking kill him," Jules makes a fist and holds it to her chest, like she's going to knock someone out.

"You always say that." Nat rolls her eyes and hugs Brynna. "Good for you."

"Yeah, well, he's a complete stubborn ass, and he's made it clear that it's just sex and he's making sure that the kids and me are safe." She shrugs, but can't disguise the sadness in her beautiful brown eyes. "But the orgasms rock."

"Here, have some liquor." I top off her glass. "You look hot tonight. We're gonna have a blast. Caleb is going to swallow his tongue when he sees you."

"Why are the guys going, anyway?" Stacy asks. "I thought

this was supposed to be girls night out."

"I don't know." Jules shrugs. "They like the music."

"I wish Will didn't have to go out of town this weekend." Meg frowns.

"We'll send him pictures." Nat assures her. "We'll take pics of us from the front row, flirting with the security guards, trying to get back stage."

"Uh, Nat." I chuckle and shake my head. "We're with the band. We don't have to flirt with security."

"Well, what fun is that?" She scowls, and we all laugh at her.

"There, your hair is perfect." Jules teases one more strand in the front and backs away. "Go check it out."

She did a good job. She's made my shoulder-length blonde hair look choppy and messy in a rocker kind of way. How she managed to do that with a flat iron and some gel stuff is beyond me.

"Thanks." I grin. "You know, if that whole investment banking shit doesn't work out, you could totally do hair."

"I'll keep it in mind," she replies sarcastically as I reach for my makeup bag and dig in, with Brynna hovering close by, giving me pointers on making my eyes smokey. Finally, after what seems like forever, Brynna, and the rest of the girls, are satisfied with my face.

"I'm getting dressed," Jules announces.

"Me too." I follow her into the bedroom and pull my tight, thigh-length silver-studded black dress over my hips. It has a deep V neckline, showing off my boobs, thanks to a really great push-up bra.

"Holy fuck, you're hot." Jules is staring at me, her mouth open. "What shoes are you wearing?"

I pull my super-strappy black heels out of my bag and hold them up smugly. "Fuck me shoes."

"Leo's gonna need some sort of resuscitation." She smirks and steps into a pair of tight blue jeans and a red halter-top that is loose with a cowl neckline that also dips down between her breasts. Red patent leather Choo stilettos complete the look.

"We're all showing off our boobs tonight." I snicker.

"Hell yes, why not?"

We join the others and earn catcalls and whistles.

"We are one group of hot bitches," Meg nods appreciatively. She's stunning in a green strapless, thigh-length baby doll dress with a handkerchief hemline. Nat and Stacy are both in gorgeous short black dresses.

Meg's right, we're a bunch of hot bitches.

"Are we ready? Leo will be shocked that we're on time."

"Let's go shock him," Jules agrees.

* * *

The place is packed. *Key Arena* is smaller, much smaller, than the *Tacoma Dome*, but it's also more intimate. I'm not surprised in the least that the guys chose to play here tonight.

This kicks off their twenty-day U.S. Tour. The Sunshine Tour. I grin at the t-shirts as we walk past on our way down to our seats. Leo already gave me mine.

As we work our way down to the front row where I can already see, and hear, our guys, a security guard approaches us.

"Which one of you is Samantha Williams?" He asks.

The girls all point to me and keep walking to their men.

God, the guys all look fantastic tonight.

"Would you please come with me?" He asks. "Mr. Nash would like a word."

"Sure." I follow him past the others, the stage and through a black door to the back stage area. It's surprisingly quiet back here, despite the flurry of activity of roadies and other people bustling about, all wearing official VIP badges around their necks.

"Right through here." He opens a door and motions for me to go in, and closes the door behind me.

"Thank God." Leo pulls me to him and kisses me madly, then pulls back and those gray eyes move up and down my body. "Holy fuck, Sam, how am I supposed to concentrate on the show when you'll be in the front row looking like this?"

I grin and turn in a tight circle. "You like?"

"I think I just had a stroke." He confirms.

"You look pretty hot yourself." He's in black leather pants and a tank from an ancient AC/DC concert. "How long till the tank comes off?"

"Probably in the first song. I get too hot," he murmurs.

"You want to show off your stars." I contradict him and laugh when he scowls at me. "The girls will be happy. They're excited to see your stars."

"What about you?" He asks and kisses my forehead.

"I enjoy the stars as well." I grin and push my hands under his shirt and rub my thumbs where the stars are, right along his V. "They fucking rock."

"No turning me on right before a show, sunshine."

"Is that what I'm doing?" I ask with wide eyes.

"You're trouble," he mutters and smiles. "I love it. Security will bring all of you back after the show. Just stay in your seats."

"Will do. You'll be awesome," I remind him.

"Honestly, the show isn't what I'm nervous about." He frowns and kisses my forehead again.

"What are you nervous about?"

"You'll see." He shakes his head and checks his watch. "You'd better get back out there. I have to get back to the guys. We have a pre-show ritual that I'd better not miss."

"Sacrifice a virgin?" I ask with a laugh.

"Nothing that dramatic." He shakes his head, smiling softly. "I'll see you in a bit."

"Okay. Break a leg." He kisses me, hard and fast, and shows me out to the hallway where the security guard is waiting to escort me back to my seat.

"This is Lionel. He's been assigned to you guys all night. If you need anything, just ask him."

"Okay." I turn to Lionel. "I'm ready."

* * *

~Leo~

Aside from Samantha, there is nothing I love more than performing. The rush of being surrounded by thousands of people singing along with songs I've written is better than any drug-induced high.

The first half of the show has gone without a hitch. The band is warm, playing flawlessly. I've been with these guys long enough that we communicate with hand movements or eye contact.

It's the best.

My voice is strong and sure, and I've never enjoyed myself more during a show. Of course, it doesn't hurt that my city and my girl are in the audience.

"Are you having fun Seattle?" I scream and hold the mic out for their response, which is a deafening scream.

I look down front and see Lionel gather Meg for me, escorting her to the wings.

Here goes nothing.

"We have a special guest with us tonight, Seattle. Back in the day, we played in bars and clubs around the city, and this gorgeous girl," I gesture to my left as Meg walks confidently on stage, a big smile on her lips and a mic in her hand, "was a part of Nash at that time. She's agreed to sing with us tonight! Megan McBride, everybody!"

The crowd cheers and applauds, the front row going ballistic. Jules is screaming and jumping up and down.

Just wait, sweetheart.

"Hey, everybody!" Meg calls out and waves and is met with more applause.

I asked her to join me on stage a few weeks ago, and she vehemently rejected the idea at first, but I roped Sam and Jules and the other girls into talking her into it.

I always get my way.

I nod back at Gary and he starts the song on the keyboard, Eric joins him on the drums, and we begin the song.

It's not one of ours. Will asked me to change the arrangement of *Kiss Me Slowly* by Parachute into a duet, and have Meg sing it with me. I lied to her and told her it was for Sam.

She bought it.

I sing the first verse, and she takes the second, we join together for the chorus.

God, my girl can sing.

The song comes to an end and the crowd is on their feet, cheering for us, and Meg's smile is simply incredible. She should perform with us more often.

She waves and turns to leave the stage, but I grab her hand.

"Not so fast, Megan." I speak into the mic and she turns back around, surprise written on her face. "So, I'm sure you don't know this," I tell the crowd, "but Megan is my little sister. She went and got involved with someone you all know and love, I think you'll recognize his name, a Mr. Will Montgomery."

The crowd goes manic, jumping and screaming and Meg scowls at me. She thinks they're going crazy at the mere mention of Will's name.

She's wrong.

"Turn around, Meg-pie," I shout in her ear, so only she can hear, and her eyes go wide in shock and then well with tears when she sees Will approaching her from behind. He's dressed in slacks and a button-down, the sleeves rolled, and he has a mic in his hand. He nods at me and I release her hand and step a few feet away to let him do his thing, but close enough so I can watch with the rest of Seattle.

"Hey," Will says into the mic his eyes on Meg's, and then he waves to the crowd, who immediately erupts in joy again.

This is a fanfuckingtastic crowd.

I glance down to the front row to find Sam's eyes on me, smiling broadly. All of the Montgomerys are clapping and whooping, the women crying. Will and I kept this a secret from all of them.

"Meg." Will begins and steps close to her, turning her so the family can see both of their profiles. "So, I obviously didn't have to go out of town this weekend." He smiles down at her and shrugs. "Leo helped me with this surprise."

Meg glances over at me, and I just smile and shrug.

"The song you just sang was also not from Leo to Sam like he told you it was." He laughs as she lowers her mic and swears a blue streak at me for lying to her and then he turns her chin back toward him. "It was from me to you. You see," he clears his throat,

"I wasn't sure where this was going to go when I first met you, all I knew was that I wanted you."

The crowd has gone dead silent, listening in rapture to Will pour his heart out to Meg.

If I didn't love her so much, I'd call him a pussy, but she deserves every pretty fucking word, and so much more.

"There's a line in that song you just sang that says, *'And it's hard to love again, when the only way it's been, when the only love you knew, just walked away.'* Well, I'm here to tell you, in front of all of these people and all of the people we love that I'm never going anywhere, Meg. I'm never letting you go. I love you more than I ever knew was possible to love someone. So," he lowers himself to one knee and Meg covers her mouth with her hands, tears streaming down her pretty face. Will pulls a small blue box out of his pocket and opens it, showing her a fucking huge rock.

Atta boy, Will.

"Megan, will you do me the honor of being my wife? Marry me, babe."

You could hear a pin drop in *Key Arena* right now. No one is even breathing as they wait for Meg's answer. The Montgomerys are standing perfectly still. Tears continue to stream down Meg's face and a few seconds feel like hours.

"Uh, Meg," I mumble into my mic. "The answer is yes, sweetie, put the man out of his misery."

The crowd laughs, and finally she sinks to her knees before him, drops her mic on the floor, cups his face in her hands and says, "Of course I'll marry you."

The crowd goes wild as Will wraps his arms around her middle and pulls her into him, kissing her long and hard.

Too long, and too hard.

"Hey, Montgomery, put the rock on her finger and get lost. I have a show to do."

They laugh and Will slips her ring on her slim finger and kisses it, then helps her to her feet. They both wave at the crowd and exit the stage through the wings to my left.

I turn back to my band, raise the mic to my face and scream,

"Okay, Seattle, let's fucking rock!"

Chapter Twenty-Six

~Samantha~

The after party is in full swing back stage. Fans who won back stage passes for autographs and photographs have come and gone. The band made it very clear that this party was just for them and their families.

There are still more than thirty of us.

"The show was ah-mazing!" Stacy exclaims and snuggles into Isaac's side, a drink in her hand.

"It was," Brynna nods and smiles at Meg and Will, sitting on a couch, Meg in his lap. "Will, that was quite possibly the most romantic proposal I've ever seen."

"I'm a romantic guy." He shrugs and offers us all a cocky grin.

Meg explodes in laughter. "You're a lot of things, babe, but romantic isn't one of them. Did Luke give you pointers?"

"Hey! I have my romantic moments!" Will frowns at her and then leans in to whisper in her ear, making her blush.

"Oh, yeah, that's right."

"I don't want to know." Matt shakes his head and then turns to Caleb, who has been dead silent all night, even during the concert. His eyes have been narrowed, his body on high-alert. "You doing okay, man?"

"Fine," Caleb confirms with a nod.

Brynna frowns up at him. "Are you sure?"

"I'm fine." His jaw is tight, but his voice is firm and leaves no room for questioning.

"Hey, Sam." Jules approaches us from across the room. "Leo was looking for you a few minutes ago. You must have been in the restroom."

"Do you know which way he went?"

"Out into the hallway." Jules points toward the door.

"Okay, thanks." I check the time on my phone as I head out into the corridor. I wonder how long we have to stay before we can tactfully leave. The guys are leaving in the morning for the tour, and I want as many hours alone with my man as I can get.

I hear voices murmuring in the hall as I turn a corner. Leo is standing with his back to me, facing Rick his manager, who is facing toward me, but hasn't seen me yet.

"You'll destroy her, Leo. She loves you."

"I loved her too, but I sure as fuck can't trust her now. What would you propose I do? The sooner it happens, the better."

What the fuck did I do?

Rick glances over Leo's shoulder and sees me. His mouth flattens in a grim line and he exhales hard. "Hey, Sam."

"Fuck," Leo mutters under his breath, lowers his head and props his hands on his hips, and my heart feels like it's going to beat right out of my chest. "Go back to the party, Sam."

His voice is cold. Angry. He doesn't turn around to look at me.

Rick shakes his head. "No, I think this is a conversation you need to have." He slaps Leo on the shoulder and pats my own shoulder as he passes by me, leaving Leo and I alone in the stark white, quiet hallway.

"Yeah, it sounds like we need to have a conversation." I pull my walls up around me. *Do not let him see you hurt, Samantha.* I walk around to stand where Rick was moments ago. Leo won't look at me; he keeps his eyes trained on the floor. "Look at me."

He pulls his head up, but instead of looking me in the eye, he focuses over my shoulder.

"Fucking look at me, Leo."

He shakes his head, clenches his eyes shut and swears under his breath again.

"Look, Sam…"

"No, fuck this. Just tell me what I did wrong."

His head whips up and finally he pins me in his stormy, gray gaze, scowling. "You didn't do anything wrong."

"But you just said you can't trust me. I heard you."

"No." He shakes his head adamantly and rubs his hands up

and down my arms. "You didn't do anything. I wasn't talking about you, baby."

"What's going on?"

"Fuck," he mutters again, sighs and swallows hard. "I don't know how to tell you this, Sam."

"You're scaring me," I whisper.

"I'm just gonna say it, but before I do, please know that I am so, so sorry." He's looking in my eyes again, worried and sad and so pissed off.

"What?" I ask, exasperated.

"It seems that someone took photos of us in L.A., at my house, making love on the balcony."

"What? How? Your beach is private."

"Yeah, well, who knows?"

"How do you know this? Have you seen the photos?"

He scowls and shakes his head. "No. Melissa is blackmailing me. She says that if we fire her for the photo leak of you, she'll post the photos online." He shoves his hands through his hair and paces away. "So, I won't be firing her until I can figure out how to handle this clusterfuck."

"Fuck that."

"What?" He turns back to me, his eyes wide.

"She is not going to bully you into keeping her damn job, Leo. Call her bluff. Fire her. If she posts the photos, so be it. We're consenting adults in a loving relationship. If anyone doesn't like it, they can kiss my ass. I won't have her turning the most beautiful moment of my life into something dirty."

He just stands there, his mouth gaping open, and then blinks rapidly. "Wait, where is this coming from? With as pissed as you were about the photo last week, I thought for sure this would destroy you. I'm not worried about me, but I won't have something like this surfacing about you."

"Look, I might have overreacted over that photo. This shit's going to happen. It's just a part of being with you." I pull my fingers down his face and offer him a small smile. "I love you, Leo. We've established that I'm yours and you're mine, and we're in this for the long haul. I refuse to have people like Melissa dictating how we live."

"This could turn into a major shit storm for you, baby."

I shrug and wrap my arms around his still naked waist. "I bet she doesn't post them, Leo. She doesn't want to ruin her own reputation in this business. She'd be an idiot to let them leak. We don't even have proof that they exist."

"You're sure?"

"The bitch is gone," I confirm. "Now, let's go enjoy our families, have some drinks, and then go home so you can give me some orgasms."

"Lead the way, sunshine."

* * *

"What time do you have to leave?" I ask quietly, not wanting to disturb the sweet silence of the early morning. We're curled up in bed. It's not quite daybreak. The cat is curled up on Leo's stomach, purring, and I'm draped against his side, my head on his chest.

We're still sweaty from early morning sex, my skin is still humming, and Leo's fingertips are brushing up and down my back.

"I have to be at the airport at nine," he whispers.

"What do you want to do until then?" I ask and trace the letters tattooed over his chest.

"I think we should go for a run."

My head whips up to look him in the face. "Seriously?"

"Yeah." He grins down at me. "I won't get to run with you for two weeks."

"I'm going to meet up with you in New York this weekend," I remind him. Even five days seems too long.

"We won't be running in New York, baby. We'll be lucky if we make it out of the hotel room." He chuckles and kisses my forehead. "Come on, out of bed. Let's go."

I follow him out of bed and we pull on our running gear and head down to the street. I realize he's wearing the same shorts and t-shirts he wore the morning of our first run.

264

"You know," I mention casually as we jog down our usual path through the city. "I can run farther than we normally do."

"Just run. I'll follow you."

"You don't want to know where I'm going?" I ask with a smile.

"Nope, I'll go where you go."

"Okay, but you'll have to keep up. I'm not slowing my pace for you." I throw him a mock glare as he laughs.

"So noted."

Damn, he's sexy. He's just as sexy to me now as he was that first morning we ran together. Even more so now that I know the man beneath the tats and the piercings.

"So, who's your favorite band?" He asks with a grin.

"I don't know." I shrug and keep my face neutral. "I like Daughtry a lot."

"Try again."

"Train."

"I will spank you."

"I might have a thing for Nash," I reply, laughing.

"We'll work on it." He chuckles.

We run, side by side, our breathing and steps matched... thud, thud, thud, all the way to the park where he pulled me onto that picnic table to rub my legs.

"My legs aren't shaking today," I boast with a grin.

"I'm not inside you. Of course they aren't."

I raise an eyebrow and then burst into laughter, shoving his shoulder. "You're such an arrogant ass."

He nuzzles my ear, breathing hard, as we stroll down to our café. "Am I wrong?" he murmurs.

"No. Just arrogant."

A waitress shows us to a booth, hands us menus and takes our drink orders of juice and coffee.

Neither of us needs to open the menu.

"How is your job going, baby?" Leo asks and leans his elbows on the table, his eyes happy, a half smile on those kissable lips.

"Good." I nod. "No assholes named Bob at this one, and it's unlikely they'll want me to do a story on my family, given that we run exposes on wines." I wink at him and reach over to grab his hand in my own so I can trace the ink on his fingers.

"Are you excited for the tour?" I ask and watch my finger on his skin.

"It'll be fun to play and be with the band for a couple weeks, but I'm already looking forward to coming home."

"It's only for two weeks. That's better than nine months." I snicker. "Nine months would kill me."

"Nine months isn't going to happen unless you're with me," he states, as though that's the end of the discussion.

I nod, just as my phone vibrates in my bra and Leo chuckles as I pull it out.

"I do love your storage system."

I stick my tongue out at him and check the text. It's from Caleb.

Family meeting, today, 6pm. Brynna's house. Mandatory.

I frown and turn the phone to show Leo.

"What's that about?" he asks, his eyes narrowed.

"I don't know," I shrug. "Probably has something to do with Brynna's security issues. I wish she'd just tell us what the hell is going on with her."

"It's probably none of your business." He reminds me with a smirk. "You're just nosy."

"I'm concerned," I disagree and then laugh. "Okay, I'm nosy."

"Call me later and let me know what's going on."

I shrug and frown. "The meeting is late today. You'll probably be busy with the sound check."

"You can and will call me anytime, baby. I don't give a fuck what I'm doing. I need you to know that even when I'm not here, you're the priority. I want to know what's happening here."

I shrug again and sit back as the waitress sets our plates before us. "It was good to see Lori last night, even if it was just for a few minutes." I throw him a sassy grin and he laughs out loud.

"Way to change the subject, brat."

I take a bite of my eggs and blink innocently, making him laugh more.

"She wouldn't have missed the show last night for anything." Leo nods. "Plus she wanted to meet your family."

"Meg seemed over the moon to see her. How do you guys

know her?" I ask and nibble my bacon. "Besides her being Gary's wife," I add.

"Meg and Lori always got along really well. It hurt Lori that Meg and I didn't speak for a while." He takes a bite of his bacon and a sip of coffee. "I've known Gary forever." Leo begins. "Aside from Meg, and now you, he's probably the closest person to me. We met Lori after a gig here in Seattle. She had been in town and came to a show, and being a celebrity, came to the after party to hang out with us. I was determined to fuck her." He laughs and leans back in the booth, his face full of humor.

"What happened?" I ask and push my plate aside and lean on my elbows.

"She wanted nothing at all to do with me." He shakes his head ruefully. "She took one look at Gary's ugly face, and it was all over for both of them. If I'd have made a play for her, he would have shoved his foot up my ass."

I chuckle and trace his tattoos on his hand again. "Poor guy, you lost the girl."

He grows quiet, and I glance up to find him quietly watching me. "What's wrong?"

He shakes his head, as if pulling himself out of a daydream, and flips his hand over to link his fingers with mine. "We've come a long way since the first time we sat in this café."

"Yes, we definitely have," I nod and tilt my head at him. "Are you happy?"

"Oh sunshine." He sighs and pulls my hand up to his lips, brushes them over my knuckles and smiles widely at me. "Happy doesn't begin to cover it."

Epilogue

~Leo~

God, it's good to be home. We left Atlanta immediately after the show last night and flew straight home, arriving at SeaTac at around two in the morning.

Sam and I still haven't slept.

Instead we've made love, cooked breakfast, fucked on the kitchen counter, and gone back to bed, lounging and enjoying each other after being apart for two weeks.

Two weeks at a time is all I'm willing to do.

"Oh, look!" Sam is sitting with her back propped against the headboard of her bed, her Sunshine Tour t-shirt on and her iPad in her lap. "There's a picture of us on *Yahoo!.*"

The cat is curled on my stomach, purring as I pet him, my other hand tucked under my head. I'm staring at the ceiling. I don't bother to look over at the iPad.

"Are we naked?" I ask, only half kidding. I'm terrified every day of the photos Melissa threatened us with showing up somewhere.

"No, thankfully not." Sam laughs and pushes her fingers through my hair. Fuck, I love it when she does that. "This is from the show in Phoenix last week. Wow, they even printed my name under it, not just 'Nash's girlfriend' or 'Luke Williams' sister.'"

I push the cat off my belly and turn over, cradling my head in my arms and sigh as Sam traces the sun on my shoulder blade.

"Oh, these are cute," she murmurs. "God, look at that bag. The new Michael Kors line for the spring is to die for."

"Are you shopping now?" I ask with a chuckle.

"Yeah, I don't spend too much time on the rags, I just want to make sure my hair looks good in the photos." She smirks. "Oh, fuck me, those shoes are going to be mine."

As she goes on and on about shoes and bags and whatever the hell else she's shopping for online, my mind drifts to later tonight. I think I'll take her dancing. She loves to dance, and watching her sweet ass move makes me crazy.

On second thought, I'd better not. I'd have to kill every fucker who looks at her.

"I think I'm outgrowing my closet," she mutters.

"Mmm hmm," I mumble, almost falling asleep from the gentle sweep of her fingers over my back.

"I think I need to look into building a new one."

"Wait, what?" I push up onto my elbows and stare up at her. "What are you saying?"

"I need a bigger closet," she repeats as I pull the iPad out of her hands, set it on the bedside table and pull her down into my arms.

"Keep going," I mutter and tuck her soft blonde hair behind her ear.

"Well, maybe we should start looking for an architect." She bites her lip and eyes me speculatively, and I want to crow in happiness, but I just nod thoughtfully.

"You want to remodel your apartment?"

"Don't be an ass." She smacks my arm and then traces my tat there. The woman is forever touching me.

I hope she never stops.

"What are we hiring an architect for, Samantha?" I ask and nuzzle her nose.

"Well, we'll probably also need a kitchen." she shrugs. "And a place to sleep."

"What else?"

"It takes months to build a house." She lowers her gaze to my chest and I tilt her chin up to meet my gaze. "I don't want to move all of our stuff into either this apartment or your townhouse. I'm not quite ready, and besides, I think we should start somewhere fresh."

"Okay."

"But by the time we find and hire an architect, approve plans, and the house is actually built, I think we'll be more than ready." The last few words are whispered.

"I'm gonna rush this process, sunshine. I'm warning you now. The contractor is going to hate my guts because I'll be pushing him to finish every day."

"I'll warn Isaac," she responds dryly.

"Are you sure?" I whisper. *Please, God, tell me you're sure.*

"Yeah, my shoes are really over-crowded in this closet. They deserve better."

"I'll give them whatever they want." I chuckle. "Sam, I want to give you the world. I love you so much, and I want to be with you, every day."

"We can start with a big ass closet and sunken bathtub," she grins and runs her thumb along my lower lip. I kiss the pad of her thumb softly. "I love you too, Leo Nash. Every damn day."

The End

The With Me In Seattle Series continues in book five,
SAFE WITH ME, Caleb and Brynna's story.
Watch for it in the summer of 2013.

Acknowledgements:

To my husband: Thank you. I love you, handsome.

My Naughty Mafia girls: Michelle Valentine, Kelli Maine and Emily Snow. Thank you for the love, the laughs and for your friendship. I love you guys.

To my beta readers: You know who you are. Thank you for being brutally honest and my biggest supporters. I couldn't do this without you.

Renae Porter: You are amazing. Thank you for another beautiful cover.

Linus Pettersson: You were such a joy to work with! Thank you for sharing your talent with my readers and me.

Sulan Von Zoomlander: I couldn't have asked for more in a musician to inspire this character. I appreciate the many hours of answering all of my incessant questions, and I appreciate your sense of humor. Thank you, for everything.

To the many authors who have become so much more than colleagues: Thank you for your friendship and your support. The indie community is wonderful.

To my publicist, Kelly Simmon of InkSlinger: You're the best and were worth the wait. Thank you for all of your hard work!

To all of the bloggers who continue to work tirelessly to support and promote my books: THANK YOU! You do so much for this community, and it does not go unnoticed. I'm so very thankful for all that you do.

And, as always, to YOU, the beautiful reader holding this book in your hands. Thank you, from the bottom of my heart, for reading my stories. I hope you enjoyed reading it as much as I enjoyed creating for you.

Happy Reading!

Kristen

I am pleased to offer you a sneak peak at USA Today and New York Times Bestselling author Lauren Blakely's sexy upcoming release, *Trophy Husband*, releasing May 21, 2013!

TROPHY HUSBAND
By Lauren Blakely

Copyright 2013 by Lauren Blakely
LaurenBlakely.com

All rights reserved. Without limiting the rights under copyright reserved above, no part of this publication may be reproduced, stored in or introduced into a retrieval system, or transmitted, in any form, or by any means (electronic, mechanical, photocopying, recording, or otherwise) without the prior written permission of both the copyright owner and the above publisher of this book. This is a work of fiction. Names, characters, places, brands, media, and incidents are either the product of the author's imagination or are used fictitiously. The author acknowledges the trademarked status and trademark owners of various products referenced in this work of fiction, which have been used without permission. The publication/use of these trademarks is not authorized, associated with, or sponsored by the trademark owners.

Prologue
Present Day

The stars twinkle and the night air is warm as we leave the Tiki Bar and walk slowly up Fillmore. At the top of the hill, I see my friend's maroon Prius that I'm tasked with driving home tonight. I point to it.

"These are my wheels." I click on the key to unlock the car. Then I reach for the door handle. But it doesn't open. I try again. Same thing happens. "Damn. What is up with these hybrids?"

"They have to calibrate to your heart rate."

"Then how the heck am I supposed to drive it home?"

"I know a trick," Chris says.

"You do?"

"Want to give me the keys and I'll show you?" he asks, holding open his palm for me.

But before I can pull away, he closes his fingers over mine, gripping my hand in his. That's all it takes. Within seconds I am in his arms, and we are wrapped up in each other. His lips are sweeping mine, and I press my hands against his chest, and oh my. He does have the most fantastic outlines in his body. He is toned everywhere, strong everywhere, and I am dying to get my hands up his shirt, and feel his bare chest and his belly. But if I did, I might just jump him right here because I am one year and running without this. Without kissing, without touching, without feeling this kind of heat.

He twines his fingers through my hair, and the way he holds me, both tender and full of want at the same time, makes me start to believe in possibilities. Start to believe that you can try again, and it'll be worth it. His lips are so soft, so unbearably soft, and I can't stop kissing and tasting him. He has the faintest taste of Diet Coke on his lips, and it's crazy to say this, but it almost makes me feel closer to him. Or maybe I feel closer because he's leaning into me, his body is aligned with mine, and there's no space between us, and I don't want any space between us. I want to feel him against me, his long, strong body tangled up in mine, even though we're fully clothed, making out on the street.

He breaks the kiss. "I wanted to kiss you all night."

"You did?"

"Yeah, that key thing was just an excuse. Sometimes you just have to hit the button a few times to get the car to open."

I laugh. "So you said that to kiss me?"

He nods. "Totally."

"I'm glad you tricked me," I whisper, as he bends his head and kisses my neck, blazing a trail of sweet and sexy kisses down to my throat, and it's almost sensory overload the way he ignites me. Forget tingles, forget goosebumps. That's kid stuff compared to this. My body is a comet with Chris. I am a shooting star with the way he kisses me. I don't even know if I have bones in my body anymore. I don't know how I'm standing. I could melt under the sweet heat of his lips that are now tracing a line down my chest to the very top of my breasts as he tugs gently at my shirt, giving himself room to leave one more brush of his lips. Before he stops.

He looks at me and the expression on his face is one of pride and lust. He knows he's turned me inside out and all the way on.

"That was so unfair of me," he says with a wicked grin. "Getting a headstart like that on all the other candidates."

How can there be any other guys after a kiss like that? It's a kiss to end all kisses, it's a sip of lemonade in a hammock on a warm summer day. It's a slow dance on hardwood floors while a fan goes round overhead, curtains blowing gently in the open window.

If he feels half as much for me as I do for him, then I want to sail away with him in the moonlight, and that scares the hell out of me. I have to extract myself before I let this go any further. I don't mean the contact. I mean the way my aching, broken heart is reaching for Chris.

Chapter One
Four weeks ago…

I used to have sucky parking karma, the kind where every single time I needed a spot, and especially if I was racing to a lunch meeting, the only one I could locate would be in the next county, and in some cases, the next time zone.

Then one year ago, a miracle occurred. No, my ex-boyfriend didn't fall back in love with me and announce it was all a joke when he eloped with some chick in Vegas at his bachelor party the night before our wedding. But another miracle transpired. Since then I have never failed to land a parking spot on the same block as my destination. I am quite sure this is the universe's way of making up for precisely how he said sayonara – via voicemail mere hours before I was about to walk down the aisle.

And because of this awesome, amazing, powerful parking karma I no longer worry that I'll drive around scouting out a spot in the city of San Francisco, even though time in this city can truly be measured by the quest for a parking spot.

One less thing to stress about is a good thing in my book, so I give my gorgeous dog, Ms. Pac-Man, a kiss on the snout as I grab my purse from the entryway table. She wags her flag-sized, blond fluffy tail and places a big paw on my leg, her way of saying goodbye. She's a good dog, she's well-trained, and she's also particularly well-mannered when I leave her home alone in the Victorian she and I share just a few blocks from San Francisco Bay. She spends the entire time I'm gone snoozing on her Pac-Man decorated dog bed. I know this because I once set up my phone camera to verify what I suspected – that she was indeed a perfect canine.

"I'd tell you to be good, but I know you will," I say, as I scratch her ears. She leans her soft head into my hand, and I smile as I pet her. Sometimes, I think this dog is the only reason I've smiled at all in the last year. Not much has made me happy, but yet here she is, ably filling that role as only a dog can.

Then I'm off to another solo Sunday breakfast, heading down the stairs, to the garage, into the car, and onto the street, driving past a local grocery store, where bag boys fill canvas sacks with organic chickens, locally-grown asparagus and all-natural, wheat-free cereals, then a membership-only nail salon that I don't go to. Because I do my own nails, in alternating colors, and today I am wearing mint green and purple.

I turn the radio up louder, and even though I should listen to angry girl rock given how my heart's been in a sling for the last year, I can't bring myself to like that kind of music. Because deep down I am still the old standards I love. So I sing along to the music – Frank Sinatra's I've Got You Under My Skin – as I motor up steep hills that burn legs while walking, then down a rollercoaster-y dip on my way into Hayes Valley. The station shifts to the King, another favorite of this retro-loving girl, and he's now crooning Can't Help Falling in Love.

My favorite song ever.

The song Todd didn't want to be our wedding song since he'd insisted on Have I Told You Lately That I Love You, the perfect tune since that's how he felt about me, he claimed.

A red Honda scoots out of the prime spot right in front of the restaurant. As I glide my orange Mini Cooper into the space, I mouth a silent thank you to the parking gods. Don't get me wrong – I'm grateful for the way they look out for me and reward me with perfect little nooks for my car, but I have other daydreams too.

Yet those ones seem so far out of reach.

Mainly, I'd like to find a guy who's not a weasel. The kind of fella who doesn't ring you up from Sin City to call the whole thing off the day before you're supposed to slip into a gorgeous white dress with that perfect '50s flair you were looking for.

"Listen, I've had a change of heart," Todd said on his voice mail because I was on another call with the cake shop. It would have been a perfect wedding. We had what I thought was a perfect life. Cramped but cozy apartment in the Mission, my business was taking off like crazy and he'd helped launch it, we'd even picked out names for kids we might have some day – Charlotte for a girl and Hunter for a boy.

Then he had an epiphany at a poker table in Vegas when he met a gymnast he married instead.

The day before our wedding.

"I don't really see myself having kids with you, or a life with you, so let's nip this thing in the bud," he said in his phone message.

So yeah. That kind of sucked.

But as I listen to this song, I find myself longing for something more in my life. For someone to join me for breakfast at my favorite diner in the city. Maybe a sweet kiss, a nice goodnight make-out session, and maybe some love too, the kind of love that lasts, always and forever, without leaving you in the lurch, I admit silently, as Elvis croons about taking my hand, and my whole heart too.

Why do I do this? Why do I listen to this music that tortures me? I thought my almost-hubs and I were meant to be, and I was wrong, but yet as The King sings about falling in love, I can't deny that there's a part of me that wouldn't mind falling in love again.

The kind where you can't help it.

The kind that takes your breath away.

The kind that's meant to be.

I know, I know. It's like asking for the moon, so I'll stop my silly daydreaming.

But, hey, at least right now I have a coveted parking spot.

I snatch my purse with its saucy cartoon of a pirate girl winking ironed on to the side and head into The Best Doughnut Shop in the City. It's not really a doughnut shop. It used to be a doughnut shop and then the owner converted it into a diner with green upholstered vinyl seats. It's my absolute favorite diner in the whole city and it feels a bit like my special place.

I tell the hostess I'm a party of one, and look, I'm not going to lie – it still hurts to ask for that solo table, even though Todd never once, in all our five years together, came with me to this diner. He said he didn't care for cheap, hole-in-the-wall eateries. Snob.

But even when I came here all by myself for Sunday breakfast, at least I was still part of a two-some, even if the other someone was sleeping in. Now, it's just me. Party of one.

I keep my chin up, as the hostess guides me to a two-top, one of the last remaining ones. The place is packed. See Todd? You don't know what you were missing. This cheap diner knows how to bring it in the breakfast department.

I sit down and smooth out my flouncy knee-length poodle skirt. Even if I'm all by my lonesome, I still like to dress up. Fashion is like a shield to me. The clothes I wear center me, make me strong and steely with their distinctive style.

I order my usual – scrambled eggs, toast and a Diet Coke. Yep, I'm one of those people who drinks soda in the mornings. I'm sure I should kick the habit for many reasons, including the fact that Todd was my Diet Coke partner in crime, and we both downed the carbonated beverage morning, noon and night. But I refuse to let the memory of what we shared ruin my favorite drink.

One minute later the waitress brings me a glass that's fizzing just the right amount. I thank her and take a drink, then reach for my laptop from my bag. I might as well work on my fashion blog as I wait for the food. As I flip open the laptop, the waitress guides a gorgeous young blond over to the two-top next to me. I scan her outfit first. The gal is wearing sparkling white running shoes with a pink swirly stripe, black workout pants and a color-coordinated pink and black form-fitting, snug workout top. There's something about her face though that's eerily familiar. Like I've seen her somewhere, but I can't place it.

She flashes me a warm smile that shows off perfect teeth.

"Hi," she says.

"Hey."

"This placed is jammed today."

"It's like this every Sunday. The food is amazing."

"I've heard great things about it. I'm so excited to finally try it."

Okay, maybe I won't need the laptop. Maybe this gal and I will chat for the next thirty minutes, seeing as she's mighty friendly. I wouldn't mind the company, to tell the truth. It beats eating over a keyboard. "You will not be disappointed. Everything's good."

"My husband said he's been wanting to go to this place for the longest time. He's just out parking the car," she says and tips her forehead to the door.

I half expected her to say her dad was going to join her because she looks like a teenager. But maybe she was a teenage bride. "Well, both of you will love it then. I'm a total regular. A devotee, as they say," I add in a silly little affected accent that makes her laugh.

"What do you recommend?"

"Anything. Except for hard-boiled eggs, because they're totally gross."

"Oh god, yes. They're so gross. Like the most disgusting food ever."

I lean closer and say in a conspiratorial whisper. "My ex used to love them. I couldn't even be in the house when he ate hard-boiled eggs."

"You want to hear something funny? My husband used to love them too. But I laid down the law. No hard-boiled eggs ever in my house. I cured him of his hard-boiled egg addiction like that." She snaps her fingers.

I hold up a hand to high five her. "You deserve major points for that."

"Oh, look. There he is," she says, and when I turn to follow her gaze, it's as if I've just had a pair of cleats jammed into my belly, and I don't even play softball. But I bet this is what it feels like when the batter slides into home and you're the catcher who's not wearing a chest protector.

Blindsided.

Because she's looking at Todd.

The diner is shrinking. The walls are closing in, gripping me. I can't breathe. This has to be a mistake. An error. She has to be joking. I have to be seeing things. There is no way her husband can be Todd. There must be another man behind him, maybe a short man I can't see. A pipsqueak little fellow right behind Todd, who's walking over to her table. But there's no mini man hiding behind him. It's just him, and he freezes when he sees me, then quickly recovers, taking the seat across from his wife.

Wife.

It's as if there's a knife in my heart, digging for all the soft spots and scooping them out. Serving them up on the table for the two of them. The girl-child I've been chatting with, my new fucking breakfast best friend, is the college-age creature from Vegas who stole my about-to-be-husband.

I've never seen her in person before. I have only seen one photo I found of her on Facebook the day after his voicemail, as I sobbed and clicked, surrounded by unopened wedding gifts sent to our apartment. Now I feel stupid for not studying her photos more, for not hunting out more pictures of her online. I stopped after that one – a faraway shot of her at a gymnastics meet since, of course, she's a gymnast – because it hurt far too much. But now with her here in front of me, I catalogue her features. Her cheeks are red and rosy, her skin is soft and smooth, her hair is natural blonde and sleek, and her boobs remind me of Salma Hayek's.

They're so freaking huge.

Fine, I'm only six years older, but I have dark hair, and weird eyes that are sometimes blue, sometimes green, sometimes gray, and my breasts are decent, but not dead ringers for cantaloupes. I'm only twenty-seven and I know it sucks to be left at any age. But the fact that he left me for a co-ed – giving himself a trophy wife for all intents and purposes – didn't help my self-esteem. I'd been with him for five years; she'd been with him for one night, and she got him all the way to the altar. I got stuck with two mixers I never use, and party-of-one as my middle name.

"Hi McKenna," Todd says in his best business-like voice.

"Oh…." It's like a long, slow release of air from Amber, as her mouth drops open, and she shifts her gaze from him to me, registering who she's been chatting with.

She recovers faster than me though, because I'm still speechless and stuck in this chair, sitting next to Amber. She is the name of all my heartbreak, of all the ways I fell short. Amber is the name that drummed through my brain for the better part of the last twelve months, like an insistent hum in the pipes you can't turn off. Amber, Amber, Amber. The woman he wanted. The woman he chose. I will never hear that name without thinking of all that she has that I don't. The man I once wanted to marry.

"You know, why don't we just get a new table?" she says to Todd.

He scans the restaurant. This is the last empty table. "There's no place else to sit," he says, and it's clear he has no intention of leaving.

What's also clear is that he's the only of us – him and me – who doesn't care that he ran into his ex-fiancé. That realization smacks me hard, but it reminds me that I need to pull myself together and channel whatever reserves of steely coolness I have in me.

"It's fine. I'm almost done anyway," I manage to say even though my food hasn't arrived.

"So how's everything going with you?" he asks as he reaches for a menu and scans it. He doesn't even look at me while he's talking. It's not because he's rude. It's because I am nothing to him. There's a stinging feeling in the back of my eyes. I tighten my jaw. I won't let them see me cry.

"Great. The blog is great. The dog is great. Life is great," I say, pretending I am a robot, an unfeeling robot who can spit out platitudes. I have to. I have to protect my heart because it feels like it's being filleted. "I see you like this place now?"

"I love it. Favorite diner in the whole city."

My throat catches, and I grit my teeth. "That's great. And such great news about the hard-boiled eggs too."

He gives me a curious look.

"Nothing. It's nothing." I affix a plastic smile when the waitress brings me my food. She turns to Todd and Amber. They order as I slide my laptop into my bag, and consider ditching the place right now. Who needs food when there are ex-fiancés and their new wives to remind you of all that was stolen from you?

"And I'll have a coffee too. No more soda in the morning for me," he adds before the waitress leaves.

The burning behind my eyes intensifies. It's just coffee, I tell myself. But he used to hate coffee. He detested it, and now he's drinking it instead of Diet Coke.

He turns his attention back to Amber. "But no coffee for you still," he says to her in a babyish voice. She smiles at Todd, who could be Amber's big brother with his matching blond hair and blue eyes. He lays a hand gently on one of hers. I try my hardest to mask the all-too familiar feeling of my insides being shred by him. God, I loved this man. I was a fool, but I loved him like crazy, I fell for him the day I met him randomly at a bus stop several years ago. He was mine, and he was wonderful, and he was the only one I wanted.

"Well, it was great seeing you," I say, and start to push my chair away.

"You're leaving?"

"Yeah. I totally forgot that I ate a bagel already today. Stupid me," I say and smack my forehead, as if I'm shocked at my own forgetfulness.

"I do that sometimes too," Amber says. "Forget stuff. I think it's because I have baby brain right now."

"Excuse me?"

"Oh," she says, and there it is again. That long expression of surprise.

Todd nods several times. "We had a baby. Two weeks ago."

My heart races into a very painful overdrive of disbelief as it pounds against my chest. This can't be happening. Todd clasps his hand over Amber's and she beams at him, and that smile, for her, just for her, threatens my precarious sense of I'm-totally-fine-with-being-ditched-the-day-before-our-wedding.

"We have a little blond, baby girl. Her name is Charlotte."

The diner starts spinning and I grab the edge of the table. I squeeze my eyes shut, hoping, praying that'll do the trick and hold in the tears that are threatening to splash all over my face right now. He changed everything for her, all the way from children to breakfast choices. And he took everything from me, including our name for a baby he wound up having a year after leaving me a voicemail that said he didn't want to marry me because he couldn't picture having kids with me.

I open my eyes. Take a deep breath. Try to keep it together. "That was our name."

"It's a beautiful name too," Amber says. "She's such a beautiful baby, and so smart too. She's with my parents right now over in Marin. But I miss her and I've only been away from her for an hour."

"We're madly in love with being parents," he adds.

That does it. He might have cut out my heart with an Exacto blade, but I won't let him know it's bleeding again. I have to get away from them.

"You should really get back to her then," I somehow manage to choke out as I stand up, and grab my bag, doing everything not to trip and fall as I leave my food on the table, and rush to the restroom, where I slam the stall door and let the tears rain down. My shoulders shake, my chests heaves, and I am sure I look like a wretched mess. After several minutes, I check the time. But I know they're still out there, so I stay inside this stall as other patrons come and go. I camp out in the safety behind this door, registering each minute.

Until an hour passes.

Then I unlock the stall, splash water on my face, and touch up my mascara and blush.

I don't feel human, but I can at least pass for one again. I open the door a crack, spotting the table where he delivered his latest crushing blow. I thought I was over him. I thought I couldn't be more over him. But seeing him with her reopened everything I thought I'd gotten over by playing Call of Duty and shooting bad guys every night for the last several months.

I head for the counter, pay the hostess for the food I didn't eat, and then I leave The Best Doughnut Shop in The City. Another wave of sadness smashes into me when I realize I'll never be able to come to my favorite diner again. He's ruined this place for me.

I'm so ready to go home and curl up with Ms. Pac-Man for a bit, so I hurry over to my car, where I see a white piece of paper tucked under the wiper, flapping in the wind. Now I have a parking ticket? Now my karma bites me in the back? No, this should be the day when I find a winning lottery ticket on my car, not a parking ticket.

I turn around to peer up at the sign. The white and red sign very clearly says Sunday mornings are free. I glance at the curb. It's not red. There's no hydrant nearby. I scan the block. Down near the corner of Hayes Street, I see the meter boy, wearing his uniform of blue shorts and a blue short-sleeved button-down shirt. I grab the parking ticket and march down the street to confront him.

He's slipping another ticket under the windshield of a lime-green Prius. "What's up with the ticket, Meter Boy?"

He turns around to face me and I feel like I've been blinded. He is shatteringly good-looking. His face is chiseled, his light blue eyes sparkle, his brown hair looks amazingly soft. I can't help but give him a quick perusal up and down. It's clear he is completely sculpted underneath his parking attendant uniform. Every single freaking inch of him. He smiles at me, straight white teeth gleaming back. He's so beautiful, my eyes hurt. It's like looking at the sun.

My ticket rage melts instantly. My resolve turns into a puddle.

"Oh, hi. I saw you earlier when you parked."

"You did?"

He's smiling at me, giving me some sort of knowing grin that unnerves me. He's probably all of twenty-one, just like Amber. He does not posses the tire that the men I see – at the coffee shops or dog parks – wear around their midsections. No, this fellow, owns a pair of noticeably cut biceps and an undeniably trim waist. Why have I not spent more time hanging around the meters in this city with its bevy of beautiful, young, sexy parking attendants?

"Hey, I've got some other cars to deal with. But call me later." Then he winks at me. He crosses the street.

"I didn't park illegally," I shout at him.

He smiles again, that radiant smile still strong from across the street. "I know."

I stand there for a moment, befuddled on the corner of the street. Call me, he said. How would I call him? I look at the ticket

290

in my hand and flip it over.

There is no check mark on it, no official signature, no indication of a parking crime. Instead, there's a a simple note: "You're gorgeous. Give me a call sometime." Then there's a number.

I shake my head. I'm floored by the turn of events. By the shift in my day from utter crap to a pick-up line. Okay, McKenna – which is more implausible? That your ex-fiancé had a baby with her? Or that an achingly handsome young meter man wants you to call him for a date?

I walk slowly back to my car, still in a daze. I reach my Mini Cooper and lean against my car for just a minute, not caring if the backside of my sky blue skirt picks up dirt – a skirt I snagged when my girlfriends Hayden and Erin stole me away for a wine country spa weekend to forget all my woes, and it didn't work, but I did score some cute clothes at a vintage shop I found next to a bowling alley on the drive home. I flip the ticket over again, looking at Meter Man's number. Then I glance one more time down the street and see him on the other side now, writing out parking tickets. He must feel my faraway eyes on him, because he looks up and waves at me. He mimics the universal sign for phone, holding up his hand against his ear, thumb and pinky out. I can't help myself. I laugh at the incredulity of this all. I read the note yet another time. "You're gorgeous. Call me."

There's a part of me that wants to lock myself inside and have a pity party. To call my girlfriends and let them help me drown my sorrows as they have done every single time I've needed them to in the last year. But if Todd can change everything about himself, maybe I can too. So I go against my natural instinct to retreat. Instead, I pull my phone from my purse and dial the meter man's number right then and there. I watch him off in the distance as he extracts his phone from his pocket.

"I'm glad you didn't make me wait."

Be still my beating heart. He's hot, he's nice and he's flirty.

"I'm glad I didn't wait either. So, what's your name?"

"Dave Dybdahl."

I try not to laugh at the odd alliteration of his double-D – wait, make that triple-D – sounding name.

"Dave, why'd you leave this note for real? You're not trying to pull a joke on me and I'm really going to have some massive parking fine?"

He laughs, then assumes a very serious voice. "I never joke about parking meter matters," he says and I'm liking that he's got a little sense of humor working underneath that fine exterior. "I saw you get out of your car before you went into the diner and I thought you were pretty. Want to go out sometime?"

I laugh again. A date. I don't have dates. I have shooting sessions with video games. I have crying fests with my girlfriends. I share a king-size bed with a lab-hound-husky.

And I have a hope that it all may change. That this life of the last year is not my life to come. That this day is the nail in the coffin on my heartbreak. That the songs I listen to could someday be sung for me. The ones about mad, crazy, never-gonna-let-you-go love. Maybe with Dave Dybdahl. Maybe with someone else.

"Why not? I'll call you later to make a plan."

"I can't wait."

I hang up the phone and stare at it again, still not sure if that conversation really just happened. I push the phone back into my bag and it suddenly occurs to me that Todd doesn't have to be the only one who gets to win here. I am single, I have a good job, an awesome job in fact, and I'm not bad looking. (Some might even say I'm gorgeous. Who would have thought that?)

Todd took my heart. He took my name. He took himself. He gave it all to Amber, his Trophy Wife. But that moment in the Best Doughnut Shop in the City doesn't have to be the last word, does it? He doesn't deserve any more tears. He doesn't deserve any more of my pain. There is no more room for sadness or hurt.

I have to move on and I finally know how.

Because my brain has hatched the perfect plan, right here, right now, thanks to this handsome young meter man. I can turn the tables. I can even the score and take up the mantle for all the jilted ladies, young and old. This is no longer about me. There is something bigger at stake here. I have been presented with a rare opportunity. This isn't just happenstance. This isn't just coincidence.

This is real parking karma at work.

Because if the unbelievably hot Dave Dybdahl thinks I'm cute, then maybe, just maybe, I could land a hot young thing, a delicious piece of arm candy, a boy toy. Maybe Dave Dybdahl, maybe someone else. Because Dave will be just the beginning of my new project.

I am going to score myself a Trophy Husband.